CRUSH'S FALL

TIGER'S CLAW MC SERIES BOOK 1

Crush's Fall
T.S. Tappin
Published by T.S. Tappin
Copyright © 2023 T.S. Tappin
All rights reserved. In accordance with the U.S. Copyright Act of 1976, the scanning, uploading, and electronic sharing of any part of this book without the permission of the publisher is unlawful piracy and theft of the author's intellectual property. Thank you for your support of the author's rights and work. This book is a work of fiction. Names, characters, places, and incidents are the product of the author's imagination or are used fictitiously. Any resemblance to actual events, locales, or persons, living or deceased, is coincidental.
Cover Design by: T.S. Tappin
Editing Services: Elisabeth Garner & Kimberly Ringer
ISBN: *9798373699181*

Crush's Fall

Tiger's Claw MC Series
Book 1

T.S. TAPPIN

Dedication:

For my PIC and her steel-covered brick wall…

Other works by this author:

Under the name T.S. Tappin
Howlers MC Series:
Bk1: Axle's Ride
*Bk2: Trip's B*tch*
Bk3: Pike's Pixie
Bk4: Siren's Flame
Bk5: Bullet's Butterfly
Bk6: Dragon's Kiss
Bk7: Rebel's Fairytale
Bk8: Rex's Release

Howlers MC Series: UP Chapter:
Bk.5: Arbor
Bk1: Whiskey

Tiger's Claw MC Series:
Bk1: Crush's Fall

Under the name Tara Tappin
On the Clock: A Spicy RomCom Novella Charity Project

Acknowledgements:

My PIC: For pushing the *publish* button the first time for me. I Heart You. I hope I did you proud with this one! Thank you for designing Lucifer and for allowing me to use you as a model for Crush.

My family: I appreciate your support and believe in me. You are my reasons why.

Kim: Without your friendship and support, I'm not sure what I would do! Good thing I'll never have to find out. Trench-coat ready for ya! HG 4ever!

Elisabeth: Your support, encouragement, and comma-lessons are essential to my writing non-process. I'll always work these streets for you! HG 4life! Huzzah!

Catalina the Niffling: Your expertise in anatomical knowledge of the removal of balls was essential to making this book accurate. The Hype Girl Squad will forever be appreciative! Heart you!!

The HypeGirlSquad Discord: For keeping up my spirits each and every day, I thank you. I'm very proud of the safe space we've created. Just remember you're awesome.

My Beta team: If not for you, none of this would make sense. Thank you for wading through the mess to find the good stuff.

My ARC team: Thank you, thank you, thank you for taking a chance with my work! You are one of the most important parts in the publication of my books. Without you, none of this would be possible.

Content Warnings

Dear Reader,

I want to make sure that no one is negatively influenced by my work, I decided to upload my book files with content warnings about what you will encounter in this body of work.

The following are those warnings:
Death
Violence
Weapons
Possessiveness
Controlling behavior
Cussing/strong language
Explicit sex
War(Mostly off page)
Drug use(Off page)
Pregnancy(Not main character)

If you encounter something that isn't listed and feel it could trigger a reader, please email me at booksbytt@gmail.com

Thank you!

T.S. Tappin

T.S. Tappin

Chapter One

Crush

Tiger shifter Meredith 'Crush' Welles wasn't the president of the Tiger's Claw MC, a female motorcycle club out of Warden's Pass, Michigan, because she was sweet and caring. Okay, she was, but she just didn't let many people know that. She hid that behind a wall of steel-covered brick. The fact of the matter was she cared too much about people, but she also thought people lacked fucking common sense and decision-making skills. On the other hand, she was pretty sure that her friend, Axle Weber, would say the same about her. As the president of the Howlers MC, the male motorcycle club the Claws were allied with, he often had to keep her from throat-chopping stupid people. Not only were they allies, but their clubs also shared businesses and spent most of their time together. They were a family.

Growing up as an independent woman in a culture of alpha males, Crush had to learn how to hold her own. She could admit that she took that to the extreme more often than not, but only when it felt necessary. If she didn't remind them often that she could stand on her own two feet, the alpha males around her would think they could run her over with their decisions and personalities. She wouldn't and couldn't let that happen.

When you combine her temper and sometimes violent nature with her dislike for idiots, it could be a dangerous situation, since in her opinion, men were idiots more often than they weren't. Her vice president, Pinky, was a lot calmer than she was and was known to be the buffer between her and others. If Pinky wasn't around, it was Axle or her brother, Bullet, another member of the Howlers.

Honestly, she owed the three of them more than she would ever admit. If it wasn't for them, she would be dead or locked up in some jail.

She wasn't sure if it was the tiger in her that made her volatile or just her intolerance for stupidity, but it didn't matter. It was who she was and how she was, and most likely, wouldn't change.

Most of the time, she listened to Axle when he made a suggestion about plans, but this time, he wasn't ordering her around this town. Frankly, he did that too often. No, this time, she was doing what her gut told

Crush's Fall

her to do. She *was* going to Indiana, and she was going to do what was necessary to protect her club, whether Axle approved or not.

The Hell's Dogs MC had fucked with her family too many times in too many ways, but she would do it for her club sister, Pumps, alone. What they did to her club sister when she was too young to know any better was unthinkable. When she was a teenager, she had dated one of them. He had emotionally, physically, and sexually abused her while she was too young to know how to protect herself. And when those fuckers showed up to force Pumps to return to them where they thought *she belonged*, they did things to people Crush cared about that earned them destruction.

Over several months, the Hell's Dogs MC had plotted to kill the Howlers, had kidnapped their family, and had raped a family member. The Howlers and the Claws had taken out quite a few of them during the last battle between them and the Hell's Dogs MC when they came to the area with the intent of taking Pumps back with them. In Crush's opinion, they were the scum of the earth.

The goal of the mission wasn't to destroy, rather to gather information, but she would be lying if she said she wouldn't be looking for a chance to end any Hell's Dog member that might still be alive.

And she wouldn't lose a wink of sleep over it.

She was bringing her vice president, Pinky, and Nails, another member of the Claws, with her. Along with Pinky and Nails, three of the Howlers were making the trip — Dragon, Ranger, and Pike. The six of them would back each other up. Everything would be fine, but if shit went off the rails, she had faith in them to handle it and get home relatively unscathed. This wasn't their first rodeo.

With the exception of Ranger, they were all shifters with heightened senses and healing abilities that made them hard to kill. Ranger may not have those same abilities, but he had skills he learned in the armed forces that made him a force to be reckoned with in his own right.

When facing an enemy of their family, blood or not, the Howlers and the Claws would use every weapon in their arsenal to end the threat.

After days of reconnaissance of the Hell's Dogs MC in Indiana, Crush and the others had learned everything they possibly could from the second-floor room they had rented in an inn near the entrance to the Hell's Dogs compound for the sole purpose of watching them. They took shifts where a couple members would keep watch, while the others rested in their actual hotel rooms across town. Once they arrived at the point where nothing new had been presented to them in hours, they had collectively decided they needed to get closer to the Hell's Dogs clubhouse. They still had unanswered questions and unaddressed concerns about the status of the Hell's

Dogs, their plans, and the exact number of surviving members.

Crush and her fellow Howlers and Claws made a plan to get closer and see what they could find out from looking in windows and such. Just like Crush suspected would happen, they didn't end up only watching. The six bikers stormed the place, a two-story house, with guns up and ready to take out anyone in their path the Hell's Dogs were using as a clubhouse.

After taking out everyone on the first floor, with Pike getting shot in the melee, Crush headed for the second floor with Dragon and Ranger on her heels. They had tried to get her to follow them, but she ignored them and darted up the stairs.

The stairs were creaky, so she didn't bother trying to ease her way up them. When she got to the landing at the top, she paused, letting Dragon and Ranger catch up. With her back to the wall, the men doing the same thing on the preceding steps, Crush took a deep breath and released it slowly, preparing herself to round the edge of the doorjamb and enter an unknown room.

She heard an unfamiliar voice yell from in the room, "We know you're fucking there, assholes!"

With no reason to wait, Crush stepped around the end of the wall and into the room, gun raised. She locked onto her target, the older, long-haired member. "Don't you fucking move," she growled. She sensed Dragon and Ranger flank her and saw their guns in her peripheral vision, prepared to use them.

"Who the fuck?" the long-haired member shouted, locking his gun on her the same way she aimed at him. He was crouched at the end of the table, with the length of it between them.

The room was a lot like the first floor. It had warped wood-paneling on the walls and stained, rotted flooring, with missing boards and several holes. The table wasn't even a proper church table. It was one of those foldable tables you pull out when you have extra people show up to a holiday meal. At least the chairs were wooden, even if they were mismatched and looked to be curb-side quality.

Leaning against the middle of the wall to the right with his arms crossed over his chest, like his clubhouse wasn't getting ambushed, was someone she recognized from the photos Dragon had printed, but she hadn't seen him in person until that moment.

When the man turned his head and locked eyes with her, her heart fluttered and then sank. The moment that dark-as-night gaze met hers, her tiger woke up and started prowling, wanting out. Her tiger responded to that man in a way Crush didn't think was ever possible. She heard Axle talk about how his wolf demanded he claim Ashlyn, but she usually rolled her eyes when he started talking like that. She figured he was exaggerating, but as she stared into the eyes of one of her enemies, she realized quickly that Axle was telling the one hundred perfect truth. *Shit.*

The man cocked an eyebrow and had the audacity to smirk at her like he didn't have three handguns pointed in his fucking direction. *Idiot!*

"On the floor," Dragon ordered.

Crush pulled her gaze away from the idiot just in time to see the long-haired man raise up the gun a bit more to aim. She fired off a shot at the man at the same time someone else did, Ranger maybe. One shot hit him in the hand, forcing his hand to release the gun. The other shot hit him directly between the eyes.

Without missing a beat, Crush turned her gun on the remaining man. He was still leaning against the wall, arms crossed, but he was staring at his friend dead on the floor. That's when Crush noticed that his cut no longer had prospect patches. On the left side of his cut was a patch that said *member* and another that said *Lucifer*. Sometime in the last twenty-four hours, he had become a full-patched member.

"Fuck," Dragon said as he stepped further into the room. "You the last member?"

Lucifer looked up from his dead friend and gave a nod. "Since I'm assuming the only way you made it up here is because the others downstairs are dead, yeah."

"You assume correctly," Ranger replied from behind Crush and to her left.

"Might as well finish them off," Dragon commented, and raised his gun to aim.

Crush saw Dragon's finger shift to the trigger, and her heart stopped. *"Stop,"* she growled, surprised by the vehemence in her voice. Sure, she used that tone with her members to re-establish her dominance sometimes, but she rarely used it with the Howlers. They weren't hers to dominate.

Dragon turned and looked at her. "What?" He looked like he was annoyed with her, but he listened.

"We can't kill him… until we know…" *Think, Crush! Fucking think!* "Until we know what he knows, we shouldn't kill him. He might know something Axle can use. We can always kill him later."

"Well, golly-gee," Lucifer commented on a chuckle, "I think that's the nicest thing anyone has ever said about me."

Crush shot him a glare. "Shut the fuck up before I rethink what I just said." He wasn't helping her out, and it annoyed her that she felt some type of connection to him. She had no problem taking that out on him, which wasn't great for him since there were still at least two guns pointed in his direction.

Dragon huffed out a sigh and rolled his eyes. "Fine. But you're in charge of securing him. I gotta go check on Pike."

"You need help?" Ranger asked. She knew he wasn't insinuating that she couldn't handle it. He was just offering a helping hand, the same helping hand he'd offer one of his club brothers. It was about respect and family. Crush appreciated that.

"Got any rope on ya to tie his hands?"

Ranger grinned. "Never go on a reconnaissance mission without it."

She snorted a laugh. "Tie his hands, will ya? Then I'll take over."

"You got it." Ranger did just that, while also warning, "I know you Hell's Dogs think you can overpower women because you're big and bad, but just a heads up, this woman won't claw your eyes out. She'll cut your balls off in your sleep because you fucking snored."

Crush bit back the laugh and gave Lucifer a saccharine smile. As much as Ranger was a jokester and was prone to exaggeration, he was being straight up at that moment. She was a female tiger shifter, after all. They weren't known for their patience or tolerance, but they were known for dragging their prey up into trees to feast.

Crush never intended to fall in love. After her literal crush on Axle Weber and the resulting embarrassment when he shot her down, she vowed to herself that she would never allow herself to develop feelings for another man ever again. Yet here she was... in love. Yup, she fell in love... with the *enemy* no less. Her brother, Bullet, was going to put a bullet in her brain when he realized what she did. Not a literal bullet. He would just angrily annoy her until she wanted to put a bullet in her own brain just to stop the irritation. Like she could help it that the man was so pretty.

And he *was* pretty. Oh, so pretty. *Yum.*

Lucifer had dark brown, almost black hair that was cut almost to his scalp on the sides but long enough on top to run her fingers through, and maybe get a grip. He had chocolate brown eyes, a full beard of a few inches, and a mustache, but the hair on his face was trimmed and groomed. She guessed he brushed and conditioned the hair on his chin more than he did the hair on his head. That hair surrounded hard but full lips that tempted her almost as much as the eight pack she suspected he had under that torn, stained t-shirt. Yeah, the man was pretty.

His name was Lucifer, though. Really. His MC brothers named him *Lucifer,* if the patch on his cut was anything to go by. No way in hell was she calling him that. She'd have to find out his real name. He had yet to hand over that information, but she was the president of her own MC, and they had ways of finding information.

Okay. Fine. She wasn't *really* in love. She was in lust. She wasn't ready to vow a lifetime to the man, but she would sit on his face and give that beauty of a beard a ride or twelve.

Now, how was she going to keep him alive long enough for them to fulfill that dream? Axle, along with the rest of his club, and probably most of hers, was going to want him dead. He was a member of the club who kidnapped, raped, and threatened to murder their family members. A member of his club wanted to take a member of her club away for gods knew what type of abuse.

Lucifer wasn't innocent. She knew that. He might have been involved in all of that, even if he was only a prospect at the time, but something about him told her he could be trusted. She just didn't know how to explain that to the rest of them without having to answer the questions.

Fucking questions.

Why would you trust him? Is it your gut or your heart talking? Is it your heart or your vagina talking? Have you lost your mind? Can't you find pretty dick somewhere else?

Always with the questions.

Answer — *My tiger told me so.* Yup. Being a tiger shifter was cool until her tiger did shit like tell her the enemy was their next prey and not in the track-and-kill category. More like the track-seduce-fuck category.

Yeah, that would go over great with her brother. Hey, Bull. You think you could not kill the man who was part of the club that raped Axle's youngest brother, kidnapped three of our family members, threatened to kill all of them, and wanted to kidnap another member? Why? Oh, my tiger wants to fuck him.

Maybe he *would* put a bullet in her brain. All of that ran through her head as she walked him out with her gun pointed at his back, after they made a stop on the first floor to do some quick clean-up. Crossing the driveway to the van, she was relieved to see that everyone else had cleared out. She was surprised and a bit unnerved that Lucifer hadn't even tried to run, but she just put it down as he knew there was no making it out of there without them tracking him down or killing him. Once at the van, she had switched out the rope for handcuffs and cuffed him to the metal bar that ran along the inner wall.

"I like the look on your face," Lucifer uttered with a smirk. "You want to look? I'm at your mercy. You could… look or… touch or… do whatever you want to me." His smirk grew into a heat-filled smile. He looked over at his bound hands cuffed to a bar in the back of the van, then back over at her. "Not that I would fight it, anyway."

Crush ground her teeth together and tried her best to stop the blush from gracing her cheeks, but she wasn't successful. "I have no idea what look you're talking about."

His chuckle was low and sexy. "Oh yeah, you do. I can practically see the sexy thoughts swirling around in that fucking gorgeous head of yours. What position were you thinking about?"

"I don't know what you're talking about," she bit out as she crouched in front of where he was sitting and finished tying his feet together, using the rope that Ranger had tied around his wrists before she cuffed him. Then she shifted to her knees and checked to make sure the handcuffs were securely fastened to the bar. Doing that brought her chest closer to his face, and she felt his breath against the tops of her breasts.

"Fuck," he mumbled under his breath. "You smell good."

Crush jerked back and cleared her throat, ignoring the way her tiger stretched and whined, wanting to play with their new toy. "You realize you're going to die, right?"

One of his brows popped up. "Has that been decided?"

"Your club has to pay for the shit you guys pulled," she spat at him, irritated that she wanted him, while at the same time wishing she could give in to her desires.

"What shit did I pull?" When he met her gaze head on, there was a fire in it that made her tiger want to sit back and purr at it.

"Whatever." She stood and headed for the front of the van. As she made her way to the front, she bent forward a bit to avoid hitting her head, groaning at the situation she was now in. Bullet and Axle were going to have her tiger's hide for this.

"Even the fucking government tells you what you did before they strap you to the injection table or the electric chair," he called from behind her, but she ignored him.

Slipping into the driver's seat, she glanced over at Pinky sitting in the passenger seat and ignored the smirk on her best friend and vice president's face. "Ready?"

"Should we gag him?" Pinky asked.

"Kinky," he said with a chuckle, "but I'm game."

"We don't have time," Crush replied, ignoring him. "We need to get out of here in case any police show up."

"What about cleanup?"

Crush shrugged. "What about it?"

"Pike's blood."

Crush grinned. "I might have quickly covered that entire area in bleach."

Pinky let out a sigh of relief.

"And started a fire in the trashcan on the other end of the bar."

As Crush put the van in drive and pulled away from the compound, the smell of smoke and the sound of windows shattering filled the air.

CHAPTER TWO

Crush

Back at the hotel, Crush didn't answer any of the silent questions swirling around her. She knew the Howlers and her club sisters were curious and wanted to know what she was thinking, but she wasn't about to lay that out for them. She was the president of the Claws, and her sisters wouldn't push it.

Instead of addressing the elephant in the room, they discussed what to do now, while Pike rested in one of their hotel rooms. He had passed out from his gunshot wound in his shoulder during the getaway. While they waited for him to recover a bit, they decided to see if they could load Pike's bike into the back of the van with Lucifer. If they could, Nails would drive the van while Pike rode along in the passenger seat. It took some effort and some shuffling, but they managed to get the bike in the back.

Crush ignored Lucifer as he tried to talk to her through the open van doors as she stomped over to her bike and mounted it. How in the world was she going to make this work? She couldn't let them kill her mate, but she couldn't put her selfish needs over the well-being of her club and the Howlers. Judging by the prowling and mewing of her tiger, Crush knew she was going to be fighting strongly conflicting instincts.

Pike came down as she stared at Lucifer in the van. She heard the Howlers talking off to the side of the parking lot, but she didn't pay attention to anything they said. Lucifer's dark eyes were locked on hers, and she was having a hard enough time fighting the urge to climb in that van and…

She watched as Pike walked up to the open door. Forcing herself to listen in, she heard Pike say, "There are some fucking rules. I'm not in the damn mood to deal with bullshit. So, you're going to accept that you're not getting away. You're going to realize I have no problem killing you without whatever knowledge you have. And you're not going to cause me even *a headache*. Do you understand? Nod your head if you fucking understand."

Crush knew Pike meant every word. Being the sergeant at arms, Pike took his job to protect the club, especially his president, seriously. That duty extended to the Claws only because Pike wanted it to. It wasn't required of him, but he required it of himself. Vixen, the sergeant at arms of the Claws, felt the same way about the Howlers. When Vixen needed a stand-in, Nails always stepped up, and she wasn't much different.

With both Pike and Nails in the van with Lucifer, it was going to be a tense drive. Crush could only hope Lucifer kept his damn mouth shut, at least until she figured out what she was going to do.

Lucifer

When they finally pulled Lucifer out of that fucking van hours later, everything hurt. His arms were aching from lack of movement. His ass hurt from sitting on the hard metal floor for hours. His balls ached from all the thoughts about the fucking badass goddess who cuffed him in the first place. Lucifer was happy to walk around. The walking eased the ache in most places, except at his crotch. There were only a couple of ways to ease that, and walking wasn't one of them.

The driver, the cute woman with long curly brown hair and observant hazel eyes, nodded to the crazy-looking man who had walked up and dragged Lucifer out. He heard someone say something about her being a part-time enforcer for her club. That boggled his mind. She was thin and fit, but he couldn't see her being too much of a danger. Now, the crazy-looking one with the long, wild hair sticking out everywhere and the unkempt beard? Lucifer would know he was an enforcer to the Howlers, even if he hadn't been wearing a patch that identified him as such.

"Who was she?" Lucifer watched as the woman walked away and around the corner of the building.

"Nails. And don't even think about it. You're not really her type, anyway."

When he was done speaking, one of the other men from the attack on the clubhouse approached. His cut said his name was Ranger. He had long, dark hair, and his eyes seemed to be constantly amused.

The two men led him over to a door in the building they stopped next to. He assumed they were in the back, because the only thing he saw was a stretch of parking lot surrounded by a tall chain-link fence with trees beyond it. Looking from side to side, he caught glimpses of other buildings, but he couldn't tell what they were.

Once inside, they brought him down to the basement and into a room that had not only a normal door but also a door made up of bars, like the door to a jail cell. Without a word, he was checked over for weapons before the wild, crazy-looking one pressed him into a chair, with more force than was necessary, and tied his hands behind his back. After that, the crazy one tied Lucifer's ankles to the legs of the metal chair he was in, like he was going to get up and try to go anywhere. If he tried, they'd just run him down, so why bother?

"Get comfortable," Ranger ordered with an evil grin, the man who had the rope and advised Lucifer to watch himself around the badass goddess. "Pres will be down when he's good and ready. Could be awhile."

"What about Sugartits? When will she be down?"

Lucifer thought he heard a growl come from the crazy one, but that could have been his imagination. Then the rope dude gave a humorless laugh, looked over at the crazy looking one, and commented, "Yeah, he won't make it long."

Crush

It wasn't as if Crush brought the man to the compound and just let him roam free. She rolled her eyes as Axle continued to pace and bitch and moan about having a Hell's Dogs member on their property when they could have just killed him and been done with it.

Crush hadn't told Axle that Lucifer was her mate. She had yet to accept it herself. She hadn't discounted killing him and wasn't even completely sure why she saved him to begin with. Yes, he was her mate, but he was also involved with the Hell's Dogs. Maybe it was because he was a prospect with the HDMC until the day of the ambush. Maybe it was because he was the last member of the HDMC Indiana chapter alive, and the last chance they had to get any information about the club's plans. She didn't know, or she wasn't ready to admit the reason to herself, but she had followed her gut and didn't regret the decision.

"Are you fucking listening to me," Axle bellowed from where he had stopped pacing to glare at her.

Leaning back against the wall next to his office door, Crush crossed her arms over her chest and met his stare with her own. "Not really," she answered honestly, shrugging.

She wanted to laugh at his anger, which had reddened his face and caused his eyes to flash silver light, a sign that his anger was at the edge of explosive. She wasn't worried about it. Axle had enough control to pull himself back. Besides, she could hold her own. It would be an interesting fight — wolf versus tiger. In nature, the tiger would take the win. When dealing with shifters, though, things weren't so cut and dry.

After he took a few calming breaths, Axle rested his hands on his hips and quietly asked, "What's going on?"

When she just stared back at him, Axle threw up his hands in irritation and huffed out a breath.

"I can't believe I have to even say this, but... Crush, whatever you say to me stays with me. Consider it courtesy from one president to another, as well as what friends do for each other. Please, *tell me what's going on.*"

Crush dropped her gaze to her feet and sighed. She didn't really want to talk about it, but he was right. If she expected him to give her time to figure things out and expected him to back her decisions, she needed to give him the information.

"Whatever it is... I can't help you if you don't trust me."

"He's my mate," she said in a voice so quiet a full human wouldn't be able to hear her.

Axle's sigh was deep, indicating he understood the gravity of the situation. "Okay. Do we know how involved he was with the Hell's Dogs BS?"

She shook her head and lifted her gaze again. "I haven't had the time to talk to him, really. I don't know if I should be the one. I mean… if he was… if he has to die, I don't want to get too… attached."

Every word was painful, like they were yanked directly from her soul. She wasn't used to showing vulnerabilities. She was the cold-hearted bitch men were afraid of. She didn't have emotions or weaknesses. The last time she showed that side of herself to Axle, he rejected her. Crush didn't blame him for that. It just made trusting others even harder than it already was for her. Showing him that side of her again sent panic through her system that she had to push down below the confusion and tension from finding her mate in the enemy's clubhouse.

She dropped her gaze again, but the toes of Axle's boots showed up in her view after a few moments.

"Crush," he said, softly, before he used his knuckle to make her lift her head and look at him. The look in his eyes wasn't the pity she expected. It was filled with understanding and support. "You're already attached. Your tiger did that for you. We won't do anything until we know who he is and what he's about." He dropped his hand, but held her gaze. "I have to believe that if he's your mate, he has to be redeemable. I have to warn you, though, I can't say the entirety of your club or mine are going to be so optimistic."

She swallowed hard and nodded, fully aware of how her club would react, at least initially. "I can't control the fact that he's my mate, but I'll deal with my club."

"I'll back you with the Howlers."

"Thanks," she bit out. She couldn't talk about it anymore. She'd had enough.

"I'll talk to him and see what I can find out."

She gave a nod and stormed out of his office. Rather than focus on her worry or her confusion, she focused on her anger at having a mate from an enemy club. How cruel could nature be? Magic? Science? Hormones? Whatever the hell created shifters. Regardless of the source, she didn't appreciate the tough spot she'd been put in.

Axle

After making his way down to the basement of the clubhouse, Axle stopped just inside the room where they were holding the Hell's Dogs member, Lucifer.

The man looked to be of average height, maybe a little shorter than most of the Howlers, but Axle wouldn't call him short. He wasn't the most muscular man, but he had obvious power, especially in his arms and chest. He could tell by the way the man's tee stretched across those areas that the man spent some time working on his physical fitness. Axle wondered if only muscle strength was important to Lucifer, or if that priority also stretched to character. If he had any chance of saving his life, it was having some kind of moral code that aligned with The Howlers and The Claws. For Crush's sake, Axle really hoped Lucifer had something good inside of him.

The man in question was sitting on a metal folding chair in the middle of the room with his arms tied together behind his back and his ankles tied to the legs of the chair.

Off to the right, Dragon was casually leaning against the stone wall, looking bored. Rock, who had relieved Ranger, was doing the same on the left. Bullet was standing just to the left of the door, his arms crossed across his chest and his feet spread and planted, but his angry eyes were locked on Lucifer.

Lucifer was staring back at Bullet, smirking, and seemed to enjoy Bullet's annoyance.

Axle wondered how much Bullet had figured out. The other possibility was Lucifer had been running his mouth about Crush. He wouldn't discount that.

Axle stepped in front of Lucifer, blocking his view of Bullet. "So, how exactly do you plan to save your life?"

Lucifer let out a humorless chuckle. "Thighs of Steel told me my death was a given."

By the very feline-like sound Bullet made, which made sense since he was a tiger shifter, Axle assumed the man was talking about Crush.

Axle ignored Bullet, but he noted the look of surprise on Lucifer's face. He just smiled and replied, "Well, I happen to be president of these assholes. If I tell them to take your head, they will take your head."

"Fucking gladly," Bullet bit out.

"If I tell them to drag you through the streets, they will tie you to the back of a truck and drag you through the streets."

"My truck is in the lot," Rock commented, like he was offering to let Axle borrow it to move a couch.

"If I told them you get to keep your life… for now, they would watch you like a dog watching a steak on the grill, but they would let you keep your life." Axle glanced behind him at Bullet, then he met Lucifer's stare again. "Unless you keep talking about Bullet's sister that way. I won't get in the middle of a man defending his sister's honor." Axle knew if he told Bullet to back off, he would, but Lucifer didn't need to know that. "So, again, how exactly do you plan to save your life?"

Lucifer was silent for a long moment. Then he dropped the smirk and asked, "If I give up everything I know about what the Kentucky chapter is planning, will you let me go?"

Axle shrugged. "Depends on what you know. If it's useful to us, we'll consider it. Your only other option is to die." Axle crouched down in front of Lucifer, his arms resting on his bent knees. "What's it going to be?"

Lucifer glanced up at Bullet, then back at Axle. "I have two conditions. First one, make him leave."

Axle didn't feel any threat from Lucifer. The man had been checked for weapons, and he was tied up. He couldn't do anything to Axle that he couldn't handle, even if he wasn't restrained. "Rock. Bullet. Leave." He didn't bother telling Dragon to leave. As an enforcer for the club, when Pike wasn't around, Dragon technically was responsible for Axle's safety. Dragon would fight him on it.

Bullet cursed under his breath as he left the room, followed by Rock.

Once they were gone, Axle asked, "What's the other condition?"

Lucifer lifted his chin a bit and said, "I'll only speak to her."

T.S. Tappin

Chapter Three

Crush

Sitting at the bar in the Howlers clubhouse, Crush took another drink of her beer, ignoring the looks from the other people in the room. Pinky, Nails, and Pumps were sitting at a table in the corner, behind Crush and to the left. Trip was sitting on a stool down the bar, leaning back against the wall. She knew Axle's VP, Skull, was at a table with Smoke and Zero, because she saw them when she walked in. They were all staring. She could feel their eyes on her.

Crush just took another drink of her beer and stared at the wall behind the bar. They all wanted to know why she saved Lucifer. They wanted to know what she was thinking. Well, they could keep fucking wondering. She was barely able to get the words out when she told Axle. She wasn't ready to go through it again.

"Since when do we let douchebags we have locked up decide who gets to be in the room when they're interrogated," Bullet bitched as he came down the hall with Rock. The sound of her brother's irritated voice set her on edge even more. He stepped into the room and took a seat on the stool a couple down from her. Rock took the stool on the other side of Bullet.

"We don't know he's a douchebag," Crush uttered before she could stop the words from coming out. *Damn it!* What was wrong with her?

Bullet scoffed and stared at her like she'd lost her mind. "He's a Hell's Dogs member," he blurted, as if that just made everything simple, easy-peasy.

"Barely. He was a prospect before yesterday." She downed her beer to stop herself from saying anything else.

Out of the corner of her eye, she saw Bullet open his mouth to say something, but he didn't manage to do so.

She was grateful when Dragon slipped onto the stool between her and her brother. "Axle wants you down there."

"What?" Crush set her empty beer bottle on the bar and looked over at Dragon.

"Axle said to send you down," he replied. "I didn't want to leave Axle down there by himself, but he Alpha-voiced me." Dragon's brows drew together. "He's never Alpha-voiced me before."

Crush's Fall

"Wh-Why does he want me down there?"

Dragon leaned a little closer and said, "Because Lucifer won't talk to anyone but you."

Her tiger purred inside her at the knowledge. She liked that he wanted to talk to her, but she hated it at the same time.

"Why?" Bullet stood and came to stand on Crush's other side. "Why does this dude have such a hard-on for you?"

She gave a shrug and shifted off the stool. "Guess I'll go down there," she mumbled, stomping away from them and down the hall.

Crush's tiger was prowling, eager to see their mate. She hated to admit she was eager to see him, too, and that disturbed her. Why couldn't she just hate him the way she would hate any other Hell's Dogs member?

She jogged down the steps and down the short hall in the basement before she stepped through the open door to the room in which they were holding Lucifer. She didn't look at him, for fear of what her reaction would be to the sight of him. Instead, she stopped next to Axle and met his gaze. "What's up?"

"He'll only speak to you. If you don't want to talk to him, let me know. I'll take care of it."

Crush cleared her throat and put her hands on her hips. She gave a nod. "Okay. I'll… uh… talk to him."

"Do you want me to stay in the room or go?"

T.S. Tappin

Crush hiked a brow and smirked. "Is Axle Weber, president and alpha, really asking me if I want to be left alone in a room with a man he doesn't know?"

Axle shrugged. "You reminded me, recently, that you are a president in your own right, and I need to respect that."

"True enough." Crush considered having Axle stay, but she didn't really want anyone to see how she responded to their prisoner. He made her anxious, and he turned her on. He pissed her off, and she wasn't sure she was going to be able to keep her head together completely. She didn't need any witnesses to that. "I'll be fine."

Axle gave a nod. Before he left the room, he turned and glared at Lucifer, making it clear he wouldn't have a problem ending the man if he didn't act right.

After Axle shut the door behind him, Crush paced the front of the room, preparing herself. It wasn't often she had to work so hard to keep her head on straight.

"I'm fine with you walking back and forth in front of me for as long as you want to," Lucifer commented.

Crush gritted her teeth in annoyance. At the sound of his voice, her tiger purred again and paced with anxiety. That wasn't helping her keep it together. She didn't want to talk to him. She wanted to untie him, *or not*, and fuck him. She wanted to claim him, mark him. It wasn't logical, but rather instinctual. It was animalistic.

If it was truly instinctual, like they were always told, then why would her instincts tell her he was the one for her? A Hell's Dogs member? A friend of drug-runners, if not one himself? She hated drugs. She despised the people who put them in the hands of children. She would never choose to be with someone like that.

Her tiger was telling her to shut the hell up with that nonsense and take him, claim him, keep him. She felt her breasts swell as his cocky smile flashed in her mind.

"Seriously, your ass looks fucking fantastic in those jeans," he commented, causing her to stumble a bit.

As he chuckled, she rebalanced and turned to face him. With her arms crossed, she took a breath in through her nose and slowly exhaled. "What's your real name?"

His gaze traveled down her body and back up, lingering on her hips, then her breasts. A grin slowly spread across his face. "You tell me yours, I'll tell you mine."

"You're not really in a position to make demands," she replied.

He hiked a brow. "Apparently, I am. It's why you're standing in the room right now, looking sexy as hell. Do you ever wear heels? Or do you just stomp on men's hearts in those boots?"

"What do you know about the Hell's Dogs?"

She watched as his tongue slid across his bottom lip. A tremble slid up her spine at the sight. She wanted that tongue used in some very specific areas.

"Give me one night with you, Sexy. Then you can stomp all over my heart in those boots. Bet it'd be worth it."

A wave of lust swamped her, nearly pulling her under. Her tiger was prowling, pushing, begging her to take him up on it. Crush closed her eyes to try to center herself.

"You want to, don't you? I can see the goosebumps on your arms." His voice dropped lower. "Just one night."

Images of him sprawled out naked on her bed, her straddling his hips, flashed into her mind. That was followed by him taking her from behind, taking her in the shower, bending her over the table. Her breath caught as she was assaulted by the vivid scenes, one after another.

No. No. She swallowed hard and shook her head. She knew he was seeing right through her, but she couldn't be distracted by her lust. Taking a deep breath, Crush slowly exhaled. At the same time, she told her tiger to sit down and shut the hell up.

Then she opened her eyes and asked, "What is your name?"

He chuckled again. "Maverick Brooks. What's yours?"

"Meredith Welles." She took a step closer. "What do you know that you think would save your life if you shared it with us?"

"Well, it depends on what you're interested in. Who they were selling to? Who their allies were? What clubs are planning what in retaliation? What women were taking which member's cock? What do you want to know?"

She took another step forward, putting her ten feet in front of him. "All of it."

When Crush saw the lascivious grin slowly form on his face, she knew she wasn't going to like the next words out of Lucifer's mouth... or would like them too much. Turns out, it was the latter.

"A kiss for a tip."

Crush rolled her eyes, fighting hard not to let him know she liked that idea. "No."

"What's wrong with a kiss? It's not like you don't want to kiss me. We both know you do." He bit his bottom lip as he stared at her mouth.

"This isn't a date."

"I dunno." He shrugged as much as he could with his hands tied behind him. "We're talking, getting to know each other better, throwing each other flirty looks, giving off signals. Sounds date-ish to me. And I'm having a great time. What about you?"

"You're twisted," Crush commented and snorted a laugh.

"Yeah, but I'm thinking that's exactly how you like 'em."

Stopping herself from laughing again, Crush shook her head and dropped her gaze to the floor.

"What? Are you scared of kissing me? Scared you might want to do it again? Scared you might want more?"

Crush knew it was a trap. She *knew* it. But she couldn't stop herself from shooting him a glare and saying, "I'm not scared of kissing you, Lucy."

And just like she knew he would, he grinned again and taunted, "Prove it."

She just stared at him for a long time, wondering what the best way was to handle it. Should she try to get close, win his trust? Should she use the flirting to her advantage? Or should she just treat him like she would anyone else she interrogated?

It was a tough decision. If she got close to him and they ended up having to kill him, it would be much more difficult for her to make it through, but just treating him like any other prisoner didn't seem to be working.

She took a few steps toward him. "Okay. Here's the deal. I will give you a kiss for every question you answer. If at any time I feel like you are just playing me, I will leave this room and tell them you have nothing to offer. Do you understand?"

He gave a nod. "But I want a kiss to seal the deal."

Rolling her eyes, Crush moved closer until she was standing about a foot in front of his knees. She bent forward, her gaze locking on his. She smirked, figuring if they were taking the flirty route, she better hold up her end. "Ready to have your world rocked? I'm about to ruin you for any other woman."

"Fuck," he quietly groaned, his gaze dropping to her lips. "Give me what you got, Babe."

Not allowing herself to second guess her plan, she went for it. She leaned closer until her lips were a few inches from his. She lingered, letting the anticipation build, making him long for it. When she noticed that his breath was coming quicker, she nipped at his bottom lip. She released his lip, only to soothe it with a caress of her tongue, making him groan again. That's when she dipped in and gave him one hell of a kiss, her tongue slipping in and tangling with his. Just when he was getting into it, his eyes closing, she straightened and returned to her pacing.

Pretending her heart wasn't about to pound out of her chest from the overdose of pleasure that had coursed through her when their tongues touched, Crush asked, "Who were they dealing to?"

He was panting slightly, staring at her with blatant desire burning in his brown eyes. She also noticed a new determination there. She wasn't sure what he was determined about, but that wasn't important at the moment.

"They weren't really dealing to anyone in Michigan or Canada. They were transporting. They were the middlemen. Leighton has set up shop in Toronto. He didn't want his GR associates to know he was expanding."

Crush knew he meant Grand Rapids, Michigan, and that Leighton was one of the leaders of a drug trafficking organization, and nodded for him to continue.

"They would want in. So, he was having HD Indiana transport to his soldier in Toronto, some guy with family connections to Leighton. I don't know how exactly.

T.S. Tappin

Leighton wanted it stable and lucrative before he moved his headquarters there."

"He was planning on leaving Michigan?"

"Not completely. His base of operations was going to move, but his Michigan business wouldn't stop. But I guess you guys or the Howlers or whoever the fuck made that difficult when you ambushed our guys."

"Were you there at the ambush?"

He raised an eyebrow. "I answered two questions."

Giving a slight smile, Crush stepped up in front of him and bent down again. She didn't tease him as much. She just pressed her lips to his and lingered. When she pulled back, he tried to follow, but the restraints stopped him.

"Damn it," he growled, panting again. "Untie my hands, Babe."

She chuckled. "Not happening, *Babe*. Were you involved in their drug business?"

He swallowed hard, his eyes flashing fire. "No. I was a prospect. I was good at being around and not being noticed. They didn't guard their conversations the way they should have. I just learned shit from paying attention and not drawing any attention to myself." He huffed out a breath. "Look. I don't do drugs. I drink. I might hit a joint or bowl every now and again, but that's it. When I found out about the drug business, I considered bowing out of prospecting, but things changed. They found out you had one of their girls. Pres and his brother, Digger, started recruiting to send a crew to get her back. Then you guys killed Digger…

or the Howlers did. Whatever. I could understand rescuing a member's woman. I understood wanting revenge for the death of a member. So, I didn't leave. The drugs were shifted to the Ohio chapter. I was fine with that. Transport through Michigan wasn't going to be HD Indiana's responsibility. The mission became taking down the Howlers, taking over Michigan."

"Christel wasn't theirs. And Digger died because he was stupid and fucked with Howlers territory and put our families in danger. Pres died because he kidnapped and assaulted our family."

"Fair enough." He sighed. "I didn't know all of that. I just knew what I heard. You can't fault me for that shit. I was a prospect. I didn't make decisions. I didn't get a vote."

She believed him, but she wasn't sure if that was just wishful thinking. Was it just the part of her that desperately wanted her mate not to be a complete asshole? It was easier to believe he didn't know the truth. Was that why she believed him?

T.S. Tappin

CHAPTER FOUR

Crush

Crush pushed her doubts aside and asked, "Who are their allies, and what are they planning?"

"I answered your question. Where's my kiss?" Lucifer's smile wasn't as intense as it was before, but there was somehow an intimacy to it. She didn't examine that for too long.

Bending back down, she braced herself with her palms high on his thighs. His thighs were thicker than they looked, harder, stronger. Instead of kissing his lips again, she went for the gusto. She bent her head to the side and kissed a path across his jaw to his ear. After giving the lobe a nibble and a suck, she whispered, "Tell me everything I need to know to protect my club and my family — that includes the Howlers. If you do, and give me everything, I'll straddle your lap and give you your next kiss from there."

He turned his head and licked along the side of her neck. "You play hardball."

She pulled back enough to look into his eyes. "You gonna tell me what I need to know?"

His attention dropped from her eyes to the generous view of cleavage she knew she was giving him. "If you sit there while I talk and promise a good, long kiss when I'm done, I'll tell you everything I know." His gaze returned to hers. "And I'll be an open book to you and the Howlers. I have no interest in bringing the Howlers down. From what I've seen since you handcuffed me in that van, the Claws and the Howlers just seem like two clubs who just want to protect the people they care about. Sounds pretty kickass to me."

Her heart skipped a beat at his words and the sincerity in his tone. She really hoped he wasn't playing her.

Crush held his gaze as she shifted and took a seat on his lap, straddling him. She rested her palms on his shoulders and sighed. "Tell me everything, so I have a chance of saving your life. We'll talk about what you're going to do after."

He didn't ask what she meant by that. He just opened his mouth and gave what she asked for. The information made fear steadily grow in her chest. When he was done, she closed her eyes and shook her head.

Crush's Fall

They were in so much trouble. She didn't know how she and Axle were going to fix things. The thought of going to war against that big of a group terrified her. Even being shifters, there were limits to the size of an army that they could take. What Lucifer was talking about was... more than she could comprehend.

"Tell me you have a habit of exaggeration," she practically whispered. It was odd for her to be that vulnerable, but she was too stunned to rebuild her walls.

"I wish I could, Crush," he said, softly. "And I wish I could hold you right now. You look like you need a hug."

"Stop trying to get me to untie your hands just so you could escape," she mumbled.

"Crush, look at me."

Still reeling from what he had told her, Crush opened her eyes and looked at him. "What?"

"I'm not trying to escape. I haven't tried to escape once. From the moment you rounded that wall and stepped into the HD church room, I have done everything you told me to. I'm not asking for you to untie me for any reason other than you look like you need a hug, and I want to be the man to do that. You could tie me back up and go back to hating my guts afterward." He smiled. "Besides, we're in a building with a shit ton of bikers upstairs... and I'm in a state I'm not at all familiar with. Where in the hell would I go?"

T.S. Tappin

Not even taking a moment to think about how stupid the move was, Crush reached around behind him, let a claw out, and cut through the fabric that had been restraining him.

"How did you—" He tried to wrap his arms around her and groaned as the ache in his shoulders and arms hit him. On the second try, he managed to get them around her.

Crush didn't examine why she was rubbing the ache out of his shoulders as he held her gaze.

"Feels a lot better, Crush. Thank you."

Resting her forehead against his, she closed her eyes and just let them be two people wrapped up in each other. She wasn't sure what was going to happen when they were forced to return to the real world, so she was allowing herself to savor the moment.

He tightened his arms around her until she was forced to slide her arms around his neck. "One last kiss, then you can tie me back up and do what you need to."

Without opening her eyes, she tilted her head and kissed him. This time, she let him take over. They kissed for a while, sometimes lazily, softly. Other times, his kisses were intense, urgent, demanding. All the while, his hands caressed her back and sides, cradled her head, squeezed her thighs. It was the best make-out session she had ever had.

It wasn't until after she re-tied his hands and was heading upstairs that she realized she still had her gun in the holster of her cut and her knife strapped to her ankle. If he wanted to do her harm, he could have killed her in an instant.

Maybe it wasn't wishful thinking. Maybe Lucifer really was the guy he said he was.

Axle

Sitting at the bar, Axle was lost in thought, trying to figure out what to do about Lucifer and how to convince his club to be okay with the man keeping his life. Honestly, Axle would feel bad ending the man since he was Crush's mate, but that wouldn't stop him from doing it if it was necessary.

He was pulled out of his thoughts by a tap on the shoulder from Pike. Sliding off his stool, he and Pike met Crush half-way down the bar.

"What?" Axle's voice was firm and calm, but the panic in Crush's eyes had him on edge.

"Not out here," she replied, her voice matching his calm tone.

"Fuck that," Bullet said as he stopped next to his sister. "What's going on?"

Crush turned her head and gave Bullet a hard look. "You will find out when your president informs your club. Right now, I need to discuss it with your president." Then she turned on her heel and headed for Axle's office. "Pinky and Vixen. I want you in there."

Axle followed her, calling over his shoulder, "Skull. Pike. My office."

It was a tight fit for six of them to occupy Axle's office, but they made it work. Axle took a seat in his desk chair, Pike and Skull flanking him on their feet. Crush and Pinky took seats in the chairs across the desk from Axle. Vixen stayed on her feet, standing between her president and VP, facing Axle.

He started the conversation. "Okay. What has you spooked?"

Crush didn't delay, and Axle watched her expression as she opened her mouth and said, "Hell's Dogs chapter Ohio and Kentucky have been in contact with the UpRiders to join them. They also recruited the Reapers from New York, Wisconsin, and Tennessee. They are planning to take down both of our clubs and take over Michigan. He doesn't know when or how they are going to attack us, but he said he knows for sure they are planning to. Ax, he said the mission is being referred to as the *Fang Extraction*."

Pike uttered, "Do they know... about us?"

Crush shrugged. "Lucifer said he once asked why they were calling it that and was told he'd find out why when he became a member. If it was just because of the names of our clubs, why wouldn't he just say that? Why would the reason for the name be kept quiet but not the mission itself from the prospects? I think it's best to assume they know."

Fuck.

Pike asked, "Ax, you don't think Hawkin passed that bit of knowledge on, do ya?"

Axle shook his head. He knew Hawkin well enough to know the man wouldn't do that. He may be a human, but he was a trustworthy ally. Owner of Milhawk Investigations, located in Warden's Pass, Mick Hawkin was a rule-follower, at least more than the Howlers were. He avoided breaking laws as often as possible. Even though they had different definitions of justice, Hawkin wouldn't go back on his word, especially without giving a warning. "He only knows about me. Besides, Hawkin is pretty strait-laced. I don't see him helping the Hell's Dogs or their allies." He sat back in his chair. "We're being watched."

"What do you want to do?"

"We need to take it to the table, but we need to relocate, reinforce, prepare… but all of that takes time."

"Joint church?" Crush stood.

Axle nodded. "Tomorrow morning?"

Crush nodded and headed for the door.

"Crush," Axle called out. When she stopped and looked back at him, Axle stood. "What are you going to do with Lucifer?"

"I don't think he had any part in the bullshit. I think he earned his freedom, but I'm not the only president around here. Talk to him. We'll talk about it at church."

Axle gave a nod. "We'll put him up in a room and have it watched."

She nodded back and left, with her VP and sergeant at arms following her.

Pike and Skull took the seats Crush and Pinky had just vacated. Skull huffed out a sigh. "What in the hell are we supposed to do to prepare? That's not a small group. Most of them may not be big chapters, but together..."

"First, we need names. We need to gather as much information about the club members and their numbers as possible. We need to find somewhere else to keep our families safe. The compound is too public. We can't protect it from a group that large. Then we need to rally as many shifters together as we can."

"Do we know that many shifters?" Pike inquired.

Axle ran his fingers through the hair on the top of his head and down the back until he was able to rest his hand around his nape, feeling his stress level build with each passing moment. "Dad would know more. Gonna have to call in Joker and Thrash."

There was a knock on the office door.

"Yeah," Axle called out.

When the door opened, Siren stepped into the room, his phone in his hand. "I don't know what's going on, but I gotta go to Florida. Pops is in the hospital. His neighbor said it's bad and I need to come down there." Siren swallowed hard. "I gotta go."

Oh, fuck. Axle stood and rounded his desk. He pulled Siren into a hug and backslap. "Yeah, brother, you have to go. But listen, keep your ears and eyes open. We'll talk once you know more about Pops, but we've got enemies recruiting allies all over this half of the country. Don't let your guard down."

"Maybe we should send some members with him," Skull suggested.

Axle thought on it for a moment. "I think it might draw attention. A single rider, no colors, could be anyone."

"I'll be fine. I'll stay alert," Siren said, then left the room.

Pike sighed. "Pixie's not getting a wedding anytime soon, is she?"

As grins lightened the faces of his president and VP, Pike chuckled. "I ordered her to marry me during sex, and she basically told me to kiss her ass with that shit. So, I still have to ask her, but it's going to happen."

It was his turn for the hug and backslap. "Happy for you, brother," Axle told him.

Skull gave Pike's shoulder a squeeze. "Fucking thrilled."

"Thanks. Think Dorothy would meet me at her shop? Gotta get a ring on my woman's finger." Dorothy was the mother of the woman Skull was seeing. They were full-humans and had no clue about shifters, but the Howlers always tried to support others within the family unit or adjacent to it. If someone needed shoes and one of the Howlers was dating an owner of a shoe store, that was where they would go.

Skull nodded with a smile. "I'm sure she'd be happy to. I'll make the call. When you want her there?"

"In an hour?"

Skull nodded and pulled out his cell, leaving the office.

Pike met the hard gaze of his president and asked, "But seriously, are we really about to organize a shifter-biker army to fight another biker army? That shit's fucking insane."

Axle let out a humorless laugh. "About as insane as the fact we can shift into fucking animals."

The next day... Crush

In joint-church, Crush let Axle address his club first. She just stared down at the tabletop in front of her. She was sitting at the opposite end of the long table from Axle. Her club was sitting and lined up on her right across the table from where the Howlers were doing the same. Crush was not about to try to make eye contact with anyone. She was still too raw for that. And what she was about to do would only make her even more on edge.

"In normal circumstances," Axle began, his president voice in full effect, "we would end this guy without hesitation, now that we know everything he knows. And ending him is still an option, but normally, we wouldn't be dealing with such complications. Lucifer is not only a new member of the Hell's Dogs MC, having only patched in yesterday, but he is also the mate of the Tiger's Claw MC president." A deep breath. "Because of that, I feel it's important that we are all on record with how we feel. First, we will vote on whether you feel this is something that should be decided by vote or by me."

The Howlers didn't wait for Axle to ask. They just started talking, and the consensus was not one of them wanted to have to make that decision. The only one who hesitated in telling Axle to make the decision was Bullet. Crush could feel his stare on her for a long while, making her anxiety and frustration grow, before she heard her brother say, "You make it, Pres."

Axle didn't take much time to think before he declared he wouldn't be ordering Lucifer's death, but if it was decided that Lucifer needed to die, he was offering the service of the Howlers.

Relief coursed through Crush, followed by a good amount of shame at wanting an enemy of their clubs to be saved. Shouldering the responsibility of keeping several people safe and trying to justify keeping her mate alive had her nearly at her limit. Feeling as if they were all scrutinizing her every movement, she cleared her throat and addressed the room. "With his connection to me, I feel... unqualified to make this decision. I couldn't do it without bias. I need my sisters to decide what we do." She lifted her gaze and looked over her club. "We'll vote. Know I will not hold your vote against you. Pinky?"

"I can't vote to kill your mate, so no," Pinky said, and shook her head.

"Same," Nails said, standing behind Pinky.

"I fucking can," Vixen growled. "His club did a lot of fucking horrible things to our family."

And so, it went. Most of the Claws voted to keep Lucifer alive, but Ginger and Foxy agreed with Vixen.

The only member left to vote was Pumps. Her connection to the Hell's Dogs would no doubt make it a difficult decision for her. Yes, they did bad stuff to Pumps, but she knew some of them from childhood.

Nervous and feeling claustrophobic in the overly filled room, Crush looked down the table at Pumps, along with everyone else. She blew a breath out and up, making her blond bangs flutter. Worry creased her forehead. "If he was a member I was familiar with, it would make this an easier decision. But there wasn't a member named Lucifer when I was connected to the club. I can't just say kill him, though, because it's a small town, and they could have recruited someone I know, so…"

"I say," Ginger began, her eyes studying Pumps, "let Pumps see him. If she cares for him, let him live. If she doesn't, or if she says he's a bad dude, we can re-vote."

Crush shrugged. "Sounds fine to me."

Axle ordered Pike and Dragon to retrieve their prisoner. The two men stood and headed out of the room. While they waited for Pike and Dragon to return, Crush made it a point not to make eye contact with anyone. She wasn't sure why she felt so damn ashamed, though. It wasn't as if she chose to have Lucifer as her mate. She didn't have much say in the matter. She didn't really know what or who made the decision about the pairings, but it sure as hell wasn't her.

Less than ten minutes later, they escorted Lucifer into the room. His hands were cuffed in front of him, but he looked unharmed. With Dragon, you never knew. Lucifer could have come in with a broken arm, and Dragon would have shrugged and said Lucifer slipped.

Crush was surprised when tears filled Pumps's eyes, and she started laughing. She didn't ask Lucifer any questions. She just said, "He's good."

Lucifer was standing near the end of the table, with shock all over the man's face. "Chrissy? *You're* the Christel they were talking about? Well, shit, it's been forever!"

After some questions from Axle and Crush, Pumps explained that she went to middle school and part of high school with Lucifer, who she referred to as 'Mav,' and they met because he beat the shit out of a boy who pulled her hair on the bus.

Lucifer jumped in with some more information at that point. Apparently, he moved and lived in Chicago for the rest of his high school years. He tried college, but decided it wasn't for him after a couple of years. Then he moved back to Reichart.

By then, Pumps had already lived through her experience with the Hell's Dogs and had escaped to Michigan. Childhood friends reunited.

With his friendship with Pumps and the pull he was obviously feeling toward Crush, Lucifer wouldn't be losing his life yet. Crush wouldn't say Warden's pass would be a carefree place for Lucifer, not for a long time. He'd have to prove himself, and the clubs weren't going to make it easy. With what was coming their way, he'd have opportunities to step up to the plate. She only hoped he would. Otherwise, she would have to end him, and Crush wasn't sure she would make it through that.

Chapter Five

Three months later... Lucifer

Lucifer watched her from across the room. Crush was wearing her typical jeans, tight black V-neck tee, cut, and black biker boots with the silver accents. Even in her casual attire, she was the prettiest woman in the room. Her dark brown hair was shiny and straight, with a fresh dye job of her purple tips. They were more of a burgundy when they first met, but he liked the purple. Hell, he would like it no matter what she did with her hair.

Her eyes were intriguing, intense. The way the brown and green swirled together made him want to stare into them for hours, *days*. The green popped when she was angry, which only made him want to piss her off as often as possible. It also made him wonder what color would pop when she was coming on his hand or his cock. He knew it would happen someday, but he hadn't quite earned the pleasure to witness it yet.

T.S. Tappin

Lucifer liked that she was tall, only a couple of inches short of six feet and thick. She was muscular, strong, and fit, but she had thighs and an ass, both of which he wanted to grip in his hands while she rode him. A desire to storm across the room, take her hand, and pull her out of the clubhouse was strong. He wanted to take her to the nearest bedroom and do all the things that had been rolling through his head for months. Lucifer had respect for her and her need to make him work for it, though, so he didn't do anything to push her on that… yet.

When she stepped away from Pinky and Kitty, and headed for the front door, he took another drink of his beer and set it down on the bar top. Then he followed her.

Picking up his pace, he caught up with her as she rounded the front corner of the strip mall across the street. Lucifer knew she was headed for her personal apartment, where she could lock him out, and his hopes for any kind of connection would be dashed.

"Crush," he said as he came up next to her and matched her pace.

She huffed out a deep sigh. "I'm not in the mood for your bullshit, Lucy."

He let out a chuckle. "What is wrong with my bullshit?"

"You're infuriating, annoying, exhausting."

"I'd like to exhaust you," he told her and stepped in front of her, forcing her to stop. They were near the rear corner, and the door to the stairwell that led up to her apartment and the church room for the Tiger's Claw MC was fifty feet away.

He looked into those eyes of her and saw the green spark as she narrowed them on him. She opened her mouth and accused, "You couldn't exhaust me if you tried."

Lucifer stepped closer, leaving only a few inches between them, and replied, "How can you know that when you haven't taken me for a ride?"

"I know men like you, Lucy. The hype is usually better than the reality."

Lucifer gripped her hips and turned Crush, walking her back until she was up against the brick of the building. He knew she had the ability to end it at any point, and he was curious about how long and how far she'd let it go on. Leaning his face closer, he lingered a couple of inches from her lips and gazed into her eyes. "I want you. I want to strip you down and fuck you until you can't breathe... *can't move*. You want it, too. I can tell by the way your eyes flare when you look at me, the way your breathing picks up when I get close. Say you want it, Crush."

She stared at him, her chest heaving and the green in her eyes popping, making Lucifer wonder if she was *actually* going to give in. Then she grabbed ahold of his tee and yanked him forward. Her lips hit his, and they were on. As he fought with her to take over the kiss, nipping and licking along her lips, he slid one of his hands around her hip to her ass and pulled her against him. His other hand slid up her side, under her cut, as her lips separated and allowed him entrance. He slid his tongue inside, caressing hers, as his hand reached for her tit and cupped it.

Her perfect breast overfilled his hand and made him yearn to nibble and suck on the mound. He swallowed her moan and found her nipple with his thumb. As he caressed it, he pressed his erection against her.

Then she was no longer in his arms. He looked to the left and saw her rounding the corner. He followed her and saw her open the door and step inside. He picked up his pace, but when he reached the door to the stairway, it was shut and locked.

"Fuck," he groaned and leaned back against the brick wall next to the door. It was going to be yet another night with his cock in his hand.

Crush

When she entered her apartment, she crossed her open living space to the window that overlooked the front of the strip mall and the rest of the compound. Looking out, it took a few minutes, but she saw Lucifer round the corner of the building and cross the parking lot in front of the mall, heading for the apartment building.

The man was fucking beautiful, and he could kiss like a fucking dream. He wasn't soft and gentle often. In the few kisses they had shared, he was demanding. Rough. Intense. The few times he was soft, it was only in preparation for another round of urgent and hard. He made her heart race and her pussy clench with just a deliberate look. She wanted nothing more than to drag him up to her bed and let him have a go at exhausting her.

She could have done that, but she knew it would mean disaster for her heart. He wasn't a kind soul, a gentle force, or a calming presence for her. She was grateful for that because it would bore her to tears. No, he was quite the opposite. He was bold, insistent, demanding. He would be a wrecking ball to the careful wall she had built around her heart.

They would battle for control of their relationship if she were to allow them to get that far. Unfortunately, she worried she wouldn't have the strength to keep the upper hand. The thought of letting him be in charge grated on her nerves and made panic rise in her chest.

But it was so difficult to deny him when he gave her that smirk and verbally poked her at every turn.

As she watched him reach the far edge of the parking lot, a dozen yards from the apartment building, she resigned herself once again that while he may be her mate, they weren't right for each other. They couldn't be, no matter what her kind said about mates being perfectly balanced.

Stepping away from the window, she pulled off her cut and headed for her bed to spend yet another night alone.

T.S. Tappin

The next night... Lucifer

In the main room of the Howlers clubhouse, Lucifer watched as Crush talked and flirted with a man across the room. He didn't know who the guy was, only that he came with the guy that Vixen was seeing. The dude was all wrong for Crush, though. He was too polished, too pulled together. His hair was short and perfect, not a hair out of place. The polo shirt he was wearing was fucking pink, and he was wearing sneakers, for fuck's sake. Everything about the guy screamed *banker*. Crush was not a banker's wife. She was a biker's woman. *His woman*. She just needed to accept that.

When the banker-in-training went to use the restroom, Lucifer made his move. He crossed the room and sidled up next to Crush. Leaning in close, he whispered in her ear, "Do you think he'll regale you with the benefits of spreadsheets while he *makes love* to you, missionary style?"

Crush stayed leaning back against the wall and only turned her head. Looking into his eyes, she smirked. "As opposed to what? A two-minute railing in the bathroom, where you fumble to find my clit?"

Lucifer loved it when she sparred with him. It heated his blood. "Oh, Sugartits, it would be the best two minutes of your life."

At the table a few yards away, Pinky spewed the drink she just took of her beer across the surface as she burst out with laughter.

Crush's smirk faded, and a scowl took its place. "If you like your balls where they are, you'll stop calling me Sugartits."

"It's a compliment." His gaze dropped to her breasts encased in another tight V-neck tee, this time white. "I bet they would be sweet as hell to suck on."

"You have a motherfucking death wish," Bullet growled. Lucifer looked behind him to see Bullet storming across the room toward him.

When Bullet made it halfway, Axle stepped in front of him and stopped him with a hand to his chest and some low words that Lucifer couldn't hear.

"I'm going to fucking kill you," Bullet called out over Axle's shoulder.

Lucifer shrugged. "Just wait until I'm done with Crush first, then you can give it your best shot."

Axle bit out a curse and wrapped his arms around Bullet, then he dragged Bullet out of the room.

"If you think Axle will always save you," Crush began, "then you're dumber than I thought you were."

"I'm not scared of your brother, Sugartits."

Crush chuckled. "But you should be." Then she walked over to the table Pinky was at and helped her clean up the beer.

Crush

When the evening began to wind down and *Jared McCarthy* began giving hints about wanting to go home with her, Crush was irritated. It didn't bother her he wanted to spend the night or that he wanted to fuck. Normally, she'd be all over it. He was exactly what she didn't want in a man, so it would be easy to fuck him and kick him out. No, it wasn't that he was a douchebag who was masquerading as a decent guy. It was that every time she thought about fucking, the guy in bed with her was Lucifer.

The last thing she wanted to do was bring Jared back to her place, get naked, and start fucking, only to have to fight her brain when it attempted to switch out Jared for Lucifer. If that was what was going to happen, she might as well go home alone and dip into her treasure chest for assistance.

Taking Lucifer home wasn't an option. He was too… *Lucifer*. She was afraid it would take one orgasm for him to demolish the carefully constructed walls she had built around herself.

Axle had been the last straw, but he wasn't the reason for her walls. The walls were up to protect herself from the bullshit *but you're a girl* comments she had heard all of her life. She used to let the walls down with men she was dating, but twice, men had demanded she *soften up* and *submit* to them as soon as feelings had gotten involved. She was who she was, and she wouldn't be changing for anyone. Instead of dropping her walls, after that, she strengthened them, fortified them, turned them into brick-encased steel.

For a brief moment, she thought she could drop them with Axle, but he had met Gorgeous and put an end to all of that. That was the day she decided she'd just be alone. She didn't need a man and wasn't even sure she wanted one for the long haul. Crush had been happy with her life since then.

Then Lucifer barreled into her life and shook shit up. Now she couldn't even get herself off without him being on her brain. That shit was not okay. Hell, he'd replaced The Rock as the cover of her mental spankbank, and her self-control in those moments was non-existent. She automatically pictured him when she touched herself. It was unfair, really. How was a girl supposed to keep her head on straight when a rough, pretty biker was constantly trying to get in her pants?

"So, what do you say?"

Crush's body jolted at the sound of Jared's voice. She turned her head and looked at him again. He was a very nice-looking man. She would even call him handsome. He would work just fine for a one-night stand, but it wasn't going to happen. It wasn't right to fuck him and think about Lucifer.

"I'm not feeling it tonight," she said and walked away.

As she passed Lucifer on her way toward the front door, she flipped him the bird and rolled her eyes when he chuckled.

Fucking Lucifer.

T.S. Tappin

Chapter Six

Three months later... Lucifer

As Lucifer entered the clubhouse, he wasn't sure how Axle would take his offer. Either Axle would be on board and all for it, or he would take Lucifer's life for even suggesting it. Either way, he was ready for whatever response he got.

He was done with waiting around for the Howlers to deem him trustworthy. Without having much opportunity to prove it, he was stuck in this never-ending loop of to trust or not to trust, and he was fucking over it.

About a week ago, Lucifer decided he needed to figure out a way to turn things around. After learning what he could about the Howlers, he determined that the best way to earn their trust was to stand up for the things they believed in and show them he believed in them, too. And he believed in keeping drugs out of kids' hands and protecting the unprotected.

It was the type of mission he could put his all into. Something he could be proud of. If that meant he was finally accepted by the Howlers and the Claws, that was even better.

At first, he wondered how he could get it across to them he was an asset to them, then it hit him. He had connections. Growing up the way he did and living the adult life that he lived, he knew people. He knew people fighting for the side of good, but he also knew people who were perpetuating the bad. If he used those connections to further the mission of the Howlers, he hoped it would go a long way to proving his usefulness and deem him trustworthy.

Lucifer knocked on Axle's office door and took a deep breath to prepare himself for whatever came out of the meeting.

After a moment, the door opened a few inches, and Pike was looking out at him. "Yeah?"

"I need to talk to Axle."

"About?"

Lucifer rolled his eyes. Sometimes, it was a pain in the ass dealing with the Howlers. Axle was one of the biggest men in the club, but the members, especially Pike and Dragon, acted like he was incapable of protecting himself.

"I need to talk to Axle… not one of his minions."

"Let him in, Pike."

Pike glared at him as he slowly opened the door and let Lucifer enter the room. He knew Pike was picturing slitting his throat, and he didn't fucking care.

"What do you need, Lucifer?" Axle was sitting behind his desk, leaned back in his chair, with his feet propped up.

"A minute alone, if you can manage to get your dog to leave the room."

Axle raised a brow. "You know how clubs work. He's doing his job."

Lucifer shrugged. "And we both know you can protect yourself against me."

Axle chuckled quietly before looking over at Pike and nodding toward the door.

As Pike left the room, he uttered, "Remember that killing you won't get me kicked out of the club, asshole."

Lucifer grinned as he waited for Pike to close the door behind him, not giving Pike the pleasure of taking him seriously. After the door clicked shut, he took a seat in one of the chairs across the desk from Axle and met the man's curious gaze.

"He's going to kill you, one of these days, if Bullet doesn't get to you first."

Lucifer shrugged. "If their egos are that fragile, they need to work on thickening their skin."

Axle rolled his eyes. "What did you need to talk to me about?"

"I think I have a way to help the Howlers. I want to earn my place here, earn the trust of the clubs. And I think I can do that using my contacts."

"You've got my attention," Axle mumbled, staring at him, studying him.

Lucifer launched into his past in Chicago and various connections he had to mafia families in the city. He also told Axle he knew of some members of Leighton's team and might be able to weasel his way in to play insider.

Elijah Leighton was a drug lord that ran the lower Michigan territory, distributing all over lower Michigan and into Canada, Ohio, Indiana, and the Chicagoland area. Leighton grew up in Chicago. His younger brother, Leo, had graduated with Lucifer and his friend, Liam Agosti. Liam and Leo were never friends, but they both seemed to get along with Lucifer. Leo hung around with Jensen Maloy and his crew. Back then, they weren't into anything but picking up chicks and partying on the weekend. Oh, how things have changed.

"I still have Leo Leighton's number. We've kept in touch, but I haven't spoken to him since the shit went down in Indiana."

Axle lowered his feet to the floor. His amused curiosity turned to focused attention as he leaned forward and placed his elbows on the top of the desk, his eyes locked on Lucifer. "You have a connection to Leighton?"

Lucifer gave a nod. "I might be able to work my way into his crew. Leo would get me a job with his brother if I told him I was reeling after my club was decimated. I could use the angle that I held a grudge against the Howlers and was willing to do what I needed to in order to get back at you."

Axle was nodding. "And you'd report back to me?"

"Every chance I got." Lucifer took a deep breath and let it out slowly. "I know you don't have a reason to trust me, but I just want a chance to prove it."

Axle was quiet for a long moment before he finally let out a sigh and sat back in his chair. "I have to run it past Crush."

"I thought *you* ran your club," Lucifer uttered.

One of Axle's brows went up. "You're walking a fucking line, Lucifer. I *do* run my club. And she runs hers. What affects us, affects the Claws. Crush has to give her approval."

"Well, then let's get Sugartits over here and see what she has to say."

Axle snorted a laugh as he picked up his phone from the desk and dialed a number. "She's going to cut off your balls, if you keep calling her that."

"That would involve her touching them, so I'm all for it."

Crush

When Crush answered Axle's call, she heard him tell someone, She's going to cut off your balls, if you keep calling her that.

She realized who Axle was talking to when she heard the reply, *That would involve her touching them, so I'm all for it.*

Crush let out a very un-catlike growl before she uttered, "What?"

Axle cleared his throat and said, "Hey. I have to run something past you. Got a minute to meet?"

"You in your office?"

"Yeah."

"Be right there." She ended the call and stood up from her island in her apartment. The club finances could wait. She didn't organize or process the financials, but she looked them over every quarter, so she had a reference when money decisions needed to be made. If she had to do the actual accounting, she would put her 9mm to her head and pull the damn trigger. She hated math.

She also couldn't handle the blatant sex interest that Lucifer oozed with every word he spoke about or to her. He didn't hide it behind pleasantries. He punched her in the face with the fact that he wanted her, and he would do anything to have her. It unnerved her a bit, which only pissed her off more.

As she descended the stairs and rounded the strip mall that held the businesses her club owned, some of which they shared with the Howlers, she hoped Lucifer didn't lay it on too thick in front of Axle. Talk about *awkward*.

She waved to Ginger's kids in the diner window as she passed them and crossed the parking lot. In the lot next to the clubhouse, Trip was sitting on his bike, making out with Darlin' who was standing next to him.

Crush shook her head and laughed as she saw Dragon come out of the tattoo shop and notice the couple. The loud growl that rang through the air was not unexpected.

Ignoring them, she jogged across to the clubhouse and entered through the front door. Not her circus, not her monkeys. If they killed each other, that would be an Axle problem.

She waved to a few of her club sisters who were hanging out in the main room as she walked through, before making a right and cutting down the hallway. She didn't bother knocking on Axle's door, since she knew they were waiting on her. She just stormed in and shut it behind her.

Pretending Lucifer wasn't sitting there, looking sexy as all hell, Crush plopped down in the other chair and gazed across the desk at Axle. "What's up?"

Axle looked over at Lucifer and gave a nod.

Lucifer opened his kissable damn mouth and started spewing all kinds of words that sent fear and anger running through her veins. He wanted to put himself in danger! Her tiger started prowling and hissing inside of her, demanding that she protect their mate, claim their mate, drag him off, and ride their mate.

Pushing down her instincts, she tried to focus on the merits of the plan and not on her hormones or her emotions or her tiger. She was president, which made her responsible for a whole list of people. She couldn't pass up the opportunity to protect them and also further the mission her club had been on since their founding.

When he was done, she looked back at Axle and swallowed hard. "What do you think?"

Axle shrugged. "I think we need to give him a chance. I mean… if nothing else, we might be able to gather some intel that has been elusive to us until this point."

She gave a nod. "I'm on board." The words rubbed against her throat coming out, making her feel raw, but it was the right decision. She knew that.

"I already secured an apartment out of town. I'll pack up the little I have and move in there for now. I'll be in touch as soon as I have a position secured." Lucifer stood and headed for the door.

Axle called out his name, and Lucifer stopped with his hand on the doorknob. When he looked back at him, Axle uttered, "Try not to get killed."

Lucifer grinned. "I've done a good job of that so far." Then he left the room.

Urgency coursed through her, pushing Crush to her feet. She darted out of Axle's office and stopped Lucifer halfway down the hall. Pushing him up against the wall with her body, she gripped his nuts in her left hand and squeezed. All the breath left his body and pain registered on his face as she stared into his dark brown eyes.

Swallowing hard, she fought back her panic at the thought of him being in danger and told her tiger to shut the hell up. Then she bit out, "Get yourself hurt, and I will cut these off."

He gave a nod as he gritted his teeth. Pressing her lips to his, she gave him a hard kiss. She let go of his nuts and let her hand graze his cock as she backed away from him. Unable to look at him any longer without dragging him back to her place, she swiftly headed down the hall and across the main room. Crush needed to get away from him as quickly as possible.

Lucifer

Bent over in pain and nausea, Lucifer was still turned way the hell on. He fucking loved the way Crush reacted to him. He knew she only threatened him because she was scared he'd get hurt. It meant she cared whether or not she wanted to admit it. It meant he stood a chance to win her over. It meant he was doing the right thing. So hurt nuts and all, Lucifer was happy as a biker in a Harley shop.

T.S. Tappin

As soon as his balls weren't fucking bruised, and he didn't feel like he was going to puke, he would be filing away that interaction in his brain for use in his private time while he was away. Who knew a woman threatening to remove your balls could be sexy?

Before he fully recovered, Axle's office door opened, and he stepped out. Axle's gaze landed on him, then he grinned. When he started chuckling, Lucifer raised his hand and flipped him off, which only made Axle laugh harder.

"Watching the two of you circle each other is becoming the highlight of my day... well, besides my wife and Nugget."

"Glad I could entertain you," Lucifer wheezed out and straightened. As Axle continued to laugh, Lucifer made his way out of the building, no matter how much it hurt to do so.

It took him another ten minutes before he could mount his new bike. Well, it wasn't new, but it was new to Lucifer. The bike he left behind in Indiana was a piece of shit that was barely hanging on. Thanks to Zero and a few of the other Howlers, he found a fixer-upper bike that was decently priced, and the Howlers helped him get it running. Now it purred and growled just the way he liked it.

When he started it and the sound from the pipes rumbled through him, he grinned. He carefully rode it over down the sidewalk and over to the door of the apartment building.

After he packed up the meager belongings he had acquired over the last six months, he would load them into his saddlebags and head out. He didn't have much, but he might have to strap a bag to his bitch seat as well.

Leaving Crush for a while was going to be hard. Even though they weren't actually together, it would bother him to not be able to see her scowling face every day. He knew she was his, and she knew it too, but they had yet to take that leap. That was okay, though. When it finally happened, it was going to be explosive.

Grinning from ear to ear, with his nuts sore as hell, he dismounted his bike and headed into the building.

T.S. Tappin

CHAPTER SEVEN

Three months later... Lucifer

After Benjamin picked him up for the meeting, and they got to the warehouse, Lucifer got a text from Leighton ordering him to help Benjamin with a pick-up. He didn't think anything of it until he got back in the SUV with Benjamin and his driver in the front seats, at which point he was informed that they were picking up a woman. Something in his gut told him this woman wouldn't be coming with them of her own free will, and that shit didn't sit right with Lucifer.

He didn't say anything, thinking of ways he could help her if this was going to go the way he believed it might.

After about thirty minutes, Benjamin began shouting instructions at the driver, ordering him to park the SUV on a trail in the woods.

The driver lifted his hand up in the air as he climbed out of the SUV and flipped off Benjamin over his shoulder as he began his trek through the woods.

"Who are we picking up?"

Benjamin's head swung in Lucifer's direction. Glaring at Lucifer, he replied, "You are on a need to fucking know basis, and you don't need to know."

Rolling his eyes, Lucifer held up his hands in surrender. What the fuck ever. He'd find out as soon as the woman got in the vehicle. If needed, he'd figure out a way to help her.

After twenty minutes of silence and Lucifer imagining all the ways he'd like to teach Benjamin a lesson on how to speak to people, Benjamin ordered Lucifer into the driver's seat. Making a promise to figure out a way to make the fucker pay, Lucifer got out of the back seat and slid in behind the wheel.

Following Benjamin's orders, he drove the SUV off of the trail and down a driveway, pulling up in front of a small house. When he put the vehicle in park, Benjamin's whiny voice ordered him to get in the backseat. Lucifer rolled his eyes as he climbed out.

After returning to the back seat, he got a glimpse at the face of the unconscious woman the driver was carrying toward the cargo area of the vehicle, and his gut sank.

Siren's woman. Fuck!

He knew Benjamin had a connection to April, but he didn't know she would be the woman they were picking up. Why would she be? Because Benjamin was a damn lunatic. That's why.

The mission just changed from an information gathering pursuit to a critical rescue. Pulling his phone from his pocket, he opened his text string with Axle and sent a quick message.

Lucifer : SOS. Will need pickup.

There was a sudden rustling from the cargo area of the SUV before April stilled. Lucifer hoped Benjamin and the driver didn't hear it, but of course, they weren't that lucky.

"We know you're awake, bitch," the driver said loudly.

"Don't fucking talk to her like that!" Benjamin's face was red with anger as he glared at the hoodie-wearing driver, obviously not liking anyone talking to who he considered his woman.

Lucifer turned and looked at her, but he knew she couldn't see his face in the dark interior, especially since it was shadowed by the hood of his sweatshirt. "Are you okay?"

April shifted her gaze to Benjamin. After a moment, she lifted her right hand and flipped him the bird.

"April," Benjamin snapped and narrowed his eyes.

"Fuck you, Benjamin."

At her bark of words, Lucifer turned to look at her again, this time shifting his hood back a bit so she could see his face. April jumped and backed away, which made sense, since she knew his name and what he looked like, but she didn't *really* know him. She also didn't know the business of the Howlers or the Claws, so she would be surprised to see him.

As she stared at him, he gave a brief shake of his head and widened his eyes. Then he winked and said, "Watch your mouth, little girl."

Staring at him with curiosity in her eyes, she mumbled, "Sorry."

Lucifer looked toward the front seats. When Benjamin turned around to face the front, Lucifer shifted his gaze back to April again and mouthed, *Everything will be fine*.

Turning down the brightness on his phone, Lucifer opened the text string with Axle and positioned it so that April could see it, letting her know the Howlers were aware and would be on their way.

Her sigh of relief settled in Lucifer's chest. She was giving him her trust, and he would do everything in his power to keep her safe.

April

When they turned off the two-lane highway onto a dirt road, April guessed they were about an hour from Warden's Pass. She watched out the front window, but she didn't recognize the area, but judging by the direction they had been driving, she guessed they were north of Grand Rapids.

On either side of the dirt road were thick woods. She didn't see any driveways, houses, or even random outbuildings. Wherever they were going, it was in the middle of nowhere.

Sitting on her butt with her arms wrapped around her knees, April tried to peer through the darkness to see anything useful, anything that would give her an indication of where they were taking her, but there was nothing. Between the dark of night and the tint, she couldn't see a thing through the windows near her.

Five minutes later, the trees opened up, and a large parking lot and a huge brick warehouse came into view. It was obvious the warehouse was no longer in use by any business or corporation by the lack of any signage or company logo, but she wouldn't call it run down either. Whoever owned it had kept the building up. The sides of the building were brick but painted a bland gray. The front doors were industrial white metal and had small rectangle windows on the top half of each. On the side of the building, there were three dock doors, but she didn't see any trucks. As for vehicles, there were a handful of cars and SUVs parked near the front doors, where there were also a couple of large men dressed in black leather jackets.

"Here."

April jumped and twisted her head around to look at Lucifer. He held out his hoodie to her. She wasn't sure when he took it off, but he must have. He shook it at her until she took it.

"Put it on," he quietly told her. "It's a bit chilly out here at night. It has pockets in case your hands get cold. I've heard women have a thing for pockets." He flashed her a grin and gave her a wink.

April smiled at him as she slipped the hoodie on. She slipped her hands in the pockets and felt something hard, metal, and oblong in the right one. Trying to be discreet, she felt around, trying to decipher what it was as Benjamin, Lucifer, and the other guy climbed out of the vehicle. From what she could tell, it was a folding knife. With that bit of knowledge, her gut unclenched a bit. Lucifer was doing what he could to help her, and Axle would ride in with the Howlers soon.

The hatch swung open, and she twisted around to look. Benjamin was standing there with Lucifer and the hoodie-wearing guy standing behind him. Benjamin still looked angry, but there was a weird affectionate look in his eye, as if he actually cared for her in a twisted way. Whatever it was, it sent a chill down her spine.

"If you just listen, sweetheart, nothing will happen to you. Okay? Just do what I tell you," Benjamin told her.

April wanted to tell him to shove his endearments up his ass, but she bit back the retort and gave a nod instead. When he held out his non-casted hand to her, she reached out and put her hand in his. She allowed him to help her out of the SUV and didn't let her hand go as he led her toward the building.

Behind them, the hatch to the SUV was slammed shut, and she heard the sounds of boots hitting the concrete as the other two followed them. When they got to the edge of the parking lot, she stepped on a stretch of gravel and cried out as a sharp rock bit into the heel of her foot.

"Shit." Benjamin huffed out an exasperated sigh, as if it inconvenienced him that she was unable to walk across gravel on bare feet without hurting herself. "Do I need to carry you?"

It was his fault her feet were bare to begin with. Her kidnapper knocked her out and snatched her up. He didn't stop and grab her shoes, so she didn't know what he expected her to do.

"I got her," Lucifer said and scooped her up in his arms, forcing Benjamin to let go of her hand. When Benjamin's face turned red and he looked like he was about to go off, Lucifer nodded toward Benjamin's cast. "Wouldn't want you to make that worse."

She briefly wondered why he had the cast, but knowing his penchant for pissing people off, it could be anything.

After shooting Lucifer a glare, Benjamin twisted on his heel and stomped toward the front door. The hoodie-wearing guy followed Benjamin. Lucifer hung back just enough to give them enough distance between them and the other guys in order for him to whisper, "I'm basically undercover for the Howlers and Claws. Just try to stay quiet and avoid attracting attention as much as possible. We'll get you out of here and back to your man."

April nodded and took a deep breath, preparing herself for whatever was on the other side of those doors. She couldn't see anything except light shining through those rectangle windows. She had no clue what was in there or exactly how much trouble she was in. All she had to reassure her was Lucifer, a folding knife, and the knowledge that Siren would be there soon. Things may be up in the air between them, but Siren would do whatever he needed to do in order to save her. She was sure of that.

Chapter Eight

Lucifer

Lucifer was instructed to take April into the office to the left of the front door and bandage her foot, so she wasn't bleeding all over the place. When he carried her into the room, he was thankful no one else was in there. It was just a normal-looking office with light gray walls that matched the color of the utilitarian desk and shelving units that were all that occupied the space. He set her on the edge of the desk and rummaged through the shelving units in the room until he found a first aid kit.

She winced when he wiped her foot off with a wet wipe of some sort. He tried to be gentle, but he knew it still stung like a bitch. After covering the cut with a large bandage, he pulled out a large elastic dressing. While he wrapped her foot with it, she opened her mouth to speak, but Lucifer stopped what he was doing and gave a sharp shake of his head, then mouthed the words, *Ears everywhere*. April instantly shut her mouth, giving him a nod to let him know she understood.

When he was done, he held up the package of pain reliever and looked at April's face. She was staring straight ahead, and he could tell she was lost in thought.

"April," Lucifer said.

She jolted and looked at him. "What?"

"Do you need pain reliever? Dickwad mentioned he hit you in the head to knock you out. Does it hurt?"

She eyed the first aid kit and the package in his hand before she shook her head and answered, "I'll be fine."

He nodded. "Keep your mouth shut out there. They don't give a shit about what you have to say. So, unless they ask you something, just keep quiet. Got it?" His words were harsh, but he gave her a smile and a wink to let her know he didn't mean the tone, but he meant the words.

"Okay," she replied, returning his smile. "How bad is my foot?"

"Might need a few stitches, but if you keep it clean, you'll be fine."

He set her on her feet on the concrete floor, wrapping his arm around her waist to help stabilize her.

Crush's Fall

She slid an arm around his shoulders and let him lead her out of the room.

When they returned to the main warehouse space, Lucifer noticed April was looking around and taking in as much information as possible. It was ridiculous to feel pride for a woman he barely knew, but he did. She was smart.

Her eyes clocked the office on the other side of the space next to an exit door, two bathroom doors to her right, and three docking bays to her left. Most of the space was empty, except for an area in the middle where some tables and chairs were set up. Around the tables were open wooden crates, with the word *fragile* stamped in red on the outside. They were used to transport the drugs for Leighton's operation. There were five men sitting around the tables, a mixture of Leighton's men and men who worked for Benjamin's father, Reynold, repackaging the blow.

Benjamin, the driver, Reynold, and two other men were standing on the other side of the tables from April and Lucifer. They were engaged in an animated conversation, arms flailing and fingers pointing, but their voices weren't raised.

They were halfway to the tables when Benjamin noticed them. He broke away from the group, causing his father to glare at him and throw up his hands. "Sweetheart," Benjamin said possessively as he approached. He practically shoved Lucifer out of the way, obviously intending to help April instead. Lucifer didn't move much, which said a lot about Benjamin's lack of strength.

April shifted away from Benjamin's outstretched hand and held onto Lucifer. When Benjamin's eyes narrowed, she pointed at his cast. Lucifer was trying to play the part of helpful stooge, but he knew he'd have to step in if Benjamin didn't back the fuck off.

Benjamin must have accepted her reasoning, because he headed back toward the group, shooting orders over his shoulder. "Bring her over here, Lucifer. My father wants to meet her."

April's eyes shot to the older man again and widened a little in surprise. Lucifer could understand the shock, since there was little resemblance between the two men. Where Benjamin had dark brown hair and light blue eyes, his father had light blond hair and eyes that were a darker color, but Lucifer couldn't tell you what color exactly. Benjamin was fit and just under six feet tall, but his father was much taller, broader in the shoulders and chest, and had a large belly, as if enjoyed bread more than most. Even the size and shape of their eyes and noses were different.

They had just rounded the table when the older man called out, "So this is the little bitch who sicced those thugs on you?"

"Father," Benjamin whined on a huff.

"Stop your whining, boy," his father ordered with annoyance. "She was working at the bar where bikers hang out, and you're surprised when you end up being jumped. She's probably one of their whores. You know how those bikers like their whores."

Glaring at the man with narrowed eyes, Lucifer cleared his throat. "I know you think you're untouchable, but bikers have been watching your ass for years, Reynold. Those bikers are no longer around… except for me."

His father opened his mouth, no doubt to let Lucifer have it, but Benjamin blurted, "Stop calling her names!" He stomped his foot. *Actually. Stomped. His. Foot.* "I'm going to marry her!"

"Not on your life!" April blurted, and Lucifer almost laughed at the surety in her voice, but instead, he sighed and looked down at her. She shrugged.

"I don't care what you do with her," his father shouted. "Marry her, fuck her, whatever. If I'm paying for your expenses, I'll call her what I like, and she's going to cut ties with those thugs."

After father and son argued some more, Reynold asked April, "Is there anything in your apartment that you care enough about to make us go get for you before you move into Benjamin's room at my place?"

When she didn't answer or seem to be paying attention, Lucifer shook her a bit at the same time that Benjamin's father asked, "Is she dim?"

"He asked if there was anything in your apartment that you care about enough for them to go and get before you move into the room at his house you'll share with Benjamin," Lucifer told her and widened his eyes a bit, attempting to tell her to just say there was nothing

97

and not piss off the old bastard any more than she already had.

"Oh." April took a deep breath. Then she replied, "No, nothing."

"Good. Michaela will outfit her with an appropriate wardrobe and get her stylist to get rid of that god awful red in her hair." Then the old man turned on his heel and approached the tables.

"Take her to the back office. She can wait there while we have the meeting," Benjamin said through clenched teeth, barely containing his rage at his father.

As Lucifer helped her cross the rest of the warehouse without putting too much weight on her hurt foot, he hoped the Howlers hurried the hell up.

When he opened the door and led her inside the room, she gasped at the sight of the two young men sitting on the floor across from the door of the empty office space. He knew she was reacting to the poor state the men were in. They had obviously been starved and possibly drugged, not to mention dirty.

Lucifer lowered his head so he could whisper in her ear, "We'll get them out, too."

Standing just outside the door to the room April was being held in, Lucifer knew the minute the Howlers arrived. Honking started in the front, causing Benjamin and four of the men to head that way. As soon as they were outside, men started running in from the backdoor, being chased by the Howlers. All hell broke loose, and Ranger came barreling in from the front with Benjamin held in front of him, held there by a hand around the front of Benjamin's throat and his gun to the man's temple.

They were facing Reynold, Leighton, and the men who had been working the table. The workers were split — one group facing Ranger and Benjamin, the other facing a number of Howlers. In front were Pike and Dragon, each holding goons in front of them in the same position as Ranger was holding Benjamin.

When Siren stormed in the front door moments later, he looked around frantically, no doubt searching for April. When his eyes landed on him, Lucifer tilted his head back toward the door behind him to signal she was in there and okay.

Siren let out a sigh of relief so deep that Lucifer heard it from across the large space.

"What is this about?" Reynold demanded.

In a growl, Axle replied, "You think we're going to stand by while you snatch-grab our family? Nah." Shaking his head, Axle eyes flashed silver light, and Lucifer was sure he imagined that. *What the fuck?*

Apparently, that was the signal to the Howlers to end everyone since the Howlers immediately burst into action.

It wasn't shocking to Lucifer, really. There was one sure-fire way to make the Howlers go nuclear — Fuck with their family. It would *literally* be the last thing you did. Lucifer knew that before he watched what happened next, but what he saw in that warehouse solidified it in his opinion.

As Reynold shouted, "What the hell?" Leighton lifted his right arm, locked his aim on Axle, and pulled the trigger. The shot reverberated through the space as Lucifer watched Dragon dive in front of Axle. Dragon's body jolted when the bullet hit, and his hand went to his gut as he crashed to the ground.

Lucifer's gut clenched at the sight, hoping it wasn't bad enough to end the man, but before Leighton or anyone else could take another shot, the space erupted into even more chaos.

One by one, Lucifer watched as the Howlers turned into motherfucking animals! One minute they were men, the men he had gotten to know over the previous several months. The next second, they were tigers, wolves, bears, and lions who were roaring, growling, and tearing people apart. *What in the fucking fuck?*

Lucifer stood frozen in place, mouth agape, shocked at what he was watching. A part of him was sure he had lost it. Maybe he had been knocked over the head and was dreaming. Maybe he really died back in Indiana, and this was some sort of fucked up place God sent the people who were fuck-ups in life. Maybe he had just lost his grip on reality. Whatever happened, there was no way he was really watching the people he had gotten to know as a make-shift family turn into motherfucking predatory animals. Well, not all of them. A few were still human, and they were heading his way.

His eyes shifted over to where Siren had been standing, who was now stalking toward Benjamin, whose entire body was shaking. Benjamin's breath wheezed out of him at such a labored pace, Lucifer was sure he would pass out before long. Siren looked the same as he always did as he glared at Benjamin — Intense, deliberate, sure. When Siren was within ten feet of Benjamin, Benjamin's frantic gaze swung around to lock on him. Gold light shone from Siren's eyes, and the sound from his chest started off as a low grumble, but quickly grew into a roar that shook even the brick walls.

Benjamin screamed like a toddler, and the scent of urine filled the air. Lucifer didn't blame him. *That shit was crazy!* In the next second, Siren turned into the biggest fucking lion Lucifer had ever seen and shredded Benjamin to pieces.

April

What sounded like an all-out war was happening just outside the room. Animal roars, gunshots, and screams filled the air moments before the door flew open and a half-dozen of familiar faces filed into the room. Lucifer was followed by Siren, Striker, Ranger, Rock, and a guy she thought was named Rebel.

When her gaze locked on Siren's, April leapt to her feet, ignoring the shooting pain in the injured one, and threw herself at him. Relief swamped her as Siren's arms caught her.

It was guttural when Siren groaned, "Sugar," into the hair on top of her head with his arms wrapped around her, holding her as tight as he could. She could barely breathe, but she didn't care.

Over Siren's shoulder, she saw Rebel stop six feet from the two young men still sitting on the floor in the opposite corner. She watched as Rebel put a hand to his chest and started rubbing as his face twisted in pain. He was connected to those boys in some way, which made her happy. Rebel and the Howlers would help them.

"Are you okay?" The sound of Siren's voice was so low and broken she could barely understand what he had asked her.

"My foot was cut on a rock, and my head hurts a bit, but I don't think I have a concussion or anything."

"You might need to stitch up her foot," Lucifer said from a few feet away. April tried to look at him, but Siren wasn't letting her move much.

"Siren, you have to loosen your grip." She ran her fingers through his hair and jumped at the sound of his purr. Then she laughed and caressed his head again.

Slowly, Siren loosened his arms and pulled his head back to look at her. "Let's get you in the van so I can check you over." Then she was scooped up in his arms, and Siren was carrying her out of the room.

As they passed Lucifer, April noticed he looked a bit shell-shocked, with wide eyes and a slight tremble throughout his body. "Lucifer? You okay?" She patted Siren's shoulder to stop him, and he complied.

Lucifer's gaze slowly swung around to her. "Yeah… uh… did you… I mean… Fucking wolves… and… lions, tigers, and bears…"

April giggled. "Oh, my."

Siren snorted a laugh, and she heard chuckles come from behind them.

"You knew?" Lucifer's question was a bit quiet, but she heard him.

"For a few hours, yeah," she confirmed, remembering the conversation she had with Siren early in the evening and how shocked she was by the news.

Lucifer shook his head like he was trying to shake reality into place in his brain. "I'm okay. I'm… just trying to process." He shrugged and huffed out a breath. "I'm a bit fucking jealous, if we're being honest."

"Saaaammmmeeee," April dragged out and nodded. "What animal would you want to shift into? I'm thinking I would want to shift into a tiger."

"That'd be the shit," Lucifer agreed.

"Then you could join the Claws, Sugar," Siren said with a grin.

"What?" Lucifer's eyes were wide again. "Are you telling me…"

Siren nodded. "Your woman isn't just a badass who could kill you with her bare hands. She's a pussycat that could remove your balls with her claws. Congratulations."

As they left Lucifer to come to terms with that bit of information, April asked, "The Claws are tigers?"

"Well, not all of them, but the club is called *the Tiger's Claw*." She pondered that, and a realization popped into her head, when she remembered the wolf tattoos she had noticed on the boys in the room while they waited. "Oh! Rebel is a wolf, isn't he?"

Siren's brow furrowed as he continued carrying her across the space. "Yes. Why?"

"I don't know how they're related, but those boys are related to him, aren't they? They're wolf-shifters too, right?"

"Yes. I wouldn't call them boys, though. Young men? Yeah. You're only a few years older than them, Sugar."

That bit of news shocked her. She'd place them in their mid-teens, but she guessed it made sense. They were malnourished.

As they continued across the space, April finally looked around. And she regretted that decision with every fiber of her being. Blood and parts of bodies were everywhere. *Gross*! She was just glad the Howlers MC was on her side.

April returned her gaze to Siren, not wanting to take in any more blood and gore. There was a tenseness to him she suspected had nothing to do with her. She didn't question how she knew that. Instead, she cupped his face in her hands and waited. Siren looked at her and forced a smile.

"What's wrong?"

"You were kidnapped because I didn't keep you safe."

April narrowed her eyes on him. If they were mates and were in it for life, she wasn't going to let him get away with hiding his worries from her. It was her job to support him and help him through. And she was going to do that, whether he wanted her to or not. "We'll return to that bullshit later. What else is bothering you?"

She watched as he visibly swallowed hard. "Dragon. He was protecting Axle… got shot… in the gut. It's bad."

T.S. Tappin

CHAPTER NINE

Lucifer

While waiting for the other van to arrive for transport, Lucifer was leaning back against the outside wall of the warehouse. He was trying to stay out of the way of the Howlers, especially with Siren doing his best to stabilize Dragon in the back of the van. He watched as April hobbled over and settled next to him, playfully bumping into him with her shoulder.

"Hey."

"Hey." He playfully bumped her back.

"You good? You look a little freaked still."

A little freaked? Yeah, he was more than a little freaked, but he was also in awe. Sure, he briefly thought about the friends he had made and what they were capable of, but he was really focused on Crush and what she looked like shifted into a tiger.

Pushing that aside to answer April, Lucifer quietly chuckled. "Nope. What else exists? I mean... it's kind of cool, but my brain's having trouble accepting it."

April giggled. "Well, you better figure it out. If you want to be with Crush, and we both know you want to be with her, you can't avoid it."

Lucifer grinned. He knew he was obvious with his desire for Crush, but he didn't give a fuck. He wasn't one for hiding his truth if it wasn't essential to keep him alive. If he wanted something, he was honest about it. And he wanted Crush like he wanted his next breath. "I don't know what it is about her, but I can't function when she's around."

April giggled again.

"I see her, and all my blood shoots to my... Well, you know. I won't say it. Siren would literally tear me apart." Lucifer looked over at her and grinned again. "Do you think he'd kill me if I started calling him a pussy?" When she began to laugh loudly, drawing the attention of the men milling around the parking lot, Lucifer added, "I mean... he *is* a pussy."

Tears of laughter gathered in the corner of her eyes. "Death wish," she choked out as he watched her try to get her laughter under control.

"What's going on over here?" Trip's arms were crossed over his chest as he approached them.

"Nothing." Lucifer winked at her but shrugged. He couldn't help himself. He liked the Howlers, but they needed to lighten up. They were too easy to tease. "We were just talking about what toys cats liked the most. There are so many options. Balls… of yarn. Feathers. Mice toys. Other balls. And do they like to eat sugar… treats? I bet they do."

An ungraceful snort came out of her before April was howling with laughter.

"We'll take a poll. We'll start with… Pike, since Siren is busy."

Trip must have caught on. He was grinning and shaking his head. "You've got balls. I'll give you that."

Crush

Crush was pacing in front of the diner when she saw the vans and bikes of the Howlers turn onto the street. She waited for them to turn into the clubhouse parking lot, then she bolted across the street toward them. First, she checked on Bullet and found him perfectly fine. Second, she tracked down Sugar, whose real name was April, and found her to have an injured foot, but she looked to be okay. Then she scanned the crowd and found Lucifer climbing off of Dragon's bike.

She didn't think. Crush just reacted, rushing over to him, and checking him over. As her hands ran over him, she didn't pay attention to anything around her. She just needed to know he was okay. Crush ran her hands over his shoulders, his arms, his chest, and down his abdomen as her eyes scanned his body. "Do you have a damn death wish? Dragon will kill you for touching his damn bike," she growled.

"He's a little too worried about the hole in his gut right now."

It wasn't until her gaze flipped up to his face that she saw the grin and realized he was fine. Instantly, she yanked her hands back.

"Don't stop now, Kitten. We were just getting to the good part," he uttered through his grin.

"Kitten? Not Sugartits?" She watched as his eyes sparkled with humor. *Fuck.* "Who told you?"

"About you? Siren and April, but that was after I watched the club turn into multiple exhibits from the zoo."

Crush crossed her arms over her chest, turned, and stomped back across the street. She wasn't at all surprised when Lucifer fell into step next to her.

"So, a tiger?"

"Go away," she mumbled.

"You don't really want that." He put his hand to her lower back, and she sidestepped to break the connection.

"I do want that."

"I don't know why you're fighting it, Kitten. You and I both know you'll be purring under me eventually," he said with confidence in his voice.

"Or cutting your balls off with my claws."

"I mean… I'm not usually into pain, but I'm willing to try everything once."

Crush rounded the corner of the strip mall and tried to ignore him. Her tiger was pushing her to bring him upstairs, strip him naked, and double check that their mate was okay, before climbing on top of him and riding him for all he was worth. It took everything in her to fight the impulse. She had nothing left in her to spar with him.

As she reached the door to the stairway that led to her apartment, he reached out and put his hand to the metal panel, stopping her from opening it. She lifted her gaze to his face and saw that the humor was gone from his chocolate eyes.

His tone was serious when he told her, "I'm okay, Kitten. Really."

"And Sugar?" Even though she saw her, Crush needed to hear him say it.

"She's fine. Might need a stitch or two to her foot. Might have a headache. She'll be fine."

Crush let out a deep sigh of relief and nodded.

He just stared at her for a long moment before he cupped her face in his palms and leaned towards her. Pressing his lips to hers, he stepped forward, forcing their bodies together. Crush reached up and curled her fingers around sections of the front of the tee he was wearing. Opening her mouth to him, she moaned when his tongue tangled with her own, sending zaps of pleasure through her body.

The kisses quickly turned feral as they engaged their teeth, nipping lips and tongues. He was groaning into her mouth as she moaned into his. Their hands explored, grabbing onto anything they could reach. His hands were on her ass, and her hands moved to fist in his hair before he broke the kiss and moved his mouth to her neck.

Crush loved the way her skin seemed to sizzle everywhere he touched her. The chemistry between them was off the charts, and when they kissed, it was like someone poured gasoline on a fire. *Explosive.* Every time his lips moved up her neck, her breath caught in her throat. It was perfect, hot, consuming, until his mouth reached her ear, and he bit out, "Let's go upstairs."

At his words, panic filled her, dumping cold water over the inferno that he had built inside of her. And just like the last time, she extracted herself from his grasp and bolted.

As Crush made her get away, she cursed herself for the urge to return to his arms and also for the fear coursing through her at the thought of giving in. She was a fucking coward, and she was well aware.

CHAPTER TEN

Two months later... Crush

After finding out what the Hell's Dogs were planning and assessing the vulnerability of the Howlers and the Claws having such a well-known compound location, Axle and Crush agreed that a new safe house or safe property needed to be acquired. They needed somewhere to send their families to if they received a threat. Axle had asked Crush if she knew anyone who would be a good fit for the search, and Crush had put Pinky on it.

Months later, Pinky and her yet-to-be-claimed mate, Xander, were sure they had a solution. Crush called a meeting with Axle and had told Xander to wait in the main room of the clubhouse while they went into Axle's office, but the man had insisted on joining them. Crush just shrugged and let him go with, knowing exactly how it would play out.

Crush and Pinky walked into Axle's office, followed by Xander and Skull. Xander had spent much of the last decade doing work as a stuntman in Los Angeles. He was returning to Warden's Pass to be close to his sister, Pixie, who was mated to Pike, but also because he met Pinky during a visit, and the two discovered they were mates. Well, at least Pinky did. Like all human mates of shifter, Xander just felt a strong pull toward her and an undeniable attraction. He had returned to Los Angeles to finish a contract and prepare to move, but when he did, communication with Pinky had been less than stellar. It looked like the two were making up, but he would have a lot of work to do to prove he wasn't going anywhere.

Xander had an offer to extend to Axle, Crush, and the clubs, but Crush knew Axle wouldn't like having an outsider in the room for any discussion that was considered club business, whether you were a mate, family of an Ol' Lady, or not.

Axle laid some papers down on his desk, looked over at Pixie's brother, Xander, and asked, "What's he doing here? This is club business."

When Pinky snorted, Axle looked over at her, but she just shook her head and waved off his silent question. Crush knew Pinky had already told Xander that exact thing before they made it over to the clubhouse, because she had heard her.

"I can help with this," Xander informed him and pointed to the paperwork, "if you decide to go that route."

Axle narrowed his eyes on the man. "You'll wait in the clubhouse's main room while we talk about this. We'll let you know if we need your input."

"Axle, I'm willing to—"

"We. Will. Let. You. Know. If. We. Need. Your. Input." Axle's tone was letting Xander know exactly what would happen if Xander pushed him on it. Axle would make sure Xander was physically unable to give his *input*.

Axle's VP, Skull, stepped in front of Xander and nodded for the door. "You heard the boss. We appreciate your patience while we look into the matter," Skull said, voice full of sarcasm, essentially shoving the man into the hallway and shutting the door behind him.

That's when Pinky burst out with laughter. "I tried to tell him," she choked out. "He just didn't want to listen."

Axle grinned at her. "You just wanted to make him squirm."

"I do enjoy a squirming man," Pinky replied, returning his grin.

He nodded at the paperwork. "Tell me about this. I need to get back to Nugget. I left her with Bullet."

Nugget was what Axle called his infant daughter, Caroline. She was fucking gorgeous. She got her mom's beautiful blond hair and her daddy's silver eyes, and her smile could melt the heart of even the toughest biker.

"You did what?" Skull gasped.

"Harlow is with them," Axle replied. "Anyway, what is this?"

Crush didn't say anything out loud, but she breathed a sigh of relief when she heard that her brother's woman was with them. At least Harlow had enough sense to know how to take care of a baby, because Crush was pretty sure Bullet was useless. It made Crush grateful for Harlow that her possible future nieces and nephews would be safe, since Harlow was her brother's mate, even though they had yet to make it official.

Crush, Pinky, and Skull crowded around the other side of Axle's desk. Spread out on the top were the blueprints and satellite photos of a property they were considering buying to use as a safe place for the clubs.

The four of them looked over the paperwork as Pinky explained, "It's a peninsula of land about an hour and a half from here on the coast of Lake Michigan. It has two pole barns and an out-of-business, extended-stay motel. The motel has eighteen units, some of them more than one bed. There is forest all around it, so no one would see the buildings from the lake or from the road. I looked up the driveway on a street-view program. If it looks the same, the trees and brush have grown so much that it just looks like any other driveway, rather than a business entry. I don't know the state of the buildings' interiors, but it's worth a look."

Axle nodded his interest, and Crush agreed. It did look like it could be the answer to their safe place problem.

Axle asked, "How much are we talking?"

"Land, outbuildings, and all? Just under a million. Comes as is, but they are willing to let us look at it before we make an offer."

Skull whistled. "I knew this would cost us, but... that's a lot of dough."

Axle nodded. "I could cover about half of that, personally, without touching my investment accounts. As for the rest, we'd have to take it from the business accounts, which means HTC would be on the deed."

Crush was a bit struck by the amount of money Axle had squirreled away, but then again, she didn't have much less than that, so she wasn't sure why it shocked her so much.

"The man you shoved out of here has a plan for that," Pinky said and shrugged. "Might as well hear him out."

At Crush and Axle's nods, Skull walked over and opened the door. An irritated Xander walked back into the room.

"Pinky said you have a plan," Axle said.

Xander crossed his arms over his chest and gave a nod. "Yeah. I do. But it means you all will have to start talking to me and stop shutting me out of rooms."

"Pinks, get control of your man before he pisses off the wrong wolf," Crush commented, noticing Axle wasn't too fond of the stunt bastard's attitude.

T.S. Tappin

"Let it go, Xander." Pinky gave the man's forearm a squeeze with her hand. "I told you it was going to be like this. Just tell Axle what you offered."

Xander huffed out a sigh. Then, he lost the attitude and explained, "I could buy the property and put my LLC on the deed. As for use of the place, I would give you guys unlimited access to it year-round. That way, there's no one directly from the Howlers or the Claws on the deed, and there's no lease agreement with any of your names on it, either. I plan to be around. My sister and future brother-in-law are your family. And my mate is your family. I'm not going anywhere. Let me help. I have the funds, I have the ability, and I want to."

"How does this benefit you if you're paying for it?"

The man's newly trimmed blond hair stuck out a bit when Xander ran his hand through it, obviously irritated with the question. Then, his sea-green eyes locked on Axle's and were determined when he said, "It benefits me every single day that I know my sister is not in harm's way, that I know my brother-in-law isn't in danger, that I know my mate has a safe place to go to after she's done kicking ass. It benefits me greatly."

Crush had to admit that she liked the man's answer. Just like Georgia and Emerson, Xander was part of the family. She hoped Pinky didn't chew him up and spit him out. That would make holiday dinners uncomfortable.

"Fine. Crush, I think we should send Pinky and Skull to take a look with a couple of other members, maybe Ginger and Top. If the place looks solid enough, we'll have our new friend here put in an offer. Everyone good with that?"

Crush nodded. It sounded good to her. "I agree. Mind taking Lucy with ya?"

Skull snorted. "But how would you survive without your mate?"

"Sorry, Boss Lady," Pinky began, "there's no chance in hell you're pawning him off on us just because you get off on finding new ways to torture him."

Crush heard Axle chuckled as she glared at her second in command. "You're a bitch. You know that?"

"Nah. I'm a pussy," Pinky, a tiger shifter, replied with a grin.

Pinky

It ended up just being four of them going to look at the property. Trying to ignore the tension in the car between Crush and Lucifer, Pinky focused on the map and gave directions to Xander.

The two in the backseat were being ridiculous. In the beginning, when they first brought Lucifer back to the compound, Pinky understood why Crush was standoffish with Lucifer, but it had been *months,* and the man had done nothing but try to earn their trust and Crush's attention. Pinky wouldn't say Lucifer was doing it in the most romantic way, but he was set on a relationship with Crush. Most of the time, she treated him like scum, on the rare occasion she acknowledged his presence at all.

"Crush," Lucifer began in the backseat, "you gonna look at me?"

"I'd like to keep my breakfast in my stomach. So, no, probably not," Crush replied, sounding bored.

Pinky rolled her eyes. As Crush's best friend, she knew that was a bunch of bullshit. Crush wanted to climb the man like a tree and camp out on his face. Lucifer's cocky attitude and often biting words only fed Crush's desires, just as Crush's ambivalence and sometimes disdain only encouraged Lucifer's affection toward her.

If you had to define toxic relationships, they would be the perfect example, but it worked for them, and it wasn't up to anyone else to tell them how to manage their relationship. Crush would deny there was a relationship, but she was lying. Lucifer was her mate. They all knew it. She just had yet to act on it.

That was the part that boggled Pinky's mind. How could Crush see Lucifer every day and *not* claim him? It was difficult for Pinky to be in the same car with Xander and not give in to the annoying constant itch to bite him and mate him. There was no way she would be able to spend every day around Xander for that many months and not act on it.

"If that happens, I'll give you something else to eat," Lucifer offered.

Xander snorted a laugh and shook his head. "Sorry," he choked out.

Pinky stared at her yet-to-be-claimed mate and warned, "If you ever talk to me like that—"

Xander shot her a wide-eyed glance. "No need to warn me. I wouldn't."

Pinky smiled at him. "Watch the road. Take a left in a mile."

"If you don't take your hand off of my thigh," Crush growled, "I will tear your fingers off and use the bones as toothpicks."

Pinky heard Lucifer chuckle and reply, "If you wanted my fingers higher, all you had to do was ask."

Xander took a left.

"Right there. Take a right at the driveway. The one that's hard to see."

Xander did as she instructed. Trees and brush lined the sides and curved over the top of the driveway as they traveled down it. About a half mile down, the trees parted, and a field was revealed with several buildings in need of repair.

"We're here."

After touring the property and seeing what needed to be done, the four of them gathered in the parking lot in front of the rundown motel.

"Should I call the realtor?" Xander asked.

"Wait until I talk to Axle," Crush replied. "Then we'll have you call."

Xander rolled his eyes. "I'll buy it. If you don't want it? Oh well. Guess I'll own property. I'll figure out what to do with it."

Crush shrugged and turned to head for the car. "It's your bank account."

Lucifer chuckled and followed behind Crush.

"You are a pain in the ass. You know that?" Pinky crossed her arms over her chest, staring at the man she would claim soon enough.

Xander looked at her and gave her a sexy grin. Stepping closer to her, he gripped her hips. "Yeah, but think of how many ways I can make it up to you."

Pinky tried to fight the smile, but it managed to form on her face, anyway. "I'll have to start making a list."

Xander groaned and laid his forehead against hers. "Please do."

Crush

Crush was motherfucking annoyed and turned on in equal measure. As they toured the property, Lucifer kept finding reasons to brush up against her, touch her, lean into her. It had her tiger purring and demanding they play with him. One look into his chocolate brown eyes told her he was game as soon as she was ready. That didn't help keep her walls up.

How could he be hot and annoying at the same damn time? It was fucking unfair.

She reached out to open the car door, but Lucifer got there first, pulling the door open and waving his arm to let her know she could slide in. She flipped him off as she took the seat. Instead of walking around the car and climbing in the other side, he slid in next to her, forcing her to move over. Before she could fully make it to the other side, he had his arm around her and kept her close.

"Stop pretending you hate it when I touch you. Your hard nipples and I both know that to be bullshit."

Crush looked down, and sure e-fucking-nough, her tits were betraying her. She crossed her arms over her chest and looked away from him. "Maybe I'm cold."

The annoying asshole chuckled. "It's eighty out here."

She didn't reply, because seriously... What was she going to say?

"Crush," he said low, his breath caressing her neck as he leaned closer.

A shiver ran through her at the sound of his voice and the feeling of his breath against her skin. She wanted to feel that everywhere, hear him say her name like that while he slid inside of her.

"Just know I'm here, Kitten. Ready when you are. Okay?" When she didn't reply, he tightened his hold on her. "Okay?"

She gave a nod, and when he loosened his hold, she slid across the car. After putting on her seatbelt, she stared out the side window and tried to calm her racing heart.

Her tiger was pacing and purring inside of her, pushing and demanding she claim him. Crush closed her eyes and took a deep breath through her nose, cursing when his scent of leather and tobacco hit her. *Fuck!*

His quiet chuckle made her turn her head and glare at his handsome face.

"You're so fucking pretty when you're pissed off, Kitten."

Crush flipped him off, only succeeding in making him laugh harder.

CHAPTER ELEVEN

A week later... Crush

Harlow, given the Ol' Lady name Butterfly by Bullet, had left the compound with the intention of keeping Bullet and his family safe from her stalking, violent, child-killing, drug-dealing, and sex-trafficking husband, which sent the Howlers and the Claws into a panic. They could handle her ex, but they didn't like the idea of her being out on her own with the fucker tracking her. Not to mention the fact that Bullet would lose his motherfucking mind if anything happened to his mate.

After she left the compound, she was kidnapped by a hired gunman, who had been instructed to bring her to an old farmhouse outside of town. Thanks to Keys, the Howlers resident tech genius, they were able to track her down. By the time they got there, Butterfly had already put her stiletto through her husband's eye... literally.

Apparently, she had tried running, but one of her husband's goons had grabbed her by the hair to pull her back. That was when Bullet and Dragon stormed the place in their animal forms. Crush could only imagine the reaction of the goons when they were faced with a pissed off wolf and a tiger there to save his mate.

Crush wasn't sitting in Axle's office to get the rundown on that. She already heard the details of the actual fight in the farmhouse as the men chatted about it when they returned. No, she was there to get details about the encounter Axle had outside after the fight was done.

Something about there being actual fucking gods who had champions they'd send out in the world to do whatever the fuck, and Axle actually met one of them.

As the Howlers were getting ready to leave the farmhouse, a group of approximately a dozen people walked out of the tree line in the back and over to the Howlers. One of them introduced herself as a woman named Lira.

Axle shook her hand and swore that when he did, he was transported to another dimension or something, where he met the God of Balance.

Crush was skeptical about the whole thing, but Axle wouldn't lie to her. She trusted his word and his judgment, so she was going with his lead on this.

There were gods, and the shifters were connected to them in some off-the-wall way? Who fucking knew? She shouldn't be surprised that something *other* was involved. Shifters could change into animals with no logical or scientific explanation as to how or why. Why wouldn't gods and magic be involved? Yeah, she was going with Axle's gut on this one.

That's what made the Howlers and the Claws such good allies. While their first priority would always be their own respective clubs, Crush and Axle were good at figuring out how to help each other and trusting each other. It helped that the trust given was never betrayed. They had open communication, even if sometimes he treated the Claws like damsels who needed the protection of the men.

"So, we were made because a demi-god had bad impulse control, and now that demi-god's siblings want to help keep us a secret?"

Axle gave a nod. "From what I've learned from them, the gods think it will end with the humans finding out about us and other creatures I didn't know existed until now. It isn't hard to figure out what the humans would do if they found out."

Apparently, the champions were sent by the God of Balance to help the Howlers and the Claws fight the Hell's Dogs and the multiple clubs they had pulled together to fight with them on their side. There was also talk about a plan to out the shifters to the world as savage beasts and make them look as dangerous as possible, and that was confirmed by the champions.

Something about an anti-shifting drug that caused shifters to go feral if used for too long. When they finally did shift, they would be uncontrollable and lack the restraint of their human side. If the shifters were outed, it was entirely possible for the other creatures to be outed too. It would be a snowball effect. Crush wasn't sure why she hadn't put together that there might be more than shifters out there, but it made sense.

Crush relaxed back in the chair across the desk from him. "What other creatures are out there?"

"I didn't ask for a master list, but vampires and witches were mentioned. I'm going to go on the assumption that anything is possible until I get confirmation that's wrong."

"Fuck. Vampires?"

"I can think of a few people on this planet who certainly drain the life out of a room, so I guess it makes sense," Axle commented dryly.

Crush snorted a laugh. "And now they want to meet with me?"

"Lira and the other champions, yes. I told her I don't run the Claws, and that you were going to want to make your own decision."

Crush smiled. "I'm glad you are aware of that. Sometimes you get a little too big for your britches."

Axle rolled his eyes but smiled. "I never do anything with the intention of taking your power or choices away. It's always in the name of trying to keep people safe."

"Yeah, but that's the thing about freewill. We have the choice to put ourselves in danger if we want to, just like the Howlers." Then she stood and turned for the door. "Well, I guess we better head out to meet with these champions so I can get a read on them."

Axle stood and followed her out of his office. There was no way they were inviting the champions to the compound until she and Axle came to a joint decision on how trustworthy they were. So, until then, they would meet with the champions out at the farmhouse.

In the parking lot of the clubhouse, where their vice presidents and sergeant at arms were already waiting, Axle and Crush climbed on their bikes. Once the pipes were roaring, they took off and made the drive out to the farmhouse.

When they arrived, there were four people sitting on the steps that led up to the porch at the front end of the house. As they parked their bikes and cut the engines, Crush looked over the people. Were the champions considered people? She didn't fucking know.

One was a man with dark hair buzzed tight to his scalp, intense dark blue eyes, and enough toned muscles to let everyone around him know he could hold his own. He had on a navy tee with the sleeves cut off, a pair of gray track pants, and navy sneakers. He was sitting on the step two up from the ground.

The other man was the same build as the first, except his skin was a warm, deep brown that matched his golden-brown eyes. His dark hair was also kept close to his scalp. He was sitting on the top step, wearing a pair of deep blue jeans, a dark gray button-down shirt, and a pair of black boots.

Sitting on the middle step was a woman who had olive skin, long, dark brown hair, green eyes, and was wearing a pair of black leggings with a pink tank and flip-flops that showed off all her curves. She could see the strength in the way she held herself.

The last person was a gorgeous black woman. She had skin the color of earth, dark and rich, and black hair that she kept cut short. Her body was that of an athlete, fit and muscular. Except for the color of her tank, she was dressed much like the woman next to her. And there was a large smile gracing her stunning face.

"Introduce us," the black woman said through her smile. "I recognize a couple from the other day, but I didn't get the honor of an introduction."

Axle sighed and pointed to his right. "This is Skull, my VP." To his left. "Pike. Sergeant at arms." He nodded at Crush. Pike and Pinky stood between her and Axle. "Crush. The president of the Tiger's Claw MC. To her left is her sergeant at arms, Nails. To her right, Pinky, her VP." He motioned to the woman who asked for an introduction. "Lira. I don't know who the others are."

"Allow me." Lira motioned toward the woman next to her. "This is Marya. She's my second. Behind her is Sol. In front of me is Storme. They are champions of other gods, but they are in the fight with us."

"Enough with the niceties and bullshit," Crush said, bored with the pleasantries. There was too much to get straight. Crush wanted to get to the point and make things perfectly clear to these *champions*. "If we allow you to fight with us, you are not in charge. My women will not follow you. His men will not follow you. You can fight beside us, but you will not command our people."

Lira raised a brow. "The gods didn't send us here to control you or command you. They sent us here to get you out of the mess you got yourselves in."

Who the fuck did this bitch think she was? Crush took a step toward Lira. Nails and Pinky stepped forward with her. Storme stood up in front of Lira.

"You trying to say we're to blame for all of this?" Crush growled.

Axle cleared his throat, trying to give Crush a warning to chill, but fuck that.

Lira stood and put a hand on Storme's shoulder, and Storme returned to his seat. "I didn't say that." Lira shrugged. "You made choices and are dealing with consequences. I'm not saying you made the wrong choices, but you made choices, nonetheless."

Crush narrowed her eyes and glared at the woman. "When people disrespect my club, I make choices. You'd do well to remember that."

Lira grinned, and Crush wanted to backhand it off her face. "You're a firecracker. I look forward to working with you."

In response, Crush showed her fangs and hissed.

"Lira, this isn't helping." Axle let out a deep sigh, obviously over the whole situation and trying to keep things calm.

"Fine. Fine. Fine." Lira waved a hand in front of her. "Yes, I understand. And I assume you understand that the champions will not take orders from any of you, either. We will need to plan and communicate. Or this will end with the world being changed forever, and shifters being hunted. So... we gonna make this work?"

Crush looked over at Axle and stared a moment, then she gave a slight nod. Axle returned his attention to Lira. "Yeah, we'll make this work. Any idea how long we have until this war?"

"As of right now," Sol began in a voice so deep Crush could barely understand him, "our intel says two months, but that could change."

"We'll find a place for you to meet with us and the club members. How can we reach you when we have it arranged?"

Marya stood and handed him a business card.

After leaning forward and taking it, he looked down at it and sounded surprised when he uttered, "A gym?"

"F.L.A.G. Fight Like A Girl Gym." Marya sounded proud. "We may be champions to gods, but that doesn't mean we don't have bills to pay."

Axle still looked confused, and Crush could understand that. "We'll be in touch," he mumbled, and slipped the card in the side pocket of his cut. Then he turned and headed back to his bike.

Crush gave the foursome one last glare before she turned on her heel and stomped to her bike. After mounting it and turning it on, she glanced at Axle and shrugged before they all took off.

Lucifer

When Crush, Axle, and their members returned to the compound, Lucifer was eating lunch. He finally was able to grab a bite to eat at the diner without feeling like a mooch. After helping the clubs and keeping Sugar safe, Skull asked him if he wanted to go to work with Trip, one of the members in charge of doing needed repairs on any of the Howlers or Tiger's Claw owned properties. Lucifer jumped on it since he was tired of being idle and depending on the kindness of the clubs to feed and clothe him.

Yes, he was *finally* able to buy his own food, and wasn't ashamed to admit how proud of that fact he was. Setting his meatball sub back down on his plate, only a couple bites eaten, he studied the look on Crush's face through the window as she got off her bike. She looked thoughtful, maybe even concerned.

"Something wrong with your food?"

Lucifer didn't look away from Crush when he answered Kitty's question. "No, but can I get a box, please?"

"Sure thing." Kitty was a Tiger's Claw member who frequently served at the diner. She was a bit older than most of the Tiger's Claw members, but she was smoking hot and knew it. To Lucifer, she was a very nice-looking woman who was a sister to the woman he was meant to be with, so he didn't feel a damn thing for her but respect.

His eyes hadn't left Crush as she stood with Pinky and Nails by their bikes. As they talked, Crush put one hand to her hip and used the other to rub her forehead. Lucifer wanted to see if there was any way to help, but he knew she'd shut him down if he tried.

"Here ya go."

Lucifer pulled his gaze away from Crush to look down at the table and found that his sandwich and onion rings were boxed up for him. "Thanks, Kitty."

As he pulled his wallet from his pocket, Kitty quietly said, "Don't give up on her."

Lucifer looked up at her and saw that she was staring at Crush through the window like he had been. He waited for her gaze to meet his before he replied, "I'm not going anywhere. When she's ready, I'll be here."

Kitty gave a smile and winked. "No doubt she's going to make you work for it, but I promise she'll also make it worth it."

He chuckled and dropped a twenty on the table. "She already has. I like her feisty."

"She is that," Kitty confirmed and patted him on the shoulder before she walked away.

As Lucifer slid out of the booth, he looked back to where Crush was standing. She was now staring over at him and looked pissed. He was confused as to why until he thought about what had just happened. Kitty had smiled at him, winked at him, and touched him. His feisty kitten didn't like that at all.

Grinning, Lucifer picked up his food and headed for the front door. When he stepped outside, he blew Crush a kiss before he headed for the apartment building.

He wasn't surprised at all that she caught up with him just inside the building as he was about to head up the stairs.

Crush

"What the fuck was that?" Crush demanded as she grabbed hold of Lucifer's bicep and yanked him around to face her. She ignored the smug look on his face as she waited for his answer.

Lucifer leaned down and set his to-go container on the stairs before fully facing her. Looking into her eyes, he asked, "What?"

"Why in the fuck are you flirting with Kitty?"

His eyebrows shot up his forehead, and he laughed. "Flirting with Kitty? Why would you think I was flirting with her?"

"She winked at you."

He nodded. "And I did what?"

"You... you smiled at her."

"Okay." He shrugged. "I've smiled at Axle, too. Does that mean I'm flirting with him?"

"Don't be ridiculous," she growled at him.

T.S. Tappin

"*I'm* being ridiculous? How about you just admit that you're jealous? And while you're at it, admit that the reason you're jealous is because I'm yours."

Crush scoffed and crossed her arms over her chest as she looked away from him. He was crazy if he thought she would admit that. And she wasn't jealous. She just didn't like him flirting with other women. He did flirt, right? She ran back through what she witnessed and tried to pinpoint what exactly he did that was inappropriate. The problem was she couldn't think of anything. Even Kitty winking at him wasn't a surprise. Kitty winked at everyone. She flirted with everyone. None of it was with intent. She had other ways of making sure a man knew she was interested, and Crush didn't see her do any of those things with Lucifer.

"Crush," Lucifer said, pulling her gaze back to him, "admit that I'm yours."

Crush stared at him, but she didn't say the words. She couldn't. If she said it to him, it would be real, and she wouldn't be able to run from it. And didn't that just irritate the fuck out of her. She didn't run. It wasn't something in her playbook, unless she was faced with a mate capable of breaking through her emotional brick wall, apparently.

Lucifer stepped close to her and reached up. He slid his hand across the side of her head to cup the back of it. Staring into her eyes, he whispered, "One of these days, you're going to stop fighting this so much. Don't get rid of those claws. I like them, and I know I'm going to love them digging in my back as I fuck the hell out of you. I'm not looking for you to change. I want you to tell me off. I want you to throw me attitude. I want every bit of that fire in your eyes directed my way. I just want to be at your side when you face the hard shit, and to be able to fuck you at the end of the day."

Before Crush could say anything, not that she knew what to say, he leaned forward and took her lips in a scorching kiss that had her pressing her thighs together to try to relieve the ache that had developed between them. When he broke the kiss, he laid his forehead against hers for a moment before he pulled away.

As Crush watched him pick up his to-go container and head up the stairs, it took everything in her not to follow him up. She wanted to, but it would just open a can of worms she wasn't ready to deal with. She already felt like she had the world resting on her shoulders. They had a damn war with the Hell's Dogs and their allies to deal with. Crush had just found out that gods existed, and apparently, they sent champions to help them fight. Until she could resolve all of that, she couldn't take on another problem, a problem she wanted, but couldn't admit to herself just yet.

Swallowing the lump in her throat and telling her tiger to shut the hell up, she left the building and headed for her place.

T.S. Tappin

Chapter Twelve

Lucifer

Lucifer was fucking cranky. After his conversation with Crush, he finished his lunch in his room and tried to take a nap, but all he did was lay there and think about her. The woman was driving him crazy, but he couldn't deny that he liked the fire between them, even when the fire was because of irritation. She would never bore him, that much he knew without a doubt.

He was tired and frustrated as he descended the steps. He knew they were facing some big shit, from conversations he'd overheard in the clubhouse. That, added to what he already knew the other Hell's Dogs chapters were planning, it wasn't a stretch to figure out that the battle was coming their way.

Lucifer felt somewhat responsible for what the Howlers and the Claws were facing. He wanted to help, but every time he tried to approach a member to figure out how he could be involved, he was shut down. He was tired of that shit, which is why he was frustrated and cranky.

When he reached the bottom of the stairs, Lucifer headed outside and across the compound to the clubhouse. He was reaching for the door handle to pull the door open, when it flung out in front of him, and Crush stepped through. She stopped and stared at him for a moment. Then she went to step around him.

Fuck that. Lucifer stepped to the side to put himself in front of her. "Can we talk?" When she let out a heavy sigh, he quickly added, "It's not about us."

Her brows pulled together, but she shrugged. "Okay. What's up?"

Lucifer slid his hands into the front pockets of his jeans and met her gaze. "I want to help. I know you all are facing an upcoming battle with the Hell's Dogs, and I want to help."

Before he even finished, she was shaking her head and crossing her arms over her chest in defiance. "No. This is our fight."

Fuck that. "I was in it before you showed up at my clubhouse and kidnapped me, Crush. I happen to be on a different side now, but you can't keep me out."

Her eyes popped green as she glared at him. "Fucking watch me, Lucy. This is a family problem."

Family? And he wasn't family? He wasn't part of the family? Lucifer felt like she slugged him. "A family problem? And I'm not fucking family?"

"Luc—"

"No, don't fucking try to explain it away, Crush. I'm not family. I fucking got it." He started backing down the steps. "When I put my life on the fucking line for the Howlers and the Claws, it wasn't in the name of family." He nodded angrily. "When I protected April and made sure she was able to come home to Siren, that wasn't in the name of fucking family. Got it."

"Lucifer," she said on a huff and dropped her arms to her sides.

"Well, if I'm not your family, I don't see why I'm staying loyal to you then." He reached the bottom of the steps and turned. As he headed for his bike, he called over his shoulder. "Guess I'll head to Heat and do whatever the fuck I want, because I sure as hell have no reason not to."

Lucifer heard her call his name, but he didn't stop to look back at her. He was fucking over it.

Skull

They weren't shouting, but their voices carried just the same. As Skull was talking to Zero and Smoke just inside one of the open bay doors of the garage, he heard pretty much every word Lucifer and Crush said, along with Zero and Smoke.

T.S. Tappin

Right around the time he heard Crush say that it was a family problem, he stepped over to the open door and looked out, and because they were all nosy fuckers, Zero and Smoke joined him.

They watched and listened as the couple fought. Crush may deny Lucifer with her words, but there was no denying the fact that they fought like an old, mated couple.

He winced when Lucifer said he was going to *Heat*, since he had no reason to be loyal to Crush. That shit had to hurt. Did he think Lucifer would actually go to Heat? Fucking no. That man was balls deep in his infatuation with Crush. He would go and drown his sorrows, but he wouldn't do it at Heat.

"Fucking hell," Zero commented as they watched Lucifer ride away.

"I don't think I've ever seen Crush that destroyed," Smoke uttered, quietly.

Skull shifted his gaze from Lucifer on his bike as he headed down the road to Crush, standing in front of the clubhouse watching him go. She looked pissed the hell off, but she also looked hurt. Her brows were pulled down and in, her chest was heaving with labored breaths, and she was clenching and unclenching her fists at her sides. Once Lucifer was out of sight, Crush's chin dropped to her chest and her arms crossed over her chest. Seeing her display any emotion other than annoyance and anger stunned Skull. He blinked, then his gaze shifted to the sky to watch for flying pigs.

Lucifer

Lucifer was halfway to Heat when the guilt hit him. He had calmed down enough to realize that there was no way he would cut Crush loose, especially not over this. She was testing his limits of what he would put up with, but he never expected her to make things easy for him.

He was still pissed and wanted to let her stew in her bullshit, but he didn't need to betray her to do that. And in his heart, going to Heat with the intention of hurting Crush would be a betrayal. As soon as there was clear road, he swung a U-turn and headed back into town. He'd let her wonder if he went to Heat. Let her wonder if he was really ending any chance they had, and then when the time was right and the fight with the Hell's Dogs was over, he'd come back and force her to face the fact that they were fucking meant to be together.

With that decision clear in his brain, he turned into the parking lot of Bobby's Bar. Time to drown his frustrations in a bottle of whiskey and some good tunes.

The next day... Axle

When Axle arrived at Milhawk Investigations with Skull and Pike, they entered the large lobby to wait for the Claws representatives to arrive. Michael "Mick" Hawkin, owner of Milhawk Investigations, leaned back against the receptionist desk when they walked in. As usual, Hawkin had his employees, Beckett Major and Teagan Banks, with him. Since the business was technically closed, Hawkin voiced they could meet in the large lobby to discuss any help M.I. could give the Howlers and the Claws with the battle that they were staring at with the Hell's Dogs and their allies.

Hawkin was just under six feet tall with assessing brown eyes that missed nothing. Often clocking everything without letting you know, he tucked that information away for when he needed it. He wasn't a bulky man, but he wasn't lanky, either. Hawkin was strong physically, and no one would doubt that, but his biggest strength was his mind.

At first glance, you would assume he was just an older man who took care of his body, but the truth was he hid his almost genius level intelligence behind that well-defined body, shaggy salt-and-pepper hair, and gray soul patch.

Being CEO of Milhawk Investigations didn't mean you'd find him in a suit, either. He always wore black jeans or cargos, a black tee, and black boots. If it was cold, or he needed to hide his weapons, he might slip on a black jacket. His less-than-professional wardrobe was part of the reason Axle felt comfortable around him.

If you chose to underestimate him, it was a choice you would regret. If he didn't make you regret it, one of his crew most certainly would.

Crush's Fall

About a year ago, he caught Axle shifting into his wolf on a camera and held that information close, not sharing it with anyone else. Because of that, Axle trusted Hawkin, even if they sometimes had different views on what justice should look like.

"Just the six of us?" Hawkin had his arms crossed over his chest as he leaned back and rested his ass on the front side of his assistant's desk. That assistant happened to be Pike's mate, Pixie, or as Mick knew her, Alyssa.

"Crush, Pinky, and Nails will be here soon," Skull answered as he took a seat in one of the steel and brown leather chairs along the side wall of the lobby.

Axle sat in a chair directly across the space from Hawkin. Pike stood by Axle. Banks and Major stood across the room from Skull. Axle smirked at the way all of them had walls at their back. Even Hawkin had a wall just a few feet behind that desk.

"I can start explaining what's going on while we wait for Crush." Axle leaned forward, resting his elbows on his knees. "Is this room listening?"

Hawkin flashed a smile before he looked over at Banks and gave a nod. Banks rolled her light brown eyes. She was a handful of inches shorter than six feet tall, with long, dark brown hair that had a natural wave to it. Her standard outfit was a black muscle shirt and a tight pair of black jeans, a ponytail, and very little makeup. She was pretty, and she looked sweet, but she could take any man in that room without breaking a sweat.

She rounded the desk. "Ears and eyes are off," she said after pressing a few buttons before returning to her spot on the wall.

Axle didn't take offense to Hawkin having surveillance equipment running without announcement. It was what Axle would do if he were in Hawkin's position. "We eliminated the charter who kidnapped Trip's ol' lady, Darlin' and my siblings, tried to kill us, tried to force Pumps to go back with them, and also ran drugs through our state. We also eliminated three of the major drug players in SW Michigan, one of whom kidnapped Butterfly, Bullet's ol' lady, also kidnapped Sugar, Siren's ol' lady, and was also trafficking women and working with another chapter of the Hell's Dogs MC."

"That's a lot of ammo you've just given me," Hawkin said with narrowed eyes. "I could go to the police with that. You know that, which leads me to believe you want something from me and are trying to build trust."

"Other chapters of the HDMC have teamed up with a few Reapers MC chapters and supposedly the UpRiders." Axle met Hawkin's gaze. "We have a war breathing down our necks. And we need all the help we can get."

Hawkin turned his head and looked over at Major. The two of them just stared at each other, but Axle knew what that meant. He often had silent conversations with his brothers.

While they waited for Hawkin's response, the door opened and Nails walked in, looking around before she stepped aside to let Crush and Pinky enter. As sergeant at arms, it was her job to protect her president. Axle always liked Nails. She was great at her job.

"Catch me up," Crush said as she slid into the chair next to the one Axle was sitting in.

Nails flanked Crush the same way Pike was flanking Axle. And Pinky sat down next to Skull.

"I caught them up on what has happened between us and the HDMC as well as Alito," Alito being Butterfly's late monster of a husband, "and the shit stains that took Sugar. I also told them we're facing a war and need as much help as we can get. That's when you walked in."

"Get him," Hawkin said to Major.

Beckett Major was a very built and broad Black man with a bald head and stood well over six feet tall, dressing much like Hawkin, except Major's jeans were blue instead of black. Crush had told him once that Major was a man that many women wouldn't turn down, so Axle took that to mean he was attractive.

Major gave Hawkin a nod, before he turned and approached a door off the back wall of the room. After punching a code into a keypad, there was a click, and Major pulled the door open.

Growls and hisses rang through the room as Riles, the UpRiders MC president, and four other members walked through the door Major had just opened. The UpRiders had been allies to the Howlers for years, until they jumped into bed with the Hell's Dogs to set up the

Howlers for ambush. It ended in a handful of the UpRiders being taken out, the Hell's Dogs being arrested, and the UpRides picking new leadership. Axle had given them another chance to prove that they could be trusted, and that the bad seeds were taken out, but seeing them in his territory without invitation or announcement crossed the fucking line. It was an unspoken rule in biker culture to announce oneself if you were going to be in another club's territory. The UpRiders hadn't done that. With the war hot on their heels, seeing the UpRiders unannounced in their territory had Axle's wolf on edge.

"Weber," Hawkin warned, "not here. Listen to them."

"Why should we? They are partnering with our enemies." Axle knew he was close to the edge of shifting. His wolf was prowling and snarling inside of him. The weight of protecting the club and their families was crushing him. Facing the people responsible for the suffering of people he loved only made it harder to bear.

Riles shook his head. "No, Axle, that's not true." He ran his hand through his hair and huffed out a breath. "I made a promise to you guys, and I meant that. I'm here to keep that. I just found out what some of my members are doing. They aren't working under my orders or the orders of my VP."

"If you can't keep your members under control," Skull said as he stood, "then we'll eliminate the club and be done with it. We've already had this fucking talk with you."

Riles glared at Skull. "My club has nothing to do with the HDMC. We have five members who were left over from BM's days, who were on board with what he was doing. As soon as I found out what they were planning on their tubing trip, the rest of us rode down to warn you."

"Why didn't you come to us?" Crush asked, arms crossed over her chest as she leaned back in the chair, looking like she didn't have a care in the world.

Shifting his attention to her, Riles answered, "Because I wasn't sure of the reception we'd get, and we can't defend ourselves against both of your clubs. So, I came to the one place I knew would give me an opportunity to have a sit down with you, without allowing you to just take me out. Hawkin wouldn't allow that in his office, and you have too much respect for him to do it here, anyway."

"How did you know about Hawkin and the respect between us?" Axle eyed Riles as he waited for an answer, watching for any indication he was lying.

"I've known Rex since he was a prospect," Riles answered, mentioning the Howlers MC member he was most familiar with, and gave a shrug. "I was around when Joker met with the former owner. Rex mentioned that Hawkin wasn't as tight with the Howlers, but there was mutual respect."

"If that's what you want to call it," Banks mumbled.

Hawkin shot her a look, but he couldn't hide the smirk.

"We already knew UpRiders were working with the HDMC," Axle said with a shrug.

Riles nodded. "They don't know that these two are on my side." Hitching a finger over his shoulder, Riles motioned to two young men, both a good six inches taller than Riles.

One of them had a head full of long, black hair, tied back at the nape of his neck. His eyes were a light blue and assessing like Hawkins. He was smart, Axle would bet on it. He looked to be fit and a bit on the muscular side, not as big as Axle or Skull.

The other kept his brown hair almost completely buzzed, but he had a bushy, full beard on his face. His eyes were a medium brown. He looked to be the more muscular of the two, but not by much. This one could have been Skull's younger brother with the same build.

Riles continued, "They are willing to infiltrate the traitors and feed us information."

"How do you know you can trust them?" Pike asked from over Axle's left shoulder.

"I practically raised these boys. I knew their dads before some shit happened. My club was unaware of what I'd been doing, but I was at every damn game, every birthday, every Christmas."

"We didn't go without because of Riles," the long-haired one interjected. "He asked us to keep that quiet when we asked to prospect, so we did… out of respect for him."

The other one nodded. "We'd do anything for Riles… because he's earned that loyalty."

Riles stared at Axle. "I hate what is happening. I want to fix this, but I need some help. If we cut out the rot, we can rebuild the relationship the UpRiders MC once had with your club and the Claws."

"We'll talk it over. Where are you staying?" This from Crush.

Riles gave a nod. "I haven't arranged that yet. We got into the area a few hours ago."

"They were telling me what they know when you texted me, Weber," Hawkin explained.

Axle looked over at Skull. "Arrange rooms for them at the hotel. Tell Mama Hen we don't want her there for a couple of nights, and we'll have someone run the place for her."

"Tell her I'll send a few of the Claws," Crush said and stood. "Give me an hour and they'll be there."

Skull nodded and pulled his phone out of his pocket as he walked out of the room with Crush, Pinky, and Nails.

"If you even so much as stain a pillowcase, I will destroy you," Axle told them, meaning every word.

T.S. Tappin

Chapter Thirteen

Axle

In the parking lot outside of Mama Hen's hotel, The Hen House, Axle and Crush straddled their bikes and watched as Skull and Pinky talked to Mama Hen in the lobby. Pike and Nails were standing off to the side on their phones.

Mama Hen was a friend of both clubs and had been for years. She was an older woman with brightly dyed teal hair and a snarky attitude. The clubs would do anything to protect her, and there wasn't a soul in Warden's Pass who didn't love that woman. If anyone crossed her, they would have both clubs on their ass. She was also the blood aunt to Kisy, Dragon's yet-to-be-claimed mate. When they found that out, it only made her more important to them.

T.S. Tappin

"I think we have to send Rex in," Axle told Crush. "He's more familiar with Riles."

Crush let out a sigh. "I trust what he was saying. I just don't know if I trust the younger men to be able to pull this off. I think we should send Ranger with Rex. See if he can get them tips on not standing out like sore thumbs."

Axle smiled. "Good thinking."

"I know I'm a woman, Axle, but that doesn't mean I'm incapable of common sense."

Axle looked over at her and raised an eyebrow. "You're crankier than usual."

Crush flipped him off. "We're facing war. It's likely that we won't make it out of this without damage. That makes me cranky."

"Lucifer doesn't have anything to do with your bad mood? I heard you turned him away, and he told you he was going to Heat then." He watched as her jaw clenched and her grip on the handlebar tightened. Axle lowered his voice so only she could hear and said, "He didn't go. He went to Bobby's and got hammered. Bobby called, and I sent Rock to go get him. He's sleeping it off in his room at the compound."

She gave a slight nod and tried to hide her sigh of relief.

"What are you waiting for?"

Crush's head turned sharply, and she glared at him. She opened her mouth, no doubt to lay into him about minding his own damn business, but she clamped her mouth shut when Pike and Nails approached.

"Vix, Ivy, and Ginger are going to guard the room. Shortcake is going to run the desk. She filled in when Mama Hen went on vacation."

"And I called Rex. I assumed you wanted him involved in this," Pike informed Axle.

Axle nodded. Pike knew him well, so Axle didn't take offense to his assumptions.

"Well... let's hope we aren't letting roosters into Mama Hen's house," Crush deadpanned.

Axle and Pike snorted laughs at the corny joke. Nails just grinned and shook her head.

Crush

Standing in the clubhouse, Crush cursed under her breath when she saw Pumps sidle up to Dragon's side and put her hand to his chest. That shit was not going to go over well with the woman who had spent most of the evening eye-fucking Dragon. Kisy may be a human, but she was feisty, and it didn't take a rocket scientist to realize Dragon had all but claimed her.

In a blink, Kisy was across the room and shoving Pumps away from Dragon. "Hands fucking off, Bitch!"

Fuck!

Pumps caught herself on a table and straightened on her usual ridiculously high heels before she turned a glare on Kisy.

Right or wrong, Crush and the Claws backed up Pumps by lining up behind her, ready to jump in if anyone else joined the fray.

T.S. Tappin

Crush wasn't at all surprised when the Ol' Ladies did the same behind Kisy. Whether or not Dragon claimed her was irrelevant in their eyes. Kisy was already one of them.

A hiss cut through the room, and Crush knew things were inching awfully close to the edge of no return. That was confirmed when Pumps's eyes began to glow, and her fangs slid down.

"Bring it, bitch," Kisy taunted and readied herself. Crush had to admit she was impressed. Kisy wasn't about to back down, and that took some motherfucking balls as a human facing off with a pissed off shifter.

"Kisy," Dragon began, but he shut up when she turned a glare on him.

"No fangs or claws," Axle stated. "Crush, tell her."

Crush let out a deep sigh, knowing Axle was right. "She's human, Pumps. Fair fight."

Pumps snarled, but she retracted the fangs before she took a step toward Kisy. "I'm about to teach you not to put your hands on people."

"When you learn that fucking lesson, I might listen. In the meantime, I'm going to teach you what the fuck happens when a bitch thinks she can put her hands on my man." Then Kisy launched herself at Pumps, tackling her to the ground, taking down a few Claws in the process.

Crush rolled her eyes before she went about helping her sisters back to their feet. Shit was about to get real if they didn't get control of the situation, but first, she needed to get the other women out of the way.

Before Pumps could get her wits about her, Kisy held her down with a hand to her throat. Fisting her other hand, she swung repeatedly, hitting Pumps in the eye, the jaw, the nose. Pumps grabbed a hold of Kisy's face and was pushing her back, while her other hand tried to block Kisy's blows.

Something crunched under Kisy's fist just as Dragon wrapped his arms around her waist and yanked her off of Pumps.

"Let me go," Kisy shouted and futilely fought to get free.

"I'm not letting you fucking go," Dragon growled in her ear.

"I wasn't fucking done!"

"You made your point, Love," Dragon replied with pride in his voice.

Then her ass was on the bar and Dragon was in her face. His eyes scanned her body, settling on her right hand. His brows drew together, and a growl came out of him when he saw split knuckles and blood.

"Fuck," Kisy spat out.

"Yeah. Fuck." Dragon gently lifted her hand so he could look at it better. "I don't think you broke anything."

"Good." Then she hissed in pain.

Dragon scowled at her hand. "Ice! First aid kit!" His barked order was immediately answered. The prospect set a baggie of ice and a large white box on the bar next to Kisy's hip.

As Dragon cleaned up Kisy's hand, Crush called Siren over to take a look at Pumps's face. He told her

Pumps's nose was broken right before he put his hands to her face, did some jerky movements, and Pumps hissed.

"Should heal just fine."

"Go clean yourself up," Crush ordered. "Then you and I need to talk."

Pumps sighed but crossed the room to go to the bathroom.

While she was gone, Crush returned her attention to Dragon and Kisy. Axle was standing next to them and was grinning. "Your man? Who said he's yours? Dragon tell you that?"

Crush watched as Kisy leaned down and licked Dragon's face from bearded jaw to temple. "I licked him, so he's mine."

She couldn't help the snort of laughter that burst from her. Kisy was going to keep Dragon on his toes. Crush loved that for him.

When Pumps stepped out of the bathroom, Crush was waiting in the hall for her. Her blond hair had spots that were darker with blood, but Crush could tell that she had tried her best to rinse it out. Her nose was already swelling and bruising, but within a few hours it would heal enough that you wouldn't be able to tell it had even been broken.

Crush leaned back against the wall and crossed her arms over her chest. "You knew he was hers."

Pumps scowled. "No, I didn't. He hasn't claimed her."

"That's not the point, Pumps. He was doing his Dom thing with her all night. He didn't even try to hide it. He may not have completed the mating or given her his property patch, but he basically pissed a circle around her."

After a sigh, Pumps nodded. "Guess I was just being a bitch."

Crush chuckled. "It seems to be a trait of the members of our club."

"You want me to apologize or some shit?"

After a scoff, Crush replied, "Fuck no. That's Dragon's problem now."

Lucifer

Watching Pumps cross the room, Lucifer grinned. Her nose looked jacked up. She took a seat next to him at the table and turned to face him. When she saw his grin, she shot him the bird.

"Shut the hell up," she grumbled.

He chuckled. "I didn't say anything."

"You were thinking it."

"That you used to be able to fight better than that? Yeah, I was thinking it. I remember the time the girl took your chocolate milk off your tray in the lunchroom, and you used that tray to beat the hell out of her. No one ever tried to take your milk again."

T.S. Tappin

"That milk is the shit," Pumps commented and took a drink of his whiskey.

"Kisy can throw hands."

Pumps nodded and looked over at him, surprise on her face. "Right? I was a little shocked."

After they shared a laugh, he asked, "Were you ever going to tell me that shifters existed? I mean, hell, we grew up together."

Pumps patted him on the shoulder. "You weren't mature enough to have that knowledge. Honestly, whether you're mature enough *now* is still up for debate."

Bullet

Now that Butterfly's stalker husband was eliminated, as well as the uncle who had been working with him, Bullet felt it was important to bring Butterfly fully into his family. He called his parents and was instantly reprimanded for not calling them sooner. Apparently, Crush, his bratty little sister had called his mother days before to inform her that Bullet's mate had shown up and he was being an idiot about recognizing it.

He was an idiot? Wait until he told their mother how Crush's mate had been in town for months, and she was pretending he didn't exist. No. Bullet wouldn't do that, because then he'd have to explain why, and the why would have his father down at the clubhouse to go head-to-head with Lucifer. As much as he would love someone to take Lucifer out of the picture, he didn't like the idea of putting his sister in that position. Whether he liked Lucifer or not, he was Crush's mate.

Once again, he was protecting his baby sister from consequences of her own choices. Only this time, he was protecting her from their parents. Sure, she couldn't pick who her mate was, but she picked how she handled the situation. If she would have just brought Lucifer over to meet their parents, Bullet wouldn't feel the need to keep it a secret.

At the end of the call, he had promised to bring Butterfly to their house for dinner, which he did. Several days later, as they sat at his parents' dining table and ate his mother's fantastic lemon white fish, his mother was glaring at him. But when her gaze shifted to Butterfly, the glare disappeared and was replaced by the beautiful smile of a mother excited for another daughter.

"It's a shame Crush couldn't come tonight," his father said as he pushed his empty plate away. "She loves this recipe."

Bullet finished chewing his bite and swallowed. "Her and Axle have been pretty busy. Running a club and businesses are pretty time-consuming." He cut off another piece and put it in his mouth.

"It doesn't help that Lucifer trails behind her like a puppy waiting for a treat," Butterfly said, lifting her glass of wine to take a drink.

Bullet's eyes went wide, and he nearly choked on the bite he had just put in his mouth. He should have talked to Butterfly about Crush and Lucifer before they arrived.

Well, the cat was out of the bag now.

"Lucifer?" The way his father said the man's name was a lot like the way he would say *murderer*.

Bullet swallowed and cleared his throat. "Uh... yeah. He's... well, he's... He's her mate, but she hasn't... come to terms with it, yet."

His mother rolled her eyes. "That woman can't stand to hand over any control... not even to fate."

She seemed calm, but Bullet knew his mother. The moment he and Butterfly left, she'd be on the phone demanding Crush bring Lucifer over for dinner as soon as possible.

Trying to be discreet, Bullet pulled his phone out of his pocket and kept it under the table as he looked down and typed out a text to Crush.

Bullet : Mom knows about Lucifer. Sorry. Heads up. Will explain later.

The reply came instantly.

Crush : I'm going to enjoy tearing out your throat.

He felt Butterfly's hand on his thigh and looked over at her. "I'm sorry," she mouthed.

He winked at her and gave her a smile. Crush would be pissed, but it would be fine. Maybe bringing Lucifer to dinner would make her face the truth. As much as Bullet didn't like it, Lucifer was Crush's mate, and he'd earned the right to be claimed.

Crush

Staring down at the message she just received from her brother, Crush cursed under her breath and sent her reply.

"What?" Pinky asked, as they sat together at a table by the bar in the clubhouse.

Crush showed her the text string and rolled her eyes as Pinky busted out with laughter.

"Sorry," Pinky said, and attempted to quell her laughter, but she failed and started laughing harder.

"Bitch," Crush muttered and took a drink of her beer.

"You know you're going to have to deal with that, eventually. Your mom is not going to accept that you're not ready for a mate. You know how she feels about mates and fate."

"I won't be bullied into anything," Crush grumbled, and slid her phone back into her pocket.

As much as she wanted Lucifer, and knew they would eventually end up together, she wasn't sure she was ready for that. The idea of giving a part of herself to him scared the shit out of her. She worked hard to prove she was capable and independent, that she didn't need a man at her side, and she worried that her reputation wouldn't survive if she gave in. With a man like Lucifer, strong and outspoken, she could already see her future — devalued and only known as Lucifer's mate. *Nah. Fuck that.*

T.S. Tappin

Chapter Fourteen

Lucifer

Hearing Crush and Pinky's conversation as he sat at the bar and ate his Chicken Bacon Ranch Wrap, his to-go order from the diner, Lucifer winced. He could practically read Crush's mind. The idea of someone bullying Crush into accepting him as her mate would only send her spiraling and pushing him further away.

He started to wonder if it was even worth it. Why was he even trying? If she didn't want him, why was he hanging around? Okay, sure, he was there for the Howlers as much as for her. He knew they were still suspicious and hesitant, but he still wanted to prove to them he was good enough.

Lucifer wanted to be the type of man that was worthy of wearing the Howlers' colors. He wouldn't kiss their asses, but he would put in effort to show them who he was and what he could offer.

It was odd for Lucifer. Part of him was solely focused on Crush, and another part was focused on establishing himself in the Howlers-Tiger's Claw family. The rest of him was of the I-am-who-I-am mindset. He migrated from one line of thought to another in a very short period of time, sometimes the two thoughts contradicting each other.

Shaking his head to clear his thoughts, he focused on eating his food and tried to keep Crush off of his mind. That lasted about three minutes before he wondered if she missed his attention at all.

Crush

When Bullet and Butterfly stepped into the clubhouse, Crush got up from her seat and made a beeline for them. She gave Butterfly a slight smile, not feeling angry with her sister-in-law at all, before she glared at Bullet and poked him in the chest, hard.

"Are you *fucking* kidding me?" She was livid, but her tiger was silent, probably because her tiger wished she'd just go claim their mate.

Bullet crossed his arms over his chest and glared back at her. "You called Mom as soon as Butterfly got to town."

"Not *as soon as*," she scoffs.

"Close enough."

"So, this is to get back at me?" She shook her head at him. "You know damn well that our parents meeting Butterfly is completely different than them meeting…"

Bullet's brow lifted. "Why?"

Crush winced and dropped her gaze to the floor. "He's…"

"Your mate, Sis," Bullet said, low. "You're just pissed because if you bring him to meet our parents, you won't be able to deny it anymore. You'll have to face it. You'll have to accept it… accept *him*."

Her eyes lifted to his face again, and she glared. "Fuck. You."

"Hit a nerve?" He had the audacity to grin.

Frustrated, annoyed, and pissed the hell off at her brother, Crush did the only thing that a young sister could do in that situation. She partially shifted her hand, reached out, and quickly dragged her claws across his face. She barely broke skin, but it was enough to get her point across.

As Bullet's eyes started to glow in anger, Butterfly stepped between them with her hands up. "Hold on. Wait. It was me. I did it! I told your parents! I didn't realize it was such a secret. I'm sorry, Crush. Really. Don't be mad at him. There's no need for this!"

The anger slowly faded out of her as her sister-in-law spoke while her brother shoved his mate behind him to protect her from Crush. She would never hurt Butterfly, and she knew Butterfly didn't mean to cause her problems.

The whole situation was fucked up. Looking at Butterfly, who was peeking around Bullet's side, she gave a nod and then stormed past them and out of the clubhouse.

Lucifer

As he watched Crush storm away, Lucifer couldn't help but watch the way her hips angrily swayed with each stomp of her shitkickers. *Fuck*, he couldn't wait to get her naked and under him. She would be wild, he just knew it.

Fully aware that her brother was standing a few feet away from him, he uttered, "I wonder if she's a tiger in bed."

Instantly, Bullet hissed and lunged for Lucifer, but he didn't even flinch. Lucifer just grinned at Bullet. Trip slammed a hand over Lucifer's mouth and shoved Bullet's chest with the other. Two seconds later, Dragon's hands wrapped around the top of Bullet's shoulders and forcefully steered a snarling Bullet away.

Lucifer knew he should be worried for his life, since Bullet could end him without breaking a sweat, but Lucifer just chuckled.

Trip dropped his hand from Lucifer's face and shook his head. "You are a ballsy motherfucker. I'll give you that."

Lucifer nodded. "Coming from you, I'll take that as a compliment."

Crush

Since her mother found out about Lucifer, she had been texting Crush, demanding to meet him. The third text message in twelve hours vibrated her phone, but she ignored it as she headed for the front door of Milhawk Investigations with her club sisters. She would introduce Lucifer to her parents if she ever decided to actually make things official. Until then, they could just fucking wait.

Walking inside, Crush was preparing herself for being annoyed, since she knew she would leave that way. She barely managed to tolerate Axle's control issues. Dealing with the control issues of the president of the UpRiders, the leader of the champions, and Hawkin was no doubt going to set her on edge.

They were at M.I. to make a plan to handle the war and to pair up champions with members of their clubs to help bridge the gap when it came to spreading necessary information among so many people under the command of several different leaders. It made sense, but it was the part of the job of president of a motorcycle club that tested her patience the most.

What they entered wasn't a conference room, but rather a wide-open, unused section of the warehouse that held the headquarters of Milhawk Investigations. At least it was clean and well lit.

Directly across from the door they entered through, Lira and her champions were lined up. To the right was the Milhawk investigations team, as well as Riles and his few UpRiders. As Crush and the Claws moved off to the left, her tiger was pacing inside of her, already reacting to the tension.

She waited there, eyeing the other groups, as they waited for the Axle and the Howlers to file into the space.

In the middle of the room was a conference table large enough for ten people. Once the Howlers were in the room, Crush and Pinky headed for the table, along with the other leaders and their seconds. The rest of the members of the clubs and the other factions hung back in their respective sections, watching and ready to act if necessary. If any of them made a wrong move, this could be a bloodbath.

After much discussion, it was decided that Axle and Lira would be in charge of the war movements, with Hawkin and his crew only coming in if necessary, or if they had new intel on the movements of the other side. Crush was okay with this only because Axle was one of the leaders. She trusted Axle enough to know he wouldn't fuck the Claws over, especially in something so important.

Crush could understand Hawkin's hesitancy to be involved. Laws were going to be broken, and while Hawkin tried to avoid doing that, he was also the type to always side with good over evil. Despite their differences, Hawkin knew the Howlers and the Claws were good people.

"Who is watching your women and children?"

At Lira's question to Axle, Crush's gaze swung over to the woman, and she glared.

Axle stared back. "Half of the Claws and a handful of the Howlers. Do you need names?"

Lira smirked. "No. I was just curious."

"Your curiosity doesn't give me the warm fuzzies about this partnership," Crush said in a deadpan voice. Her glare didn't lessen even when she heard the Howlers and Claws chuckle.

Lira continued to smirk, but her second replied, "I thought the majority of you were fuzzy."

Trip snort laughed.

Ranger grinned at Dragon. "I think I like her."

He would, Crush thought.

"Relax, soldier," the second said with a grin. "I don't go for your type. I prefer my partners to have bigger balls and wear them on their chests."

A-motherfucking-men. Maybe these bitches weren't so bad after all.

"Which god do you represent?" Ranger asked flirtatiously. "I need to know which one I'll be praying to tonight."

Axle chuckled but said, "Shut it, Ranger. We need to finish the meeting, not find you a date. And no, we can't do both."

"Pres, not all of us have women waiting at home for us."

Trip laid a hand on Ranger's shoulder and looked at the back of Axle's head. "Yeah, Bro. Have a heart."

"Right," Ranger agreed, nodding. "I just want love."

T.S. Tappin

Dragon shook his head. "The two of you are going to get yourselves or the rest of us killed someday with your fucking mouths."

Trip and Ranger both opened their mouths to retort, but Axle turned around in his chair, and Crush could imagine the no-nonsense glare Axle was giving them when he bit out, "Not. Another. Word." In response, both of them snapped their mouths shut. *Smart.*

Lira waved a hand over her shoulder, and her crew stepped forward and lined up. "Let's sort out these partnerships."

For the next thirty minutes, Axle and Crush worked with Lira to place champions with members of the Howlers or the Claws and organize the general logistics for the war.

As they left Milhawk Investigations, Crush noticed a bruise on the jaw of her club sister. Halo tried covering it with makeup, but Crush's shifter sight was able to spot it pretty easily. When they reached the clubhouse, she pulled Halo aside. Standing near the back of the clubhouse in the parking lot, Crush pointed to Halo's jaw. "Explain."

Halo let out a sigh. "It's not a big deal."

"Then explain."

After staring back at Crush for a long moment, Halo replied, "I didn't just take it. He has a matching bruise."

Crush bit out, "As he should." She forced herself to take a few deep breaths. Her tiger was demanding she end the prick, but Crush knew better than to blindly follow the orders of her tiger. If she did, the world would be ashes by now. Instead of taking off on her bike to do away with Halo's boyfriend, she met her club sister's gaze and asked, "Want me to teach him how to treat you right?"

Halo grinned but shook her head. "Not yet."

"If you change your mind—"

"I know where to find you."

As much as it grated on Crush's moral code, she didn't go after the man and let Halo decide how to handle the situation. She calmed her tiger by vowing that they wouldn't let it go next time. No, they would end him and make it painful.

T.S. Tappin

Chapter Fifteen

A week later... Axle

Axle had spent thirty minutes on the phone with his father, Joker, the former president and now retired member of the Howlers, getting all the flight information for when the retired members would arrive in Michigan. He was worried about the war and needed guidance from his father, but a part of him was also worried about having the retired members returning. Putting even more of his family in danger didn't sit well with him. He knew better than to push Joker on it, though. His father would be pissed if he suggested they stay out of it.

When Axle took over the club, Joker and the rest of the older members moved to Florida to allow for the younger members to take over management without too much of a power struggle. It had been time for a change, so the older club brothers set up a retired chapter in their new state.

Axle tried again to convince his father to let the Howlers pick them up, but Joker wasn't having any of it. He told Axle he'd rent a car at the airport. Joker was coming with Griff and Thrash, Dragon and Rebel's fathers, the following afternoon. Joker had somehow convinced his Ol' Lady, Tweetie, to stay home with the other Ol' Ladies. Tweetie wasn't Axle's birth mother like she was Trip's, but she was his mom all the same. He didn't want her anywhere near Warden's Pass when there was a biker war going on.

Before he hung up the phone, Axle promised to keep Joker updated as to the movements in the meantime, then he and Crush made their way to the cafeteria where they were meeting with Lira and the other champions. Skull, Pinky, Pike, and Nails were already there.

When they entered the room, Axle was surprised that it was so quiet. Usually, there was talking going on when there were group events in their building. The silence was a bit unnerving to him.

There were four rectangular tables in use, each able to seat six to eight people. Three of the tables were filled with champions. At the fourth table, Lira and Marya sat with Pinky and Skull. Pike and Nails were standing off to the side, watching.

Axle and Crush took the seats between Skull and Pinky. He gave Lira a nod. "Thanks for getting all the champions together."

"We're here to help," Lira responded.

Crush crossed her arms over her chest and relaxed back. "In order to be effective, we need to know what weapons we have at our disposal."

Lira gave a nod. "That's understandable. What I need you to know going into this conversation is that each of the champions gets to decide what they are comfortable doing. We will not be forced to use powers we aren't comfortable using."

Axle shrugged. "That's understandable."

"Great." Lira took a deep breath and looked behind her. Two women raised their hands. "Along with Marya and myself, Rebekkah and Mezanya are Aileron Aegis champions. That means we serve Colvyr, the God of Stratera — the God of Balance and Calm, usually just referred to as the God of Balance."

"The guy in the boat shoes that I met."

Lira faced him again and nodded. "Yes. Our specialty is of the air. We are bird shifters. We have enhanced speed, agility, strength, hearing, and sight."

"Bird shifters?" Crush sat up and looked intrigued, a slight smile on her face.

"Yes," Lira chuckled. "Hawks, eagles, and ravens, mostly. Some falcons. We're a bit larger, just like you guys and your animal forms."

"That's kinda kickass," Crush admitted with a shrug.

T.S. Tappin

"Ordys is the lead champion of the Sagacity champions. Along with Rozzat and Vega, he serves Raghnall, the God of Sapientiam — the God of Wisdom and Thought, also referred to as the God of Wisdom and Judgment."

Axle looked over and saw Ordys, Rozzat, and Vega each give him a nod.

"They are dragon shifters. Their specialty is, as you can probably guess, fire. They have enhanced strength and speed, but they're also cunning and pretty good at persuasion. That's why their biggest weakness is their ego."

"Dragon shifters," Pike uttered from behind Axle. "That's insane."

"Maybe," Ordys began with a chuckle, "but it's true."

Lira smiled. "Next, we have two sets of champions, the Dolor Ayre and the Pangloss Eyne. They are closely connected, since their gods are twins. Rue is the God of Negans, the God of Negativity. Mattyx is the God of Positivum, the God of Positivity. Their champions are the ones that would be considered your gods since their champions are shifters of the water and the earth." She turned her head and nodded to the table behind her and to her left. "Luna, Sky, and Orion are Dolor Ayre. Sol, Storme, and Aurora are Pangloss Eyne." Each of the champions gave a wave, as their name was said. "Along with either pessimism or optimism, they have enhanced strength and hearing, but they are also really great at tracking, as you probably already know."

Axle wasn't surprised by any of that. It was basically any of his shifter brethren on steroids.

"Then we have Iri, Winona, and Chantel." She nodded to the table where the three champions were sitting. "They are Stehppes and serve Teko, the God of Accio — the God of Action. Storms, shadows, stealth, and security systems are their thing. Locks mean shit to them. I think you all might have some of their skills in that department. They are impulsive. But they have been pretty firm on not using their storm and shadow powers. It fucks with the weather systems." She shrugged as if she didn't quite understand that, but she also didn't care to. "They have the strength that the rest of us do."

Crush nodded. "And what type of animal or whatever do they have?"

"Snakes and reptiles," Iri said from his spot at the furthest table.

"Kickass," Pinky commented from next to Pike.

"And lastly, we have the Atax Aya. They are the vampires and other hybrids, only vampires here, though. Steve, Spike, Poindexter, and Aires." The middle table shot grins their way, showing off the fangs they let slide down. "They serve Aella, the God of Chaos. They are the spirit or energy god and can affect your energy, your spirit. Atax Aya are the masters of persuasion, manipulation, rumors. They aren't allergic to garlic or the sun… or even religious relics and are just like shifters, except they don't change form. Their eyes glow red, and their fangs come down, along with having enhanced hearing, strength, smell, etc."

Marya took a deep breath and said, "Basically, we have much the same abilities as you. Ours are just more enhanced. The abilities we have that you don't, we try not to use because it can have a wider influence on the world around us."

Axle nodded. After glancing around at the champions again, he uttered, "Thank you for sharing that information with us. We appreciate your trust. Now... let's get down to planning this war as much as we can with the limited information we have."

The next day... Crush

Crush was pissed the fuck off at her club sister, Lace. She wasn't the worst Crush had ever seen her when they got to Lace's place, but she was definitely drunk. Lace was the ex-wife to Rock, a Howlers member, and they had two kids together, but she fell into addiction not long after having their second child. Rock tried to get her clean, but her sobriety never lasted long. Crush hated to do it, but she had put Lace on probationary member status after the second time she caught Lace stealing from one of the registers at their businesses. Probationary status prevented her from being alone at any of the businesses and deemed her unfit to vote in any club decision. Hell, they didn't even trust her to know club business.

Crush's Fall

When they received information that the war was imminent, Crush, Pinky, and Nails headed to Lace's off-compound apartment to get her and bring her to the compound where they knew she would be safe. She had been on a sobriety kick as of the last few months, but Crush should have known it was about time for a relapse.

With bloodshot eyes, Lace swayed and stumbled through her apartment. Who knew what else, besides alcohol, was in her system? After everything Rock and the Claws had done over the years in an effort to get her clean and sober, Lace was once again throwing it all away. It made Crush want to cut her loose from the club, but Lace was family, and Crush just couldn't do it.

The three Claws decided they would just bring her back to the compound and let her sleep it off while the rest of them answered the emergency text Skull had sent her.

Skull : Explosions at HTC owned props. Gigi dead. Maybe others.

She didn't know everything, but she knew enough to gauge that the war was upon them, and shit was already messy. Crush didn't know Georgia well, but she liked her. The men of the Howlers loved that girl like she was their blood baby sister. This was going to destroy them. It was most likely going to be up to her and the Claws to keep everyone on track to take care of those responsible, because it was quite possible the men would be distracted with grief.

Crush and the girls were crossing the parking lot of Lace's apartment building across town from the compound when it happened. Shots rang out from a row of trees at the back of the lot. Crush took cover behind a car and pulled her gun from the holster inside her cut. As she looked around to check on her crew, she found Lace on the ground a few feet from the rear end of the car Crush had been hiding next to, blood coming from the left side of her abdomen.

"Lace," Crush shouted and tried to get to her, but if she did, she would put herself in the line of fire. "Lace!"

Pinky had dived behind the car that was on the other side of the lot. Lace was between them, out in the open. Crush wasn't sure where Nails was at. Then she heard it.

"Fuck you," Nails shouted. Her yell was followed by a series of shots.

Crush lifted enough from her crouch to look over the trunk of the car, just in time to see the bullet go into Nails's left thigh.

Pinky rushed out to catch Nails as she fell. Not willing to let her members continue to be harmed, Crush rushed out and stood in front of them.

"Get them out of here, Pinks," she ordered.

"I can ride," Nails forced out through gritted teeth.

Crush faced the woods, ready to defend her crew, but the shooting ceased. Eight men, wearing leather cuts, stepped out from the tree line and stopped.

The one in the middle looked like he was having the time of his life if the light in his eyes and the grin on his face was anything to go by. His hair was shaggy around his craggy, bearded face. "Give yourself up, and we'll leave your members alone," he said. He either spotted her president patch or knew who she was. Taking her out would have the most effect on the Claws and would put them at a disadvantage. The fuckers were strategic and were playing the long game.

Crush didn't trust him for a second. "Get them out of here, Pinky," she repeated.

"I need a car."

Lace moaned and tried to reach for her pocket. Crush didn't dare look back to see what was happening. Then Pinky said, "Awesome, Lace." There was more moaning and some grunting. "Boss, her car is one car past you. I have the keys." The words were said low enough that she could hear it with her shifter hearing, but the assholes wouldn't be able to.

Crush started marching forward, slowly, praying Pinky would get Lace and Nails into Lace's car and out of the lot before the men started firing again. She was surprised when the men let her club sisters go without any further resistance. The men just watched with their guns pointed at them.

As soon as her girls were gone, Crush darted for her bike, which was parked closer to the men than to her. She was almost to it when she was tackled by at least two men. A third man kicked her gun out of her hand.

As she struggled to get the men off of her, another man walked up and looked down at her. His patch said *Craggy Bastard.* Through a chuckle, he said, "Stop fighting." Then another man stuck her in the arm with a needle, and seconds later, Crush could feel her tiger begin to fade.

Kisy

In an abandoned office building on the edge of town, Kisy glared at her captors as they tied Crush and Pixie to some office chairs. Thinking about how she even ended up in this position drove her nuts.

It was her fault. When she got the text from Dragon to head to the clubhouse as soon as possible, she had told the rest of the employees to head home on a paid leave. One of her coworkers, Sarah, waited to walk out with her, even though Kisy had insisted she go. When they walked outside, there were five bikers, wearing cuts that didn't have the Howlers or the Claws patches.

Kisy instantly stopped in her tracks. Sarah had been distracted while she dug her keys out of her bag, leaving her vulnerable. They grabbed Sarah and held a gun to her head.

"Take her," one of them said, pointing to Kisy. "She's one of their Ol' Ladies. We might be able to use her. Have this one set off the bomb." He nodded toward Sarah.

Bomb? Kisy didn't know what they were talking about, but she knew they were the enemies that

Dragon was worried about. If they thought she'd go without a fight, they were fucking wrong. While they were discussing what they were going to do, she slipped her hand into her bag and pulled out a can of pepper spray.

She was only able to catch two of them in the eyes before being disarmed. One of them grabbed Kisy, holding her arms behind her as another was still holding a gun to her coworker's head while she sobbed and begged to be let go. The last biker took her bag and pulled out her keys.

"You are the reason she's about to die," he said to Kisy as he pointed at Sarah.

Even as Kisy fought to get free and yelled at all of them, they dragged Sarah to the car and forced her in. One of the men turned their gun on Kisy and ordered Sarah to start the car. As she fumbled with the keys, the bikers quickly backed away from the car.

Kisy kept yelling at Sarah to not do it and to let them kill her, but she wasn't listening. She was running on fear. Kisy prayed that they were somehow wrong and there was no bomb, but as soon as Sarah turned the key, the car exploded.

Feeling the heat from the blast, Kisy cried out for Sarah and for the Howlers. She knew they'd come for her, and they would put themselves in danger to try to save her. But what shook her to her core was how easy it would have been for her to be the one to come out to the car and turn the key, expecting to drive to the compound. Her life had been saved by a few minutes of convincing her employees to leave early.

Was it saved? Or were they just going to kill her when it was most damaging to the Howlers?

A few moments later, a car pulled up to the edge of the building, far away from her burning car, and the bikers forced her into the backseat. Kisy fought them the entire car ride, but she hadn't managed to get away. Then they forced her into an office building across town.

From what she could see as they entered the lobby, the two floors were open, with the walkways, balconies, and stairs in full view of the entire building. Around the open center were cubicles on both floors. Judging by the dust on all the flat surfaces and trash strewn across the floor, the building had been empty for a while. There were desk chairs tipped over and desks shoved into strange positions. The only area that seems to be mostly free of trash was the staircase.

The men practically dragged Kisy up the stairs because there was no way she was going willingly. Once on the second floor, they tied her up to a metal handrail that ran along the top of a glass railing that lined the interior balcony.

Pixie and Crush were about five yards from her and were being tied to visitor office chairs, the kind they lined lobbies with. As the men finished tying them up, Kisy met Crush's gaze and winked.

Crush gave her a confused but curious look, and Kisy just waited. Once the men figured the women were secure, they walked off to the side and began talking. There was a group of eight bikers, but a few others had been there and left. She wasn't sure how many were in Warden's Pass, but she counted eleven total who had passed through the office space since she had been brought there.

Kisy remembered Dragon mentioning how good the hearing of shifters was and figured she'd give it a try to get a message to Crush. While the men were talking, and not paying close attention to them, Kisy said in a low tone, "I can get out of the ropes."

Crush nodded.

She didn't want to reveal her cards too quickly, though, so she waited. Maybe twenty minutes later, the majority of the bikers left, leaving three men to watch the women. When one of them got a little too close to Pixie and put his hand to her baby bump, Kisy bit back her words of disgust and went to work on the knots securing her hands to the handrail.

It didn't take long for her to loosen them enough to pull her hands out. While the other two were smoking over by the stairs, looking at something on a phone, Kisy got to her feet and walked over. She stood next to the handsy biker. After a moment, she said, "You know Pike will kill you for touching her, but he'll cut your hands off first."

The man jumped back and loudly cursed. Then she was grabbed and dragged back to the handrail. The other bikers came over and helped him tie her back up.

Kisy met Crush's gaze and was treated to a slight smile and a nod of appreciation.

CHAPTER SIXTEEN

Lucifer

Lucifer had just stepped out of the bathroom at the clubhouse when he came to a halt at the sight of Axle, Skull, and Trip standing in the hallway, obviously waiting for him. The expressions on their faces told him to brace himself, because he wasn't going to like what they had to say.

"What?" The question came out as a demand, and he didn't give a fuck.

The way things were going down, anything could have happened, but he was pretty damn sure it wasn't that someone won the motherfucking lottery. Hell, there were explosions at Axle's house and at two of the club's businesses. Dragon was in lockdown in the basement because he found Kisy's car blown to hell and charred outside one of the businesses, and there were fucking human remains inside. And Georgia... *Fuck*. The only reason she was a target was because she was Axle's sister-in-law. Her mate, Emerson, watched her get in her car, turn the ignition, and get blown up. They had only been married for a few weeks and were getting ready to go off to college. Talk about a life cut short way too soon. Lucifer wouldn't be surprised if Emerson never recovered.

Whatever the three of them had to say to him, he would rather they got it over with. He didn't even want to imagine what it could be. The possibilities were too terrifying and the fact that they were coming to him in that manner meant that it was personal to him, which reduced those options down to a few horrifying possibilities.

"They took her," Axle said, quietly.

Lucifer stepped forward and came face to face with Axle, staring the man down. "Who. Took. Who?"

Axle winced but didn't back down. He met Lucifer's hard stare and answered, "The Hell's Dogs took Crush, and we don't know where yet."

He staggered back a step, feeling the words like a body blow. The rage and fear that instantly filled him swirled in his gut, picking up momentum like a fucking tornado. Opening his mouth, he let out a gut-wrenching yell. His throat raw, his body on fire with rage, Lucifer turned and pulled back his arm, but when he swung forward, he hit the palm of Trip's hand, instead of the wall where he was aiming.

"If you have a broken hand, you can't use it to pull the trigger when we find the motherfuckers who took your woman," Trip said, low.

"Find. Her." He was panting with rage and panic, but he needed to pull himself together. Trip was right. He had a mission now and needed to focus on it.

Crush

If Crush had to guess, the bikers holding them captive were worried their location had been leaked or compromised. It was the only reason she could think of for them to switch locations. They left Kisy tied up back at the office building, but Crush wasn't worried about her. Kisy was resourceful, which is how she managed to get out of her bounds numerous times, right under the noses of the kidnappers. She'd find her way out.

When Crush saw where they brought her and Pixie, she was pissed. If they hurt Bobby just so they could use Bobby's Bar as a place to torture them, Crush would kill them with her bare claws and enjoy stringing their intestines up like Christmas lights.

Bobby's Bar was a staple in their lives. The owner, Bobby, had been a friend to the clubs for years, especially to the Howlers. Hell, half of the Ol' Ladies and a couple of the Claws had worked at Bobby's Bar, at one point or another.

She told one of her kidnappers, Rage, as much as he manhandled her through the back door of the building and down the hall to the main room of the bar. Seeing Bobby sitting on the floor in front of the bar, Crush took a calming breath. He looked scared and quite pissed, but he also looked unharmed.

"Let him go," she ordered on a growl, attempting to intimidate the man in the only way she could at that moment.

Rage rolled his eyes. "I know you can't shift, bitch."

That fucking shot they gave her had prevented her from shifting, but it hadn't suppressed many of the other shifter-given skills. Her strength was dimmed, but not completely gone. Her eyesight and her hearing were perfectly fine, which is how she was still able to hear Dragon's howl of despair earlier when it was obvious Kisy and Pixie hadn't heard it. She wasn't quite sure what happened to cause it, but she could guess that it had something to do with Kisy being taken.

It had to be the Variulisis they were warned of — a shifting blocker that had adverse effects on a shifter over time if they were given repeated doses of it. No one knew how long the drug stayed in your system, or at least, no one knew and had been willing to share that information with them.

"That doesn't mean I can't kill you with my bare hands." Crush turned and got in his face. "Uncuff me, and we'll take care of this."

"Not a chance," Rage replied, a smile growing on his face. "How's my nephew? Heard he rushed in to save my boys."

Holy shit! Crush took a step back and stared at him. Could it be? She studied his facial features, and it only took her a moment to see it. Fuck! Rage was the biological uncle of Rebel, a Howlers MC member. What had they done to him to get him to join the HDMC? Better question — how was he okay with trying to eliminate a club his nephew was a member of?

"Yeah, that's right. Looks like the pretty kitty is finally catching on." Using her shock against her, Rage swung his leg around and knocked her legs out from under her. Once she was on the ground, he forced her over next to Bobby and ordered, "Now, don't be a fucking problem, or I'll have to kill you."

"Let Bobby and Pixie go, and I won't put up a fight," she promised. She knew it wouldn't work, but she had to try.

"I'm not letting an Ol' Lady go," Rage stated, and let out a belly laugh. "I'm not that fucking stupid. She's more valuable than you are."

"The Howlers will not negotiate with you. They will kill you for even looking at her with the wrong expression on your face. But fine, just let Bobby go."

Rage stared at her for a long moment. Then he asked, "How do I know he won't just run to the Howlers and tell them where we are?"

Crush turned her head and made eye contact with Bobby. "If they let you go, promise me you will not go to the Howlers or anyone the Howlers know and tell them anything. If you do, I will personally make sure you pay for that. Do you understand?"

Bobby visibly swallowed and nodded his head. "Y-yes. I-I won't say a-anything or g-go to them or a-anyone."

Crush looked back at Rage. "You've killed one of their women, kidnapped two more, caused havoc for them and for the Claws by taking their president. What in the hell do you need a bar owner for? Just let him be. Hell! He didn't even know shifters existed until you opened your mouth about my shifting."

Rage shrugged. "Fine. Like I care." He motioned toward the front door with his hand. "Go."

Bobby hesitated for a moment and looked at Crush with apology in his eyes.

"Don't worry about us. Go."

As tears filled Bobby's eyes, he climbed to his feet and bolted out the front door before Rage could change his mind.

Crush looked over at Pixie, who was standing with one of the other bikers just inside the room. She looked okay, but her tied hands were covering her baby bump, protecting the bundle inside. As she had numerous times in the last couple hours, Crush was grateful Pixie's hands were restrained in the front instead of the back. It was bad enough that she was kidnapped while pregnant.

The biker next to Pixie took her bicep and forced her into a chair. Then one of the bikers locked the front door and stood in front of it to block the exit. Two more blocked the hallway that led to the backdoor.

Crush still didn't know what the HDMC planned to do to them, but at least she avoided having Bobby's death on her conscience.

Lucifer

For over an hour, he had panicked and paced the clubhouse. It wasn't until Axle got the call from Mama Hen that Kisy was in fact alive and well, not blown to bits like Dragon had thought, that he started to hold out hope Crush would be okay. Then he reminded himself his mate was a bad bitch, and when she returned, they were going to talk. He was done with the games and the bullshit, but first, they needed to rescue his woman.

From information from the champions and the undercover UpRiders members, they received intel about where Crush and Pixie were being held, but rather than doing something about it, the clubs and the champions were sitting around the clubhouse talking. *Talking.*

The Howlers had rushed to Mama Hen's Inn to pick up Kisy and bring her back to the compound, where they began to ask her questions about what happened.

As he listened to Kisy tell them what she knew, his impatience rose until it was nearly impossible for him to keep from blowing his motherfucking top.

Lucifer was sick of it. While the Howlers, the Claws, and the champions sat around trying to figure out what to do to save Pixie and Crush, Lucifer was losing his damn mind and none of them seemed to notice. Hell, he didn't know how Pike could fucking stand it. Instead of rescuing the women, they were arguing about whether Kisy could go with them when there were more important things to worry about.

After approaching the bar, he took another drink of his water, set his glass down on the bar top, and headed for the door. They could sit and talk all they wanted. He wasn't wasting any more time while his woman was being held captive by some piece of shit bastards. Hell fucking no. He was going to get her.

Kisy's eyes gravitated toward him, and their eyes locked for a moment, then Lucifer winked at her before he stepped through the front door.

It didn't matter that Crush hadn't admitted that she was his woman yet. They both knew she was, and that's all Lucifer needed.

After pulling his old HDMC cut out of his saddlebag, he put it on. When he had put it in there, he wasn't sure why he was holding on to the damn thing, but now he was glad he had. Ready to go, he hopped on his bike and headed out to where the two UpRiders told them the women would be.

One look at those two young UpRiders who had been willing to go undercover and report back to the Howlers, and Lucifer knew they could be trusted. They were like him. They put their faith into a group of men and had been let down. They wanted to belong to a good group of like-minded men with decent morals.

Half of their club was exactly that, unlike the club that Lucifer had joined.

Lucifer had been sold a pack of lies when he prospected for the Hell's Dogs MC Indiana. He didn't find out the full story of why they were doing all the shit they were doing until he met the Howlers — until the Howlers and the Claws saved his life. And he would continue to repay that kindness to the Howlers and the Claws for the rest of it.

That was the thought on his mind as he pulled into the parking lot of Bobby's Bar. He slow-rolled to the back, looking around as he went, taking in everything and looking for a sign of trouble. When he got to the back of the building, he parked near the rear door and killed the engine.

Taking a deep breath, he felt for his gun in the holster under his tee in the back. Feeling the outline of his handgun, he was reassured. It was time to rescue his woman.

He yanked open the back door and came face to face with another HDMC member, who aimed a gun at his chest. Lucifer couldn't tell which chapter the man was from, but it didn't matter, anyway. He took a chance and held out his hand. The man dropped his gun hand and slipped his gun back into his holster, then he shook Lucifer's hand.

"I was sent to relieve you. They want you at base," Lucifer told him.

"Me?" The eagerness with which the man stepped past him disgusted Lucifer. He didn't even ask Lucifer any questions.

Once the guard had disappeared out the back door, Lucifer headed down the hall and met two more men at the archway to the main room of the bar.

The two of them looked him over. Then they turned around and looked over at another man. One of them uttered, "Slice, they sent a new one."

Lucifer waited for them to wave him through. He stepped past the two men and looked around. He spotted Pixie, first, sitting on a chair at the closest table. She looked okay, but irritated. That didn't surprise Lucifer. Pixie was feisty.

Crush was sitting on the floor near the bar. She looked pissed, but her face was paler than usual. He didn't like that. His gaze met hers, and he asked, "You good?"

"I'd be better if I was with my club."

As Lucifer nodded, Slice blurted, "Who the fuck are you?"

Lucifer grinned as he yanked his gun out of his holster and aimed at the man's head. "I'm her man, and you fucked up." Then he pulled the trigger.

After taking him out, he turned and quickly dispatched the other two before they could pull their wits together to do anything about it.

Then he went to work on untying the girls, Crush first. Once Crush was freed, he gave her his gun and went for Pixie's ropes.

Crush's Fall

"You good, Pix?" Lucifer rubbed Pixie's wrists to help her circulation.

"Yeah, just fucking pissed," she gritted out and stood. "Bunch of fucking assholes."

"I agree," Lucifer said, and chuckled.

"Let's get the fuck out of here. I only have my bike, but we'll figure it out."

Crush bent down to one of the guards and yanked a set of keys from the dead prick's pocket. "I'll take his."

Lucifer shrugged, took his gun back, and led the women down the hallway to the rear door. He carefully opened it and stepped out, gun up and ready. No one.

He lowered his gun and waved the girls out. He was approaching his bike when the sound of a large pack of bikes roared into the lot and around the building. When the Howlers and the Claws stopped and killed their engines, Lucifer loudly said, "Well, it's so nice of you to join us. I see Kisy won." He looked over at Kisy on the back of Pinky's bike and winked at her.

When Pike stormed toward them and wrapped Pixie up in his arms, Lucifer looked away and gave them their moment. His eyes landed on Crush, heading for Ginger and her bike. Lucifer jogged over and took her hand. He yanked her around and met her gaze. Looking into the eyes he loved so much, he stated, "We need to talk, and we need to do it now."

"Later," she said.

"No. Now," he turned and started for his bike, pulling her along with him.

He couldn't keep doing it. The push and pull had been fun for a while, but he was done wasting time. They needed to make a go of it, or she needed to let him go. And she didn't have long to decide because he wasn't going to keep going through this.

CHAPTER SEVENTEEN

Crush

As Lucifer dragged her away, she glanced around and noticed that Kisy had a Tiger's Claw prospect cut on. She had a moment of curiosity about how that went down, but she wasn't against it. Kisy had proven herself to be worth her salt. She had already put Crush's and Pixie's safety above her own. Crush had no doubt that the woman would make a good member of the Tiger's Claw MC.

Those thoughts were brief, because her attention shifted back to Lucifer as he climbed on his bike and demanded she get on behind him. Looking into his dark brown eyes, she knew he wasn't going to put up with her fighting him on it. He meant business, and now wasn't the time for their bickering.

Without a word, she climbed on and wrapped her arms around his waist. Seconds later, they were riding out of the parking lot.

Lucifer's body was stiff as hell the entire ride to the compound. It made sense. She knew he was at his end with the bullshit. She could almost guess the exact words that would come out of his mouth when they had their talk.

After they arrived at the clubhouse and dismounted his bike, he grabbed her hand and started pulling her across the street and around the side of the strip mall, heading straight for her apartment.

She felt panic rise in her at the thought of him in her private space, but again, she knew he wouldn't put up with her fighting him on it today. Resigned to having the conversation she didn't want to have, she let him lead her up the stairs to her apartment door.

"Open it," he ordered in a low tone. He didn't sound angry, just determined.

Crush took a deep breath and punched the code into the keypad to unlock the door. As soon as the lock released, Lucifer was opening the door and dragging her inside.

"You can stop dragging me now," she protested. "I haven't fought you for a second."

"Only because I didn't give you a chance to," he replied, but let go of her hand. Standing in the middle of her open living space, he turned to face her. His eyes bore into hers as his chest suddenly heaved with his hard breaths. "Either we're doing this, or you need to cut me loose."

"We're facing a war, Lucy. We can't have this conversation now."

Anger and stubbornness sparked in his eyes. "We're having this motherfucking conversation *now*. For *months*, I have let you push me away, pull me close, push me away again, and I'm fucking done. I almost lost you, Kitten," he shouted, his voice breaking on one of the nicknames he had given her. He shook his head and looked away. After taking a deep breath and exhaling slowly, he looked at her again, frustrated tears glittering in his eyes. "I could have lost you. It would have *killed* me. Knowing you were in those motherfuckers' hands made me crazy. It also made me realize that I've lost you in smaller doses many times since I met you… and it's slowly eating away at me. So, this is what we're going to do. I'm going to help with this fucking war, whether you fucking like it or not. When this is over, I expect a fucking answer. I won't wait long. Either you claim me and make this shit official… or you cut me loose, and I'll find someone else."

The emotion in his eyes and voice broke her resolve to push him off yet again. He was right. She couldn't keep dragging him along. It was unfair to both of them. She needed to deal with her shit and figure out if she was capable of having a mate. If she wasn't, she needed to be honest with him about that and let him go so he could find happiness.

Crush couldn't even contemplate him with another woman, but that was a problem for another time.

"Do you understand what I'm telling you?"

His question pulled her out of her thoughts, and she shifted her gaze back up to his face. Nodding, she answered, "Yes."

Another deep breath came from him before he stepped forward, cupped her face in his hands, and pressed his lips to hers. Like usual, it quickly ignited, turning into a desperate battle of who would have control over their kisses.

One of his hands left her face, only for his arm to wrap around her waist and his hand to grip her ass, pulling her hips against him, letting her feel the effect she had on his body. Not to be outdone, Crush fisted a hand in the hair on top of his head and yanked back, breaking their kiss.

As Lucifer chuckled, she attacked his throat, nipping and kissing, licking and sucking.

His other hand joined the first at her ass, and his grip tightened as he groaned and rubbed his erection against her. "Fuck. I don't think we have time for this."

Crush sighed and pulled back, releasing her grip on his hair. "You're right. We don't."

He laid his forehead to hers and gave her a smile. "Let me know when you make a decision, but we can't be doing this until you do."

Crush didn't know what to say, so she just nodded and tried not to whimper as he released her and stepped away.

It was only then that she realized her tiger had been silent through the entire interaction. She hadn't really felt her tiger since the asshole injected her. *Fuck!*

What if her tiger was gone? Was that possible?

Ten minutes later, Crush was in Axle's office, and they were discussing whether she should join them in the fight. Having been injected with Variulisis, Crush didn't know what other effects, if any, it would have on her besides disabling her tiger and her shifting abilities. It scared the shit out of her to think they damaged her tiger in some way, but she didn't have time to sulk and worry. They had family to protect.

Looking across his desk at her, Axle uttered, "I think it's the only way, Crush. If you're there, the Claws will be distracted, worried about you. You don't want that, and neither do I."

Crush wasn't happy, but she knew he was right. "I'll keep Ginger and Minx here with me." Satisfying her ego wasn't worth putting her sisters or the rest of her family in danger. Speaking of the rest of her sisters, she needed to know what was going on. "Any news on Lace?"

Axle sighed. "She's not doing well," he answered. "The doctor said he could make her comfortable, but he doesn't think she's going to make it. The drugs and alcohol in her system are making it too hard for her body to heal the way it should."

Crush cursed under her breath. It wasn't a complete shock. Lace had been heading down that road for years, but that didn't make it hurt any less. More than anything else, Crush felt an ache in her chest for Lace's ex-husband and her children. "Rock is going to take that hard."

"Yeah, he already is. He's with her now, saying his goodbyes. I'm not having him come with us. Nails is doing pretty good, but she's pissed she's too injured to come with."

"She would crawl onto the field of battle if we let her." Crush stood and headed for the door, intent on giving the orders to her club.

Axle followed her. "Do you want me to have Flash and Keys stay here?"

Crush shook her head. "Ginger, Minx, Rock, and I can handle it."

As they reached the doorway to the main area, he asked, "What about Lucifer?"

"If you fucking try to tell me to stay here," Lucifer began as he leaned back against the wall next to the opening to the hallway, "I'll just follow."

Axle turned his head and looked at Lucifer. "You aren't a member yet."

"I don't fucking care." One of the benefits of not being a member was not having to take orders from the fucking president. Axle could request whatever he wanted, but Lucifer would do what he wanted to do.

Axle rolled his eyes. "Whatever. I don't want to hear you whine if you get hurt."

Lucifer chuckled. "You wouldn't want to hear that either way."

Axle ignored him and gave out a loud whistle, bringing everyone's attention to him. "Gather around! We've got shit to talk about before we go!"

Axle

Once everyone was close and listening, Axle laid out the plan. "The champions are luring the assholes to the field at the Aikman Farm. We're going to hide out in the woods. Once they have them there and engaged, we're going to close them in and take them out. Sound good?"

The room erupted in howls and roars.

"Great. We'll park our bikes on the hiking trail a mile down the road. Lira's been keeping me updated. If we head out now, we should have just enough time to get our bikes hidden and hike through the woods. Mount up!"

Axle noticed Crush stop Ginger from following the others out and begin a conversation. She motioned over Vixen.

Leaving her to give the orders she needed to give to her club, Axle looked around. He saw Dragon and Kisy talking to his dad as they walked out of the room. Dragon had his arm around Kisy and looked at ease, but Axle knew better. Dragon was not okay with Kisy going along, but he knew that fighting his woman would be useless. That woman was a force to be reckoned with, and while she frustrated the hell out of him, Axle admired her. The look on Griff's face said he did, too. His slight smile was a rare sight, but whatever Kisy was saying had brought it out of the old burly wolf.

Still dealing with his injured arm, Striker was staying behind as well with Rock at the apartment building. Axle hated that they were losing Lace for so many reasons. Most of all of those reasons were Rock and their kids. It was going to hit them hard.

Axle didn't allow his brain to go near what Emerson was going through or what it would do to Gorgeous when he shared the news about Georgia. It would hit her the same way reality was hitting Rock and Emerson.

He hoped this was the last day he'd have to share news like that, but he doubted it would be.

With a resigned sigh, Axle headed out to join his club and lead them to the war that had the very real possibility of hurting or killing his family.

Lucifer

That shit was insane, Lucifer thought as he rode back to the compound with the rest of the Howlers and the Claws after their side had decimated the Hell's Dogs and their allies in battle. He knew about shifters. He knew about the champions, and the fact that there were other creatures out there — Vampires, other kinds of shifters, witches, etc. He even knew Ordys was a motherfucking dragon, but it was one thing to know it, and it was another thing to see it. When the big dark green beast opened his jaws and shot fire out, Lucifer was struck dumb for a hot minute. It was terrifying and awe-inspiring all at the same time.

It wasn't as if he stood around and just watched the shifters and others work, but he caught enough glimpses of them in action to get a good picture of the force they were working with. He was fucking glad he was on their side.

Seeing the injured and the dead was something he wasn't prepared for, though. He had thought of the Howlers and the Claws as family for months now, but that was solidified in his brain when his heart broke for each and every injury. He didn't want any of them to feel an ounce of pain. Lucifer couldn't imagine being more *in*. Patched member or not, he was one of them. He would fight for them, again and again, stand by them, defend them. They were Lucifer's family, and they would continue to be, no matter what Crush decided.

Crush... Fuck. Axle had filled him in on the injections and what it could mean for Crush. The truth was they weren't sure of the full effect yet. They were working with limited knowledge and a whole lot of hope. He couldn't imagine Crush without her tiger, though. Even never having seen her shift, he knew her tiger was an integral part of who she was as a person. If that was taken away from her, Lucifer feared the effect it would have.

He meant what he said to her, though. She had a decision to make, and while he wouldn't demand an answer right away, he would before too long. They had dead to honor and bury, and brothers and sisters to take care of and heal. Lucifer suspected they also had a town to address and police to deal with after the events of the day. No, he wouldn't demand an answer right away, but there would come a time when she would need to make that decision and stick with it.

If she chose to set him free, Lucifer wasn't sure how he was going to continue to be around her without having the possibility of being with her, but he'd figure it out. He wasn't giving up his new friends, his new family, his new home just because he was rejected, even if that rejection came from the woman he felt was meant to walk at his side.

Turning onto the street of the compound, Lucifer swallowed down the lump that had formed in his throat. He wouldn't spend the next however long it took her to decide being an emotional basket case, either. He was a fucking man, for fuck's sake.

When he rode into the parking lot of the clubhouse and parked with all the others, he looked over and saw Crush coming out of the front door. She walked over to Axle, but her eyes were glued to him.

He gave her a wink to let her know he was okay before he got off his bike and headed for his room. Lucifer needed privacy to process the hellscape that had been his day.

The next morning... Crush

The Howlers and the Claws were scheduled to meet up with Lira and the champions the next morning. They decided on the farm since the police were still holding off on questioning them. Crush didn't know how Axle swung that, but she was sure Hawkin had something to do with it.

The world had learned that shifters were a real thing, between videos that the Hell's Dogs had released as well as Dragon running through the streets in his wolf form with glowing eyes when he thought Kisy had died. Most people in the world thought the videos were edited, but the police in Warden's Pass couldn't discount what multiple witnesses had told them about the wolf with glowing green eyes. They weren't sure how to handle the Howlers and the Claws, suspecting that there were more than just the one shifter, since they also weren't sure they would be able to overpower or control them. Or at least that was Crush's guess as to why they weren't pressing the issue for interviews and interrogations.

When they pulled up at the farm, Crush was shocked. The large field behind the farmhouse looked like it had been tilled and ready for planting. It wasn't the scorched-by-dragon-fire ground that Axle had told her to expect. There was no lingering evidence of a battle or even a disturbance.

Crush and the uninjured Claws joined the Howlers and champions at the edge of the field.

"Okay. So, this is the message from the gods," Lira began, "The world has learned of shifters, thanks to those fucking videos HDMC put out before they killed the feral shifters they were using. Rebel took out the lone survivor, right?" She looked over at Rebel, who nodded. "But those videos are not being brushed off as altered. Because of that, we are offering to station a group of champions here, if you would like. I suspect a lot of visitors to Warden's Pass — some curious, some excited, some with nefarious goals."

Axle looked over at Crush. Then he shook his head. "You're welcome to station a group here, but this is our town. We will protect it."

Lira gave a nod. "Consider it backup."

Crush narrowed her eyes as she looked at Lira. "You know more than you're telling us."

"I can only give you what the gods have permitted me to," Lira confirmed without actually confirming.

"Motherfucking piece of shit gods. What good are they if—"

"Okay!" Pinky blurted, then her hand was over Crush's mouth, and she was giving them a fake smile. "Thanks for the backup."

Crush mumbled, "I will fuck you up for that, Pinks."

Pinky just rolled her eyes.

"Anyway," Axle cut in, probably to keep Crush from killing all of them. She felt like doing just that. Her emotions were out of control, and she wasn't sure exactly what sparked it, but enough was going on in her life that there was a laundry list of things it could be. While she mentally dealt with that, Axle continued, "We appreciate your help in all of this. If you need anything from us, give Crush or me a call. But please understand that we have a lot of deep shit we're dealing with right now and could use some privacy in that."

Lira inclined her head, sadness in her eyes. "As are we. Understood."

Crush swatted Pinky's hand away and shot her a glare. Without another word, Axle and Crush led their clubs off of the field and back to their bikes.

It was one thing to let the champions help in a crisis, but the Howlers and the Claws closed ranks when it came to dealing with death in the family. It would be handled and processed in the privacy of their ranks. Their dead deserved the respect, and they would get it, even Riles.

T.S. Tappin

CHAPTER EIGHTEEN

Crush

The two days after the war were a whirlwind of emotion and activity for not only Crush, but every member of her club family. On top of helping the injured and making sure everyone had everything they needed, they were hit with losses causing grief that wouldn't soon fade.

Axle's sister-in-law, Georgia was probably the hardest loss to take, because she wasn't a member of one of the clubs and hadn't taken any part in the feud between them and the Hell's Dogs. She was an innocent bystander, who just happened to be connected to Axle, and the Hell's Dogs took her out in an attempt to incite the Howlers and the Claws into battle. It worked. Her death made it impossible to resolve anything without bloodshed, and a lot of it.

Crush couldn't imagine the pain that Georgia's mate, Emerson, was in. Having to watch as his mate was blown up and not being able to do anything to stop it had to be the toughest thing a person could go through. He and Georgia had only been married for weeks. They were young, not even out of their teen years, and had just started planning a life together.

She knew Axle was worried about Emerson, too. It wasn't unknown for the surviving mate to take their own life to avoid feeling the excruciating pain of having to live without their other half. Everyone in both clubs and the Ol' Ladies were not only keeping an eye on him but were also keeping him close.

On top of that, they lost Dragon's dad, Griff, a member of the retired chapter. Crush knew Griff went out in a way he would have wanted to go — protecting his son — but that didn't make the loss easier to take, especially for Dragon and his sister, Darlin'.

They also lost three Tiger's Claw MC members — Ivy, Lace, and Lash. Crush was taking those losses, especially Ivy and Lash's, as a personal failure. Her mind circled around to the same stuff it had been telling her since the day of the war. She wasn't there in battle to save them. Having been injected with that fucking anti-shifting drug, she was held back at the compound to keep her club sisters from being distracted during battle. She couldn't help but wonder if she would have been the difference to save them had she been fighting. She didn't bother mentioning that to her club sisters or Axle, because she knew how they would respond. They would have told her there was nothing she could have done, and it wasn't her fault, but that was just platitudes.

While still grieving, Crush and Axle had to meet with the mayor of Warden's Pass to address the questions and concerns the town no doubt had after finding out about the existence of shifters. They decided it was best to keep the meeting as private as possible, so Axle arranged the meeting to happen at Milhawk Investigations. Hawkin was nice enough to allow them the use of one of his conference rooms for the meeting, no doubt in an effort to stave off any more conflict in the town that would happen if a plan wasn't formed and executed quickly.

During the talk, they agreed to a town hall gathering at the high school, where Axle would address the town about shifters and explain how they weren't a danger to the community. It grated on Crush's nerves that they would have to explain it after shifters had been a part of the community of Warden's Pass for decades and had never been a problem. If she managed to endure the town hall without taking the head off any of the citizens of the town, she would consider that a win.

When Crush and Axle returned to the compound, they gathered the able-bodied members in the clubhouse and went over what happened during the meeting with the mayor and the plan for the town hall meeting at the high school.

The Howlers and the Claws were a united front on how they wanted to handle addressing it with the community. To the rest of the world, they would always be a united front. If there were disagreements, they handled them internally and didn't let that leak to the outside world.

After the explanations, Crush walked over and pulled a box out from behind the bar. It took a lot of money to get the package overnighted, but it was necessary, in her opinion.

Kisy didn't have to go head-to-head with their kidnappers. She didn't have to put her neck out there for Crush and Pixie, but she did it without a moment's hesitation. In Crush's opinion, Kisy showed more loyalty to the clubs and strength in one day than most prospects do in a year.

As she opened the box, Crush said, "There is someone in this room who went above and beyond what is expected of someone who is not patched into the clubs. She put herself in danger to protect us and our family." Crush turned and looked over at Kisy. "The point of prospecting is to prove you can be trusted. It's to prove you will put the club above yourself. It's to prove you would do anything to protect the club and our family. You've already done that. So give me your prospect cut."

Looking a bit confused, Kisy stood and made her way across the room to where Crush was standing. She removed the prospect cut she received the day before and handed it over.

Crush laid it on the bar and reached into the box. She pulled out a new leather cut with the Tiger's Claw MC colors on the back and a member patch on the front and handed it to Kisy. "Your *Kisy* patch is on order, but I didn't want to make you wait for your cut since you have more than earned it. If you still want to be in the Claws, put that cut on."

Kisy turned and looked at Dragon, and he gave her a slight nod. Crush wasn't sure how Dragon would react to her patching Kisy in, but she was happy to see that he was approving. He may not be completely happy about it, but it was obvious he would agree to anything that made Kisy happy. He was a man of worth, even if he was able to scare the shit out of the devil.

With a giant grin on Kisy's face and tears in her eyes, she slid that cut on her shoulders. The second the leather settled, the room erupted into cheers and Dragon scooped her up in his arms. He pressed his lips to hers as he slowly twirled her around in a move that was so unlike him that Kisy broke the kiss to laugh.

Lucifer

Leaning against the entryway for the cafeteria from the main room of the clubhouse, Lucifer watched as Crush gave the cut to Kisy. While the rest of the people in the room had their attention on Kisy and Dragon, his gaze stayed locked on Crush.

The smile that grew on her face was stunning, but it was a veil over the sorrow he knew she was feeling. She didn't have to voice it for him to know that she was experiencing not only grief but also guilt, especially for the loss of Ivy and Lash. The members of her club were sisters to her, and she was their leader, their protector. She would feel a great sadness and responsibility for their suffering.

He wanted to go to her. He wanted to be the person she turned to, the person she gave her anguish and the weight of her emotions. He wanted to help her through the tragedy. In order for that to be a possibility, though, she'd have to accept him as *hers*, but she had yet to do that. Instead, he shoved down the urge to support her and turned away. With a heavy sigh, he headed down the hallway to go to his room in the apartment building.

Crush

After the town hall the next day, they had a memorial in the clubhouse for their dead. It was what you would expect a memorial to be, but it had a biker twist. After the crying and ceremony, they partied like it was their last night on earth.

Through it all, Crush kept looking for Lucifer to check in on her, but he didn't. She saw him a few times, but it was as if she didn't exist. It had been two days since she caught him looking in her direction. She hated that things were that way between them, but she just told herself it was probably for the best. With Lucifer's ability to break through her walls, he would hold the cards, and she was afraid of handing over that power to him.

The first time she felt her tiger again since they injected her with that fucking drug, it was because her tiger was just as pissed at her as Lucifer was. Prowling and hissing inside of her, the cat let her know just how much of an idiot she was, but fear kept Crush from throwing caution to the wind.

Feeling her tiger again, even if it felt muted and lost in a fog, filled her with relief. Her tiger had been a major part of her for her entire life. Living without it was like living without her soul. Her full physical strength had returned relatively quickly, but it had taken her tiger a few days to make her presence known. It started with jolts of strong emotion, slowly building to glimpses of her tiger snarling at her or pacing.

Her emotions were out of control, and she couldn't stop thinking of Lucifer. Every time a new feeling overwhelmed her, she had the urge to give it to him, lay it out, and let her mate carry the weight, but then panic would pull her back and remind her why that wasn't a good idea, even if she wanted it to be with her whole heart.

But when she climbed the stairs to her apartment every night, Crush was bombarded with an ache in her chest, a longing to feel his arms around her, a need to hear his voice. In those moments, she knew it was only a matter of time before she would give in and give herself to Lucifer to destroy or cherish at his whim.

Lucifer

The morning after the memorial, Lucifer decided to go for a ride to clear his head. He had spent the night tossing and turning after drinking with the men for a few hours. He drank more than he usually would have with the intention of it making him pass out and help him get some sleep. It didn't.

Lucifer gave up trying at around five in the morning, and took a shower, got dressed, and headed out of the building. When he stepped outside, he turned to head to where his bike was parked in the lot next to the clubhouse, but he stopped when he heard some noise coming from behind the strip mall. Curious, he reversed course and headed that way.

When he stepped around the back corner, Lucifer didn't understand what he was seeing at first. Crush was outside the door that led to her apartment stairs. Around her were stacks of boxes and bags of all different colors and sizes. She was just standing there with her arms crossed over her chest, staring down at the mess.

His ego told him she didn't want him or his help, and he should leave her alone. Hell, he hadn't even caught her looking at him in days. Either she hadn't made a decision, or the decision she made wasn't one he was going to like. Lucifer wasn't ready to hear her tell him to fuck off for good.

His heart told him she was his, that she needed help, and that he should be the one giving it to her. Physically or emotionally, there had to be something he could do to make her load lighter. Knowing she was hurting, she had to be after everything the clubs had been faced with in the previous days and the loss of loved ones, he couldn't stand by and not at least *try* to do something. It was that thought that pushed him forward.

He took slow steps toward her, but he didn't try to hide his presence. Since Crush was a shifter, her advanced hearing and sense of smell would make that attempt pointless. Instead, Lucifer just remained quiet and strolled toward her, keeping his eyes on her.

He was halfway down to her when Crush lifted her head and looked down at him. There was a scowl on her face, but somehow, he knew it wasn't for him. It was for whatever was running through her mind.

Sliding his hands into his front pockets, he came to a stop a few yards from her. "Hey," he said, low.

"Hey," she replied, her voice missing the snarkiness he had fallen for. It didn't even hold her usual bland annoyance. It was lifeless. That only made his chest feel tighter and had his heart ache more.

"What are you doing? What's all this?"

Crush shrugged. "Ivy's parents… They can't afford to come up here to retrieve her belongings, and they refuse to accept money from us." She swallowed hard and looked away from him. "I couldn't sleep, so I packed up her room. I figured I'd bring all of her stuff up to the church room, where I could pack it properly, before I shipped it to them."

"Sounds like a good plan."

Crush was quiet for a long moment. He was just about to ask her why she wasn't doing that when, in a voice he could barely hear, she said, "I didn't realize how hard it would be… to see her things and… not have her here."

Fuck. Lucifer fully understood that. Grief was a monster that repeatedly took potshots at you over time, randomly bitchslapped you, stabbed you, punched you when you least expected it. The smallest things packed the biggest punch, causing the most pain. Seeing Ivy's belongings piled up with no one to use them anymore probably felt like a knife to the heart.

"Would you like me to bring them up for you?"

Immediately, she replied, "I don't need you to carry anything for me. I'm not a helpless fucking twat."

Lucifer swallowed down the chuckle that threatened to come out and calmly said, "I know you don't *need* me. You've made that perfectly clear. And I wasn't trying to say you aren't capable. Hell, without your shifter strength, by sheer stubbornness, I'm positive you could do anything… except maybe let me in. I was simply offering to do something for you that is obviously causing you sorrow."

Her eyes lifted again. If he didn't know better, he would have sworn he saw tears twinkling in the lidline of her fucking beautiful eyes, but he *did* know better. Crush didn't cry.

"If you wouldn't mind helping, that'd be great," she mumbled.

In response, Lucifer reached down and grabbed the biggest box. Shifting it to one arm, he grabbed the handle to the door and yanked it open. After she grabbed a few things, she stepped through the open doorway and headed up the stairs with Lucifer on her heels.

As he helped her, he considered bringing up their talk and asking if she made a decision, but he decided against it. He didn't want to add more pressure to her already heavy load of grief, responsibility, and stress. There would be time for that soon.

T.S. Tappin

Chapter Nineteen

Crush

Once they were finished carrying all of Ivy's belongings up to the Tiger's Claw church room, Lucifer helped her organize the stuff on the long, large table so it would be easier for her to wrap up. She appreciated his help. She also appreciated the fact that he didn't push her on all the issues lying between them. That mountain was insurmountable in her estimation.

Okay, that wasn't true. They only had one problem, and that problem was her. When her tiger started to return to her, the only feeling she got from *her* was annoyance, and Crush knew why. Their mate had been close for months, and the only reason he wasn't claimed was Crush's fear. And that was exactly what it was... *fear*. She was scared to let him see her vulnerable. It would give him power over her emotions. But if she was being honest with herself, he already had that power.

Lucifer already made her feel things that sent her spinning. All it took was a look, a smirk, or one of those fantastic fucking kisses, and she was fighting the urge to drop to her knees in front of him.

She was the president of her club, for fuck's sake. She shouldn't be that weak. Crush was supposed to be strong, confident, and powerful. With Lucifer around, she was a mess, stumbling through her life, desperately avoiding making any connection with him.

Crush had her reasons, but she knew they were all bullshit. Since the ultimatum he laid at her feet, she had come to realize that none of it had any real substance. It was fear and ego, plain and simple. But was she strong enough to get past that?

"What's got your mind reeling, Sugartits?"

The nickname had her hackles raised in seconds. She turned and glared at him. "And why would that be any of your business?"

Lucifer's eyebrow slid up. "It's not. Doesn't mean I won't ask." He shrugged and picked up a throw blanket from the pile of linens on the table.

Crush watched as Lucifer did the absolute worst job of trying to fold it. For a moment, she told herself she could just refold it later, but when he grabbed the fitted sheet and began to ball it up, she snapped. Reaching out, she yanked it from his hands and un-balled it.

Chuckling, Lucifer went to grab the next sheet in the pile, but Crush bit out, "Don't fucking think about it."

"I am capable of folding," he told her, those fucking dark brows pulled together in a scowl.

"No, you are not." She pointed to the blanket. "That is what I would call a hot mess."

"You're being ridiculous." He scoffed and shook his head as he turned and moved further down the table.

Crush just stood there, staring at him, fuming about the fact that he thought her standards for folding were ridiculous. She was irritated and angry, but she was also turned on beyond belief. He didn't shy away from her, even when she was angry. He didn't get intimidated by her status in the club or the fact that she was capable of shifting into a large predatory animal and tearing him apart. Hell, he wasn't even afraid of hurting her feelings. Lucifer was honest, up-front, and fearless. It only pissed her off more that those things are what made him perfect for her.

"Lucy," she growled, ignoring the fact that a greenish-gold light was shining from her eyes, illuminating the side of his face.

"Yeah, Sugartits?" He said the words before he turned to look at her. When he did, he froze in place, but she didn't miss the way his breathing picked up or the slight opening of his mouth.

She just stared at him for three beats. Her tiger was prowling inside of her, urging her, demanding that she claim their mate. She wanted to. So badly did she want to, but there was a lot they needed to discuss and boundaries they needed to work out before they could take that step. That didn't mean she couldn't take advantage of the lust in his gaze as he stared back at her.

Crush watched as he swallowed hard and turned his body to fully face her. The bulge in his jeans and the desire written on his face was more than she could take. Having to face the death of her friend only made her crave the feeling of being *alive*. He was offering her that with every look, had been for months. All she had to do was reach out and accept it. Her tiger hissed at her to stop holding back, and that was it. Her control snapped, and she lunged.

Lucifer wasn't a stupid man, so he didn't turn and run. Instead, he opened his arms, braced his feet apart, and caught her. Her lips slammed against his, and the fight for control of the kiss began. As his hands slid down to her ass, his teeth took hold of her bottom lip and pulled just enough to elicit a groan from her.

"Does this mean you've made a decision?" The rough edge to his voice seeped into her veins and sent a ripple of pleasure through her.

"It means I'm willing to see if we can work through the issues and set boundaries."

He kissed her long and deep, before he broke the kiss and asked, "What issues? The way I see it, the only issue is you giving up this game that you don't want to have me in your bed."

"Game?" She slid a hand up and grabbed a fistful of his hair, yanking back a bit.

A grin grew on his face as he maintained eye contact with her. His hands flexed on her ass, and she felt his cock growing against her abdomen. "Yeah, game." Then he cursed under his breath. "Fucking hell, you're so damn hot when you're pissed."

"Issue number one," she retorted, and tightened her hold on his hair.

He chuckled. "Sugartits, you're the only one who thinks that's an issue."

"You realize I could kill you with one swipe of a claw, right?"

Still chuckling, he shrugged. "I've always liked living on the edge. I've never really been into blood-play, though I'd be willing to give it a shot, if that's what you need."

She huffed out a breath. "I'm being serious, Lucy."

He stopped chuckling, but he kept grinning at her. "No. You're being scared, Sugartits. Unless you have sexual boundaries, I don't see what we could possibly have to discuss."

She let go of his hair and reached between them. As she unfastened his jeans, she replied, "There are things with the club that you need to respect."

He rolled his eyes. When she finished with his jeans, he went to work on hers. "Like I don't already know that? Crush, I wouldn't overstep when it comes to your club."

She just stared at him as he unfastened and unzipped her jeans. Apparently, Lucifer was done with the conversation because he took her lips in a bruising kiss and slid his hands around her hips and into the back of her pants. Cupping her ass, he yanked her back against him and deepened the kiss. For once, she allowed him to take control for a moment, instead focusing on how she felt about his words.

As he worked his magic with his tongue, she desperately held on to her *thinking* brain instead of letting her *fucking* brain take over. What were her other concerns? What else did they need to talk about? *There were other things!*

Club business!

She broke the kiss and took a deep breath. "Club business. I can't..." She swallowed hard. "I can't tell you everything."

Lucifer just raised a brow. "I was in a club, Sugartits. I know that."

"And you have to stop calling me Sugartits."

He snorted a laugh. "Yeah. I won't be doing that." Lucifer nipped her bottom lip. "You like it, and you know it."

"Lucy," she growled.

With his lips just a breath away from hers, he replied, "You stop calling me Lucy, and I'll stop calling you Sugartits."

Scowling at him, she answered, "No deal, Lucy."

He chuckled. "Like I said... you like it."

Crush snarled and shoved him back until he was flattened against the wall. Dropping to her knees in front of him, she started tugging on his clothes. His cock sprung free from the fabric as she yanked his jeans and boxer briefs down to his knees, and it bounced a bit as she eyed it and licked her lips.

"I'm gonna blow just from you looking at my cock like a tasty snack," Lucifer gritted out as he reached out and threaded his fingers into the hair on the back of her head.

Wrapping a hand around the base of his erection, Crush was pleased that she could barely get her fingers around him. If nothing else, the length and girth of him would give her something to work with. "We'll see how tasty you are," she replied before she leaned forward and licked around the head of his hard cock. The hissed breath she heard from him made her grin. Curious to see what else she could wring out of him, she wrapped her lips around the head and sucked him in.

When he hit the back of her throat, she moaned, causing him to curse in a hoarse breath and tighten his hold on her hair. Reveling in it, she pulled off and did it again, repeating the movement with a quicker pace each time.

"Fuck, Crush. Yeah, Sugartits. Feels… so… good." He punctuated each of the last few words with small thrusts of his hips.

Crush felt her wetness grow and drench her panties. She knew he would have that effect on her. Hell, even the look in his eyes could have her on the edge of an orgasm. It made sense that being the cause of his pleasure would heighten that.

"Don't want to come in your mouth," he panted, and stared down at her with his dark eyes ablaze.

She stroked him a few more times with her mouth, letting her tongue drag over the vein on the underside with each pass before she pulled off and grinned up at him. "If you want something other than what I'm giving you, Lucy, you're going to have to take it."

His brow shot up, but it was joined with a look of pure intent as he pulled a little on the handful of hair, causing her head to tilt further back. Staring into her eyes, he dropped to his knees and took her mouth in the hottest kiss he'd given her yet.

It was wet and messy, wild, full of desire and demand, lacking in finesse or seduction. It was all about need, *burning hot need*. She understood that more than she would ever tell him.

Her tiger was quiet again, but most likely, that was because she was finally letting Lucifer in. They were crossing that line from tracking and circling each other to catching each other. Now, it was time for them to devour each other in the most satisfying of ways.

As his tongue played with hers, he eased her cut off her shoulders and tossed it onto the table. He did the same with his jacket. As he gripped two hands in the front of her shirt, he broke the kiss but didn't move back. Gazing into her eyes, he yanked, ripping her shirt down the front.

"Lucy," she growled and looked down to find her black-lace-covered breasts on show.

Crush's Fall

"Like you don't have a hundred more," he mumbled as he cupped her breasts and dropped his mouth to the top curve of one of them.

Crush's head dropped back at the feel of his lips and tongue on her skin. She couldn't help it. It felt amazing. It felt right. It felt like they were exactly where they were intended to be — worshiping her.

One of his hands slipped around her ribs. She fully expected him to release the clasp of her bra, but he didn't. Instead, he pressed against her spine, causing her to arch her breasts toward him.

"Could spend hours doing this," he said, and slid his tongue along the top edge of her bra.

Crush's thighs were trembling with the need to have him inside of her. As much as she loved what he was doing, she needed more, and she needed it *now*.

"Another time," she said, and started untying her boots. She needed them off and out of the way so she could slip out of her jeans.

"Now," he retorted, his arm a steel band around her.

Could she have broken the hold? Yes. He was strong, but she was a shifter. His strength would never match her own. She didn't break the hold, though, but she wouldn't admit to herself that it was because she felt safe in his arms. *Nope. Not admitting that.*

"Later," she insisted and shoved off one of her boots.

She thought he agreed as he released her and went to work on the other boot. Once both boots were off and aside, Crush got rid of her torn tee and her bra.

Then she twisted and dropped to her back on the carpet. Shoving her jeans and panties off, she watched as he did the same with his own boots and clothes.

Fuck. He was the hottest man she'd ever seen. He wasn't overly bulky like Axle, nor was he slim and fit. He was the perfect balance of muscle, athleticism, and pure sex appeal. His golden skin was embellished with tattoos snaking up his arms, over his shoulders and across his collarbones. He also had tattoos along his right side that ended just below his armpit. None of them seemed to be of anything in particular, just a collection of swirls and ropes and barbed wire that showed what a twisted, complicated man he was. With the smattering of hair on his chest and that happy trail, along with the muscles and tattoos, he was gorgeous. *A masterpiece of the Gods.*

Before she could gather herself and make a move, Lucifer was on his stomach on the floor in front of her. He shouldered his way between her thighs and set about devouring her like a starving man. After licking up her slit and swirling around her clit, causing her to fist her hands in his hair, he sucked on one lip, then the other, moaning his pleasure. She wanted to moan too, but her breath was caught in her throat. The man knew what he was doing.

"Fuck, you taste so damn good, Sugartits," he uttered before he began fucking her with his tongue. His hands gripped her hips, holding her against his mouth.

"Lucy," she managed to croak out and yanked on his hair, forcing him to look up her body at her. "I want your cock."

"Eventually," he replied, and attempted to get back to what he was doing. Her hold on his hair prevented him, though.

"Now."

He grinned. "Crush, you can try all you want to order me around outside of the bedroom, but when it comes to fucking, I'm—"

"If you think you're in charge *ever*, we're going to have a problem."

He chuckled. "Or a really exciting sex life." Holding her gaze, he snaked out his tongue and flicked her clit, making her thighs quake and her breath hiss out. "Yeah, this is going to be fun." He went back to what he was doing, and she let him. They could argue about dominance later. Her nipples were hard, and her pussy was wet and pulsating. She was aching for him, yearning to feel him inside of her. In that moment, she needed that orgasm like she needed air to breathe.

Twirling his tongue around her clit, he slid two fingers inside of her, curling them just right to rub against her g-spot with each pass.

"Lucy," she moaned as her hips moved with him, rubbing her core against his face, seeking that needed climax.

"Yeah, Sugartits, rub that pussy all over my face," he said before he wrapped his lips around her clit and sucked, sending her careening off of the cliff into the orgasm.

Her thighs clamped around his head as she arched back and let her pleasure wash over her. She knew she was saying something, but damn if she knew what it was. All she knew was her pleasure and Lucifer.

When the pleasure started to wane and Crush fell back down to reality, Lucifer didn't give her time to do anything but hold on. He shifted until he was over her. With her thighs around his waist and holding himself up with one hand, he palmed his erection with his other and stared down at her.

When he didn't enter her, she slapped at his chest. "What in the fuck are you waiting for?"

Lucifer

Crush glared up at him. "What in the fuck are you waiting for?"

Lucifer grinned and bent down. He nipped her chin and replied, "I was giving you a chance to stop what's about to happen, but since you obviously don't want that chance..." He slammed into her with one hard thrust, her pussy clamping down on his erection in a death grip. "Fuck."

Once again, her head flew back and her body arched, a clear sign that she was enjoying him. Eager to keep those feelings flowing, Lucifer pulled back and slammed in again, repeating that motion, while trying not to lose his fucking mind with how amazing she felt.

He'd had sex before, *a lot of sex*, and he'd enjoyed it immensely. During all of that sex, never had he ever felt like his world was falling apart and falling together all at the same time. Never... until Crush.

Looking down into her eyes, he wanted to tell her. He wanted to open his heart and pour it all out for her, let her know how she affected him, what she meant to him, but he didn't. She wasn't ready for that. Instead, he soaked in the greenish-gold light her eyes were giving off and took solace in the fact that he was her mate, whether she had admitted it or not.

"Lucy," she breathed.

In that moment, he knew she saw in his eyes what he didn't allow himself to say.

"Come for me," he replied and picked up the pace. "Give it to me, Sugartits." Choking down the lump of emotions, he forced himself to focus on the sensations.

Her slick, hot, tight pussy was everything he thought it would be. She was perfect, even with her death threats and her actual claws. She was the woman he wanted to fuck every single day for the rest of his life.

He reached down and shifted her thigh higher on his side, giving him more room to move. Twisting his hips at the end of every thrust had Crush panting under him and clawing at his shoulders with her nails. The bite of pain fueled his own pleasure, building it, amplifying it until he was sure he would die when it crested.

Three thrusts later, Crush's pussy began to contract, and she sucked in a deep breath.

Quickly, he demanded, "You scream my name when you come." And for once, she was a good little pussy and did just that.

After fucking her through her orgasm, he finally allowed himself to give in to the climax that had been tingling in the base of his cock. He buried his face in her neck and sucked on the skin there as he emptied himself inside of her.

He didn't just give her an orgasm during that round of sex, he gave her his heart. He just hoped she didn't throw back in his face when she realized it.

Chapter Twenty

Crush

Shit. Crush knew she was done. As she stared into his eyes while he gave her the best orgasm she had ever had in her life, she knew she would never turn this man away and mean it. She would always call him back to her, need to see him, need to hear him say *Sugartits* in that sexy way he did. She was addicted, and there would be no rehab program.

She shuddered in pleasure as his lips trailed up her neck to her ear, where he whispered, "Don't shut me out *now*. I won't let you."

Before she could say a word, there was a knock on the door. Pinky's voice came from the other side of the wood, "As much as we hate to interrupt, we were supposed to have church fifteen minutes ago. Should we come back?"

"Fuck," Crush spit out and shoved him off of her. As she scrambled to get dressed, having to use one of Ivy's tees since he destroyed hers, she didn't dare look at Lucifer. She knew it wasn't just embarrassment that had her being shy. It was vulnerability, a rawness of emotion she wasn't ready to hand over to him.

She yanked on her clothes as he did the same. When they were both pulled together, she headed for the door, but he stepped in front of her. With his hands on her hips, he softly said her name and waited. Crush swallowed hard and steeled herself, pulling her walls back up, then she lifted her head and looked into his dark brown eyes.

"We'll talk later."

She knew what he was saying. He wasn't going to let her pretend it didn't happen. Lucifer would make her face it. He would make Crush own up to the fact that he was her mate. He would make her admit it. Crush was scared to death about it, but she had no intentions of denying him. It was undeniable — Maverick 'Lucifer' Brooks was her mate.

She gave a nod. "We'll talk later."

He nodded back. Leaning forward, he gave her a hard kiss before he turned and yanked the door open. Sliding his jacket back on, he strolled out of the room, through the sea of Tiger's Claw MC members lining the hall and stairwell.

Crush's Fall

Once he was about halfway down, she heard Kisy say, "There you are. Trip is out front. He was just looking for you. Said he had an emergency maintenance job he could use your help with."

Fuck. If he was going to work with Trip with her scent all over him, the entirety of both clubs and everyone they knew would know what happened by the end of the hour.

Crush swallowed down the annoyance and shoved away the panic. There was nothing she could do about it, and she had church to run.

Her sisters began to file into the room as Crush took her seat at the head of the table. She didn't bother hiding from them. There was no point. She met each one of their smirking faces with a stare. Crush wasn't trying to intimidate them, but she wasn't allowing the embarrassment to take over. She fucked Lucifer. She was a grown ass woman, and she could fuck who she wanted.

"Is this Ivy's stuff?"

Crush looked at the piles of stuff on the table at Pinky's question and nodded. "I have to pack it properly and send it to her parents. Lucifer was helping with it."

"He was packing something, but I don't think it was Ivy's record collection," Kisy commented as she took her seat.

The room went dead silent for a few seconds before it erupted into howls of laughter.

"He looked like the cat that got the cream," Shortcake said through giggles.

"Or was that Crush?" Nails asked.

"Was it grrrrrrrrrrreat?" Ginger inquired, giving Crush a sly grin. "I bet it was grrrrrrrrreat."

As the girls went around the table giving her shit, Crush let them have their fun, but when she was done, she silenced them with a long, hard stare.

"I'm not going to pretend nothing happened in here," Crush stated.

"That's good because it smells like pussy in here... more than normal," Halo uttered, getting a glare from Crush that did nothing but make the little shit smile.

"Lucifer is my mate. We all know that, so let's not pretend he's not."

"*We* haven't been pretending," Pinky said and raised a brow. "That was you. Are you claiming him at the table?"

After a long sigh, Crush gave a nod. "It doesn't leave this room. I will address it with him when I'm ready, but yes, I would like to claim Lucifer at the table. Pinky, call a vote."

"My pleasure, Boss Lady." Pinky looked around the table. "I think it's a given, but this vote will be for Lucifer to be claimed as Crush's Ol' Man. My vote is aye."

"Same," Nails answered.

"Aye. Happy for ya, Prez," Ginger called out.

"Fucking hallelujah," Pumps cheered on a laugh.

They continued around the table, ending with Lucifer being confirmed as the Ol' Man of their president. Not one opposing vote.

Crush swallowed down the lump of emotion clogging her throat and choked out, "Thank you."

Pinky stood and crossed the room. She pulled open a drawer under the built-in bookcases and pulled out a leather cut. When she returned to the table, Crush saw that it was a TCMC property cut, already adorned with the *Crush's OM* and *Lucifer* patches. "I ordered it months ago."

Lucifer

Lucifer knew the moment it registered to Trip what he had been doing before they met up. The fucker grinned like a fool, pulled out his phone, and texted. Before long, the word would be spread far and wide. He knew it made him an asshole not to stop Trip, but he didn't want to stop him. He wanted everyone within a hundred-mile radius to know that Crush was his woman, and he was her man.

As he climbed on his bike, Lucifer shook his head at Trip's gossiping ways. The man really was a twelve-year-old at heart.

"So," Trip began as he mounted his own bike, "was she?"

Lucifer looked over at him. "Was she what?"

Trip grinned. "A tiger in bed."

Bellowing with laughter, Lucifer flipped Trip off. When he got himself under control, he simply replied, "I'm not an unhappy man."

"Fair enough." Trip started his bike, and they were off to fix whatever disaster was waiting for them.

After spending hours replacing the furnace at one of the rental properties and another hour installing new blinds at the property management offices, Lucifer was ready for a shower. He was sweaty and covered in dirt and dust, probably smelled like shit. Yes, getting cleaned up was in order. He didn't want to do it alone, though. He wanted his woman under the hot water so they could pick up where they left off.

Lucifer backed his bike into a spot and pulled out his phone to text her.

Lucifer : Need to shower. Want you with me.

Her reply came a few seconds later.

Crush : Busy

Yeah, fuck that.

Lucifer : Don't care. It's later.

He wasn't going to let it go. Whether she wanted to face it or not, they were together. That's what she solidified when she let him enter her. She was giving him more than just her fucking body. It was time she acknowledged that.

For a moment, he wasn't sure she would answer him, since her return text was a lot slower this time, but she eventually replied.

Crush : Give me ten. I'll meet you at my place. 9567

Her door code. Lucifer grinned and sent back confirmation that he understood.

Ten minutes was all he'd have to wait. Then he could have his woman against him again. Yeah, he wanted to fuck her again, but he also knew they needed to talk. He was done fucking around. He was done with acting like they weren't anything to each other. And he was *way done* with her not claiming him as both her mate and her Ol' Man.

He didn't expect her to suddenly be sweet and adoring. Shit, that would bore him to tears. He wanted her feisty and liked her that way. But while she was cutting him with her claws, he wanted her mark on him and her property patch on his body. To him, it was only fair.

Once they got that squared away, though, he sure as hell wanted to be deep inside her as many times as he could manage. They had a lot of months to make up for, and that shit started today. In ten minutes, to be exact.

He would shower with her at her place, but eventually, he'd need to get dressed again, and he didn't want to put his dirty clothes back on, so with a grin still on his face, he made his way to his room and grabbed a change of clothes and the present he bought for her when he saw it at a shop in Grand Rapids. It was perfect for her, and he knew it belonged around her neck. Hopefully, she'd like it, even if he doubted she'd ever admit it to him.

Axle

"Are you sure?" Axle stared at his brother as Trip sat down in a chair on the other side of his desk.

Trip nodded. "Positive. Her scent was all over him… and the only way it would be *that* strong is if he fucked her."

"Well… good for him," Axle said with a nod. "For her, too."

"I think it's time," Trip commented. "I know you've been considering it. He's more than proven he's worth it. He's stuck his neck out for us. He's good with the women, treats them like sisters. *And* he's Crush's mate. She's finally letting him in… and I think we should, too."

Axle let out a deep sigh as he took in Trip's words and mulled them over. "Bullet's not going to like that."

Trip shrugged. "He'll get over it. Lucifer's her mate. We all know it… especially Bullet."

"Yeah… and? You're Darlin's mate. That doesn't mean much to Dragon when he's pissed."

Rolling his eyes, Trip replied, "Look, I know I handled that all wrong. We weren't open about it from the beginning. Lucifer hasn't hidden it *at all*."

"True." Axle thought it over some more. Most of the club had come to terms with the fact that it was more of a *when* than an *if* when it came to Lucifer prospecting for the Howlers. And more than likely, his prospecting time would be shorter than most since he had already done so much for them without the prospect cut. He sighed again and said, "If she mates him or claims him as her Ol' Man, we'll bring it to the table."

Crush

Staring at her phone, Crush was lost in her thoughts. She forgot that she was sitting next to Pinky at the bar in the main room of the clubhouse.

"So, what are you going to do?"

Crush jolted at Pinky's question. She quickly typed out her response and shoved her phone in the pocket of her cut.

When Pinky started chuckling, Crush flipped her off.

"We need to talk."

Pinky nodded. "Sure. Yeah. In the shower."

Crush leaned forward and dropped her head to the top of the bar. "I'm a slut."

"Only for him," Pinky said through a laugh and patted Crush on the back.

"I won't turn into one of those women who ooh and ahh over their men," she grumbled against the beat-up wood surface.

"So… you're admitting he's your man to more than just church?"

"Fuck all the way off, Pinky. For real."

"I hear congratulations are in order," Axle commented from the other side of the bar.

Crush lifted her head and glared at him. "Who told you?" When Axle just stared at her with that motherfucking bastard grin, Crush hissed, "Trip."

"He is a bit of a gossip."

"Just like his big brother," Pinky said into her beer bottle as she lifted it to her lips to take a sip.

Axle glared at her. "I don't gossip. I just need to know everything that's happening in the club so I can—"

"That's bullshit, and we both know it," Crush blurted as she slid off the stool. "Every member of my club has known for hours because I claimed him at church this morning, but not one of them have said a word. *One* of the Howlers finds out, and it spreads like wildfire. Admit it, Axle. You lot are the biggest gossipy bitches around."

Instead of addressing her accusation, Axle hiked a brow. "You claimed him?"

Suddenly realizing what she revealed, Crush crossed her arms over her chest and looked away from Axle. After a long moment where she beat down her panic and frustration, she met his gaze again, and replied, "Yes, but I haven't told him yet. We didn't... we didn't have time to sort stuff out."

Axle's expression cleared of any amusement. He gave a nod. "Understood. I'll see what I can do to get Trip to shut his mouth."

"That's a feat of monumental proportions," Pinky commented with a snort.

"Right?" Axle nodded at Pinky.

Leaving them to commiserate about how hard it was to deal with Trip, Crush headed out of the clubhouse and across the street.

As she rounded the building, headed for the door to her stairs, her stomach was in knots and her hands were shaking. It may be a foregone conclusion that they were mates, but what that meant for their lives was up in the air.

Whether or not they would spend their lives miserable or in mated bliss depended heavily on the conversation they were about to have. She sent prayers up to whichever fucking God was listening in that moment and asked for guidance. She wasn't known for her tact or diplomacy, and she sure as hell wasn't good at intimacy or vulnerability. If left up to her, it could very well turn into a shit show.

T.S. Tappin

Chapter Twenty-One

Lucifer

Lucifer took the stairs up to Crush's front door two at a time. He couldn't wait to get their talk out of the way, so they could move forward and finally *begin*. He wouldn't be okay with being her dirty little secret for long, not that he was a secret. Her entire club knew exactly what was going on between them. He suspected the Howlers did, too.

At the top of the stairs, he punched in the code she gave him and swung her door open. He was a bit surprised to see Crush standing at her kitchen counter. She had her hands planted, palms down, on the top. Leaning over it, she just seemed to be staring down at the surface.

Confused and a bit concerned, Lucifer set his clothes and the small box down on the arm of her couch and made his way over to her. Standing at her side, he bent down a bit, trying to catch her eye.

"Crush?"

"I won't change."

More confused, Lucifer replied, "Okay."

"I mean it, Lucy. I won't change. I am who I am."

He let out a sigh. "Did I ask you to?"

"No, but I'm sure you will."

Lucifer turned and leaned his ass against the edge of the counter. Crossing his arms over his chest, he stared across her kitchen. "Why are you so sure I'll ask you to change?"

"Why wouldn't you? What man wants a woman… like me? I'm not sweet or affectionate or…"

Lucifer rolled his eyes and barked out a laugh. "Sugartits, the kind of affection I want is exactly what you give me. It's the glare and the death threats that do it for me."

Crush turned her head and glared at him, which only caused him to laugh harder. "Be serious, Lucy."

"I am." He shrugged. "I don't want you sweet and innocent. I want you feisty."

"Are you trying to tell me you wouldn't rather I be kissing all over you and cuddling up next to your side?"

Lucifer grinned. "You will. The kissing might involve your teeth, and you might have a knife to my neck as you're cuddled up to my side, but it will happen."

"I'm not joking around here, Lucifer," she growled and shoved away from the counter.

He followed her as she stomped through the space toward what he assumed was the bathroom door. As she walked, she started removing her clothes. Not wanting that to stop, Lucifer started removing his own and continued to follow her lead.

She was down to her boots and jeans when she swung the door open and stepped inside.

Lucifer kicked out of his boots and laid his jacket and tee on the back of her couch. Unfastening his jeans, he stepped into the bathroom and found her completely naked while turning on the water for the shower.

"I'm not joking." Lucifer yanked down the zipper of his jeans before shoving them and his boxer briefs off. Yanking his socks off, he said, "And I'm getting fucking sick and tired of being compared to every other man that has ever been in your life."

"You better watch yourself," she growled back at him, standing there with her hands on her naked hips.

"They aren't in your life anymore for a damn reason, Crush. *They. Weren't. Who. You. Needed.*" He picked up his clothes and tossed them out of the bathroom, so they didn't trip. That done, he met her stare and demanded, "Claim me."

"What?"

"I'm done fucking around, Crush. I'm done with your damn fear. I'm done with you pretending that you don't fucking need me in your life. I'm. Fucking. Done. *Claim me.*" Lucifer took the three steps needed to bring him against her. He shoved her hands away from her hips and replaced them with his own on her hips. Pushing her back against the glass door of the shower, he gazed into her eyes and informed her, "I'm not leaving here without your property patch."

Her eyes flashed greenish-gold light at him before she got control of herself. "You don't make those decisions."

"Claim me," he repeated.

"Or what?"

He lowered his head and nipped at her bottom lip. "Tell me you don't want to and mean it."

She winced, and her eyes closed. He knew he was right, but her reaction only proved it to be true. "Lucifer," she practically breathed.

"Claim me," he said, softer but no less insistent. "I don't want you to change who you are. I fucking love the way you spar with me. I love the way you go head to head with me over every fucking thing. And I *fucking love* the passion you give me when we fuck."

"You can't love me," she said, low.

"I love you," he replied and meant it. "I fucking love you." When she shook her head, he cupped it in his hands and used his naked body to keep hers in place. "Crush, I love you."

"I…"

He shook his head. "You're afraid. I get that. I understand it. You expect me to try to take over. You expect me to try to control you. You expect me to try to turn you into the perfect Ol' Lady. But you're missing the point, Crush. You already are the perfect Ol' Lady for me. You already are exactly what I need. I don't want to take over anything... except the occasional scene in bed." He chuckled. "I'm not Axle, though. I don't need or want to give you orders and have you follow them. I need you to fight me. I need you to challenge me. I need you to not bore me to gods-damn tears." He pressed his lips to hers and whispered against them, "Claim me."

After kissing the hell out of her, he pulled back and pressed his forehead to hers.

Looking into his eyes, she admitted, "I already did."

"What?"

She shrugged. "I already did. This morning. During church."

"Then where in the hell is my property patch?"

"You'll get it when I decide to fucking give it you," she bit out and put her hands to his chest, giving him a shove. She didn't really try, though, or he would have been on his ass. He knew that.

Unable to stop the smile from growing on his face, he took her hand and maneuvered them into the shower.

Crush

Crush loved her shower. Her apartment may have been studio style and small, but it was outfitted the way she wanted it, especially the bathroom. She wasn't a bath girl. She liked scalding hot showers. Because of that, she had a glass and stone shower installed with high-power shower heads. Others could keep their rainfall showerheads. She wanted waterpower.

The glass door of the shower had a horizontal bar handle and swung out into the room. The other three walls of the shower were a tan and gray stone that had been polished to a smooth finish that was comfortable against the skin. That was important to her, since she tended to lean against that stone and let the water beat against her after a long day.

Following Lucifer into the shower, Crush realized that smooth stone was about to be important for another reason.

He gripped her hips and positioned her with her back to the spray. Without asking, he grabbed the bodywash and squirted some in his large hands. Crush just watched as he worked the soap into a lather.

In the next moment, his lips pressed against hers as his soapy hands slid up her sides and over to her breasts. As he cupped her breasts in the palms of his hands, he forced his tongue past her lips and tickled hers.

Crush moaned and opened up to him, allowing him to kiss her properly, but she wasn't about to stand there and let him do whatever he wanted. She would be an active partner in their shower games. To make that point, she nipped at his tongue as she pushed him back against the wall of the shower opposite the showerhead.

When his back hit the stone, he broke the kiss and grinned at her. "There's my feisty woman."

Crush rolled her eyes. "Shut up," she ordered as she dropped to her knees.

One of the great things about Lucifer being her mate was it didn't take much to make him ready. His erection staring her in the face proved that. Without a second's thought, she wrapped her hand around him and stroked. Looking up into his chocolate brown eyes filled with lust, she smirked before she leaned forward and swallowed him down, chuckling when he groaned, and his head fell back against the stone.

As she bobbed and sucked, she noticed the tension in his thighs and his abdomen. He was holding back. She didn't want that. She wanted the aggressive, forward, pushy man who had been brazenly demanding her attention for months.

Glaring at him as she continued her rhythm on his cock, she unleashed her claws and raked them down his thighs, careful not to break skin. The action had the effect she desired. As he moaned her name, his hands went into her hair and fisted as his hips slammed forward and he began to fuck her mouth.

"Is that what you want?" His growled question went straight to her clit as he rolled his hips and continued to fuck her.

She moaned around his cock in answer. Retracting her claws, she held onto his thighs and let him do what he wanted.

It wasn't until she released one of his thighs to snake her hand down between her legs, with the intention of playing with her clit, that he changed what he was doing.

In the next moment, he pulled her off his cock and forced her to her feet with a tug of her hair.

"Fuck, you're so damn hot," he gritted out as he turned her and slammed her against the stone wall.

Crush chuckled. "If you were about to come too fast, just say that."

Lucifer grinned, wrapped his arms around her, gripped her ass, and lifted. Crush bit her bottom lip to stop herself from grinning back at him as she wrapped her legs around his waist.

"Sugartits, if you think I don't have the stamina to fuck you, that sounds like a challenge." Staring into her eyes, he slid into her and set a hard, fast rhythm, curling his hips just right to scramble her brain with each stroke and stealing her ability to breathe normally.

As she sucked in a breath, the greenish-gold light came from her eyes, bathing the room.

"Yeah, you like that," he bit out, putting more power in his thrusts.

Not wanting to be outdone, Crush did her best to pull her senses together enough to move her hips in tandem to his, building and enhancing the sensations for both of them. They were on the edge. She could tell he was right there with her, and she wanted to be the one to push them over that cliff. She wanted to be the catalyst for his bliss in more ways than just being the body he used for his pleasure.

Wrapping her arms around his shoulders, she unhooked one leg from his waist and extended it, searching for something to use for leverage. The ball of her foot and her toes came in contact with the handle on the door. Using that, she intensified her movements while taking his mouth in a deep, wet kiss.

Three strokes later, they moaned together as each of them went sailing off the edge into euphoria, a wave of pleasure taking them under, just as the handle of the door clattered to the floor.

Lucifer

Leaning against the back of the couch, with a towel around his waist, Lucifer watched as Crush ran a brush through her hair. He loved the purple ends and how they looked with the natural dark brown of her hair. More than anything, he liked to get a good grip on her tresses as he plowed into her. She seemed to like a bite of pain with her orgasm, and he was more than happy to give that to her.

Hell, whatever she wanted, he would give her. If she wanted him to tie her up and spank her ass, count him in. If she wanted him to gag her and fuck her ass, *yes, please*. If she wanted him to gaze into her eyes and fuck her slow but hard, he would do it. Lucifer wanted to experience it all with Crush. The dirty and the sensual. Anything and everything there was for two people to do, he wanted to do it with her.

"Quit staring at me like that."

He grinned. "But I love you."

She winced. "And quit saying that."

"But it's true. I love you."

She turned to face him and glared. "Stop it."

"Why? It's true. I—" Then he ducked to avoid the brush that came flying, hard and fast, at his face.

"Okay. You've told me. Now… stop saying it."

Lucifer snatched the brush from where it landed across the room and made his way into the bathroom. Walking up to her, he handed it over. Gazing into her eyes, he replied, "I won't stop saying it, but I can stop saying it *for now*… as soon as you admit that you feel the same way about me."

She glared up at him. "What if I don't?"

"You do."

"You don't know what I feel."

He rolled his eyes. "Yes, I do."

She continued to glare at him for a long moment before she huffed out a breath and turned away from him. Shoving her brush into a draw of the vanity, she mumbled, "Fine. I fucking love you, too."

Lucifer grinned and smacked her ass. "Good girl." He just barely dodged her fist when she turned around and swung at him. Proud of himself for being quick enough to make her miss with the first swing, he wasn't prepared when she swung with her other hand and caught him in his left eye.

"Fuck!" He covered his face with his hand and bent down as pain radiated through his face and head. "That fucking hurt."

"You deserved that." With his uncovered eye, he watched her bare feet walk out of the bathroom. "I'll get you some ice, you damn baby."

Even though his face was throbbing, he couldn't stop the grin from growing on his face. He felt like the luckiest man alive.

T.S. Tappin

Chapter Twenty-Two

Crush

After getting dressed and icing his eye a bit to bring down the swelling, they decided to grab food from the diner before they addressed everything else that needed to be talked about. The bruising on the outside of his eye wasn't too bad, but there was a noticeable red area on his actual eye. She felt a little bad about hitting him, but she wouldn't tell him that.

Everything was fine while they waited for their food, but she should have known better than to think they would make it out of the diner without questions.

"What happened to your eye?"

At Kitty's question, Crush winced and shot a glare at Lucifer to let him know to keep his mouth shut. Of course, the fucker didn't. Grinning back at her, he opened his mouth and answered, "I told Crush that I love her."

Kitty snorted a laugh. "You seem happy about that."

"Oh, I am. It wasn't the mark I wanted, but it'll do."

Crush flipped him off and snatched the bag with their to-go containers off of the counter. Not waiting for Lucifer, she turned and stormed out of the back door of the diner, heading for her place.

She heard him chuckling behind her as she climbed the stairs. Ignoring him, she entered her place and approached the island. Setting the bag on the top, she began to pull out the containers, full intent on not acknowledging his amusement or presence.

Crush felt him against her back before she felt his breath on her neck. She internally cursed at the way her body trembled and ached to have him inside her again. When her tiger began to purr and swish its tail, she told it to shut the hell up.

"Stop it."

"Stop what?"

"Being pissed at me."

"I'm not."

"Yes, you are." He nipped at her earlobe. "So, stop. Or don't. I can still fuck you while you're pissed." He ran the tip of his nose along the outside edge of her ear. "On second thought, stay pissed. It will only make the fucking better."

Crush swallowed hard and pretended he wasn't having an effect on her, but the truth was her pussy was wet and her nipples were hard from just the sound of his voice. She couldn't let him know that, though. Why? She no longer knew why, but that wasn't going to change anything.

After setting out their food, she flipped the top off her chicken chili and picked up a spoon. "Grab me a pop from the fridge, will ya?"

Chuckling again, Lucifer did as she asked. The second he stepped away from her, her tiger began to whimper. Fuck. It was like she was strung out on his touch, desperate for her next hit, yearning for the oblivion of a climax only he could give her.

"Can I see my cut?" He set a can of pop down next to her left hand and slid something around her neck before he rounded the island and took a seat on a stool on the other side.

Glancing down, she saw a semi-thick silver chain that was long enough to end in her cleavage where a heart-shaped Tiger's Eye Stone pendant laid. It was surrounded by silver and had little devil horns jutting from the top. It perfectly encapsulated the two of them — strong and resilient. Her tiger quietly purred at the sight of it as a few of the bricks in her wall of protection crumbled to dust.

Choked up by the sentiment and raw, Crush fell back into her typical surliness. He didn't deserve it, but she couldn't let him see how much the necklace meant to her. It would give him leverage she wasn't ready for him to have.

She took another bite of her chili as she watched him open the plastic container holding his meatball sub and fries. After she chewed and swallowed, she answered, "No. I haven't decided if I'm giving it to you."

He looked over at her and raised a brow as he popped a French fry into his mouth. The look on his face clearly meant to say, *Who in the hell do you think you're fooling? And don't for a minute think I don't know you love my gift.*

She fingered the pendant as she looked down at her bowl of chili. "We have traditions, Lucy."

"Is my patch going to say Lucy?"

Because she was still raw and feeling backed into a corner, Crush shrugged and replied, "It's what I call you." She knew damn well that it said *Lucifer*.

Seemingly unbothered, Lucifer popped another fry into his mouth and chewed. After swallowing, he said, "You're welcome for the necklace, by the way. We need to talk about the mating."

"Mating," she croaked and almost choked on her bite of chili. Coughing, she slammed a hand against her chest. When it looked like he was about to get up and come around to her, she shook her head and opened her pop. After taking a drink, she cleared her throat and took a deep breath. "Mating?"

"I'm your mate, Crush."

"Yes, but… mating?"

He looked at her like she lost her mind. "Yes. That's what happens. You find your mate and you complete the *mating*."

"Don't patronize me, Lucy," she growled. "I fucking know that."

"Then what's the problem?"

"The problem is you seem to be making all the decisions here," she shouted. "That's not fucking okay with me."

"You made the decision the second you launched yourself at me this morning. I told you I'm done playing your fucking games." His dark eyes stared hard at her, unwavering. "I fucking meant it. I'm your Ol' Man, so fucking claim me right. I'm your mate, so fucking mate me right. Or. Let. Me. Go. You may be the boss around here, and I'm cool with that, but you won't lead me around by my dick. I will go head-to-head with you. I *will* make you face shit you don't want to face. I'm *not* here to be your fucking slave. I'm here to be your *partner*." He lifted his sandwich. "Get the fuck over your bullshit and make a real decision. And I mean *now*, Crush, because if you don't fucking want me, I'll go find someone who will."

That did it. The thought of him wrapped around someone else, touching them, kissing them, fucking them… Crush couldn't take it. She rounded the island, grabbed him by the arm, and pulled him off the stool. He was barely able to set his sandwich down before she was pulling him over to the couch and shoving him down.

Her tiger was snarling at the thought that someone else would be that close to their mate, and Crush fully understood it.

Once he was sitting on the couch, she started stripping off her clothes. He wasn't a fool, so he

T.S. Tappin

unfastened and shoved his jeans over his hips before he yanked off his tee. Naked, she straddled his lap and slammed her lips to his. As their tongues explored and teeth nipped, one of his arms snaked around her waist, and his free hand cupped her ass, his fingertips digging into her skin.

Crush wrapped her arms around his neck, the fingers of one of her hands sliding into his hair and fisting. Their kiss was desperate and messy as she lifted her hips and adjusted so the head of his cock sat at her entrance.

Without hesitation, she dropped her hips down. Lucifer broke the kiss to groan as he entered her. "Fuck, Crush," he breathed.

Kissing along his jaw, she lifted and dropped again, soaking in each moan he gave her. When she lifted and dropped again, he slapped her ass, sending a burst of pleasure to her core.

When her mouth reached his neck, she nipped the skin on her way down. "You want my mark?"

"Hell yes," he groaned, helping her lift and drop with his grip on her. "Mark me, Crush. Make me yours, Sugartits."

"It's forever, Lucifer." She continued her movements with her hips as she pulled her head back and looked down into his eyes. "Permanent."

His eyes were clear as he smiled up at her. "Good."

Her tiger purred its approval at his answer and intensified the demand to complete the mating.

She lowered herself onto him and stayed there. Her heart was pounding, but it wasn't from exertion. It was from fear. "I'm…"

He nodded. "I know." His arms moved so he could cup her face in his hands. "I know, Crush." He gave her a soft kiss that had tears filling her eyes. "I don't want you to change, and I won't try to control you. I'll tell you that as many times as you need me to, but you don't have to be afraid of us. Babe, I just want to be yours."

Staring into the chocolate depths of his eyes, Crush searched for any bit of deception. There was nothing. He meant every word. She was going to do it. She was going to face her fears and put her vulnerable heart in his hands. She would give him her commitment, but that also gave him the ability to wreck her. The only thing she could do was have faith that he would do everything in his power to avoid that.

Slowly, she began to roll her hips and nodded, unable to voice her decision. Her tiger gave a purr, but laid down and quieted, obviously worried she'd back out if pushed too far.

After kissing her lips again, Lucifer dropped his hands to her hips, helping her maintain the rhythm. Keeping his gaze locked with hers, Lucifer lowered his head and wrapped his lips around her nipple, sucking gently. Her breath caught in her throat as she felt that all the way down in her clit.

"Fuck, your pussy feels so damn good," he growled against the skin of her breast, before kissing the pendant hanging down the center of her chest. "Want

T.S. Tappin

to feel it tighten around my cock. Want you to milk me as you sink your fangs into my skin and make me yours for the rest of our fucking lives."

His words urged her on, making her move her hips faster, her clit rubbing against him with every movement.

"God damn, Crush," he bit out, staring at her. "You are sexy as fucking hell, taking what belongs to you. I'm going to fucking blow." He shifted the grip he had on her hip so that his thumb could reach her clit. Circling her clit, he pushed her to the edge of climax. "Do it." He slapped her ass hard with his other hand.

As the sting shot right to her clit and made her pussy clench, Crush opened her mouth and let her fangs slide down.

"Yes," he moaned.

Then she struck, sinking her fangs into the flesh of the left side of his neck where it met his shoulder. The second her fangs entered him, his hips lifted, slamming against her core, his hands holding her tight against him as they both succumbed to their orgasms. As he called out her name, she felt him slide into his place in her heart, fill her, make her whole.

She kept her fangs inside of him until her climax eased. Then she pulled them from his flesh, threw her head back, and let out a roar.

The answering roars and howls were her sisters, honoring her choice and rejoicing in the addition to their family. For once, Crush allowed the grin to spread across her face as she dropped her head forward and pressed her forehead to his.

"That was the coolest thing that's ever happened to me," Lucifer mumbled, sounding drunk.

Crush chuckled. "*I* am the coolest thing that's ever happened to you."

"Fair enough," he said back before he took her lips in a deep kiss.

After a moment, she pulled back. When his lips followed hers with the intent to continue, she put her fingers to his lips. "I have to close you up." She dropped her mouth back to where she bit him and began to lick away the blood and seal the wound. The way his hips moved and the deep moans coming from his mouth let her know she made the right choice. Being hers was something that completed him the same way it completed her.

Lucifer

Twenty minutes later, Lucifer was holding Crush's hand as she dragged him into the clubhouse. He wanted nothing more than to stay naked with her on her couch, but he would let her drag him anywhere if she was willing to hold his hand. Fuck, he was a damn pussy.

When they entered the main room, the space erupted into cheers from the Howlers and the Claws who filled the room. The Howlers and their families were off to the side, allowing the Claws to be front and center, obviously acknowledging that they were there to witness, not to participate.

In front of the rest of the Claws, Pumps stood, wearing her typical jean shorts and barely-there top, along with sky-high stiletto heels. Her blond hair was down, and her lips were painted her favorite red lipstick. Lucifer knew she was beautiful, but he never really looked at her as anything other than a close friend or a sister. In that moment, all he saw was the black leather bunched up in one of her hands.

When the crowd quieted down, Pumps spoke. "I asked Pinky to let me do it, since I've known you the longest, and she gave me the honor. And it *is* an honor, Lucifer. By tying yourself to Crush, you tied yourself to us. By having her back, you have ours. By protecting her, you protect us. By loving her, you love us. We're a package deal. And we understand we're getting more out of the deal than you are."

He was surprised when Crush's grip tightened on his hand. He looked over at her to find her looking at him with love in her eyes. For the first time, she was showing him everything she felt. His breath caught, and it took everything he had to look over at Pumps again.

"Take this as a vow from us to you… that should you need anything from us, we will endeavor to provide it. As your sisters, we will hold you up should you fall, we will lift you up should you ever have doubt, we will fight for you should you ever have need to tag us in. But most importantly, we will hold your hand and have your back should you ever face trial. You will not face life alone, because we are honored to call you *brother*."

When Pumps held out the hand gripping the leather, Lucifer swallowed hard around the lump that had formed in his throat. He took the cut from her hand and didn't bother looking at it. He just slid it on to his shoulders before he turned and cupped Crush's face in his hands. Not giving her an opportunity to stop him, he slammed his lips to her and kissed the fucking hell out of her for their entire family to see.

The whistles, hoots, and hollers registered, but only barely over the quiet moan Crush gave him as his tongue tangled with hers.

"While they make out like teenagers," Pinky began, "we have another brother to welcome. Dragon! Where are you?"

"Ah hell," Lucifer heard Dragon grumble.

"It's time for your branding, Dex," Kisy said on a laugh.

Bullet

Annoyed. That was the overwhelming feeling Bullet was experiencing as he talked to Crush. His sister wanted him to congratulate Lucifer, which he could do, but she also wanted him to welcome Lucifer to the family. *That* is where his annoyance was coming from. The last thing he wanted to do is admit to that man being family. Sure, technically, he was, since he was

T.S. Tappin

Crush's mate and officially her Ol' Man, but that didn't mean Bullet wanted to acknowledge that to the man.

"Bullet, you owe me that," Crush growled as she stood in front of him with her hands on her hips. "Don't make me call Mom and tell her that you're being stubborn."

Bullet snorted. "You won't call Mom. If you did, she'd demand you bring him over, like she's been doing since she found out about him. You won't risk having that conversation *again*."

"Okay." She shrugged. "I'll tell *Butterfly* you won't congratulate him. How do you think your mate would feel if I told her you won't give my mate the same respect that I willingly gave her?"

Scoffing, Bullet crossed his arms over his chest. "When I met *my mate*, she wasn't our enemy."

Crush crossed her arms over her chest and smirked. "When you met *your mate*, she pointed a gun at you. I would have had every right to hate her, but I gave her a chance, which is all I'm asking you to do."

Fuck. She was right. His tiger was snarling and pacing inside of him, irritated that he was going to have to do what she wanted.

"Fine." Crush turned around and called out, "Butterf—"

Bullet silenced her with a hand over her mouth and growled into her ear. "Fucking fine, you brat. I'll congratulate your damn mate." He dropped his hand as his sister turned and smiled up at him.

"Thanks, Bull. You're the best."

Rolling his eyes, Bullet crossed the room to the bar where Lucifer was doing shots with a few of the Ol' Ladies. "Lucifer," he said, trying to get the man's attention.

After throwing back another shot of what looked like vodka, Lucifer spun around on the bar stool and met Bullet's stare. "Hey, bro-in-law. What's up?"

The title grated on Bullet's nerves, increasing the snarling of his tiger, but he shoved it down. "Just wanted to say... congratulations."

Lucifer chuckled. "Crush make you tuck your tail and come tell me that?"

Bullet took a deep breath, telling himself that killing his sister's mate wouldn't do anyone any good.

"It's okay that you caved. Thanks, man." Lucifer patted him on the shoulder and turned back around.

Telling himself and his tiger that beating the hell out of the man wouldn't be worth it either, Bullet stormed away from the dickhead. When he reached the table where Trip and Dragon were sitting, he saw the grins on their faces.

As he took his seat, he uttered, "Fuck you both."

Crush

Laying in bed that night, Crush felt Lucifer's fingers drawing shapes on the side of her neck. "What are you doing?"

From behind her, he pressed his lips to the spot his fingers had been caressing. "Is this where you're getting it?"

"Getting what?" She turned her head enough to look back at him.

"My name tatted."

"That's a Howler tradition," she replied, and rolled over to face him.

He slid his arm around her and pulled her closer. "Okay. It doesn't have to be your neck, but I would like something."

Crush studied his face and was shocked to see a bit of shyness and vulnerability in the way he wouldn't meet her gaze, instead he kept his eyes on her shoulder.

"It means that much to you?"

He shrugged.

"Lucy." When his eyes finally met hers, she repeated, "It means that much to you?"

He swallowed hard but nodded. "Yeah, but I won't try to force you."

"How about here?" She leaned back enough to put her fingertips to her skin above her left breast. "I'll get a tattoo that says *Maverick*." She then gripped his arm and pulled it from around her. Taking his hand, she put it to her inner thigh. "Here... there's where I'll get *Property of Lucifer*. That work for you?"

The groan that came from him was guttural. He shoved her to her back and was inside of her before she could take a full breath.

As he slammed into her over and over again, he vowed, "I'll put your name anywhere you want. Damn, I fucking love you."

T.S. Tappin

Chapter Twenty-Three

A few days later... Crush

After sending her mother *another* text telling her she'd bring Lucifer over soon, Crush hung out in the tattoo parlor with the Ol' Ladies, Pinky, and Kisy while she got her Ol' Lady tattoos, declaring her connection to Dragon. When she was done, Ginger began to clean them up as she smiled and commented, "He'll have to borrow Rock's truck if he plans to take you back to the house tonight." Since Kisy got the tattoos on each of her inner thighs, riding a motorcycle would prove difficult and painful until the tats healed.

"I don't think they'll make it that far," Gorgeous uttered and yelped when Dragon's sister, Darlin', smacked her arm. "Damn it, Dani! That shit hurt."

"Then stop talking about my brother fucking!"

T.S. Tappin

"I didn't say anything about that!"

Crush snorted a laugh, because Gorgeous was most definitely talking about that.

Pixie moved to the seat closer to Kisy and rolled her eyes. "Those two can be more like sisters than best friends."

"I like it," Kisy replied. "But Gorgeous isn't wrong. As soon as Dragon sees these, he's going to carry me up to our room here and—"

"LALALALALALALALALALALA," Darlin' blurted as she plugged her ears with her fingers, not wanting to hear about her brother's sex life *again*. Crush completely understood that sentiment.

Sugar grinned and said to Kisy, "I like you."

"I like you, too," Kisy replied.

From her position leaned back against the wall by the door to the room, next to Pinky, Crush absently played with her pendant and asked Kisy, "Where are you getting your TC colors?"

The question brought proud tears to Kisy's eyes. She looked from Crush to Pinky and back. "Full-back piece," she answered.

"Righteous," Pinky said, and grinned as she nodded her approval.

"Kick ass," Peanut agreed.

Ginger smiled at her as she stood and pulled off her nitrile gloves. "That will be an honor to do for you, Kisy. Give your body a week, and I'll get you taken care of."

Kisy looked around the room at all the women. "Thank you… to all of you. I didn't always fit in with my family, and now I have a new family that feels more like home than home ever did."

"Oh, fuck," Pixie uttered as tears started streaming down her face. "Fucking pregnancy hormones!"

Crush gave Kisy a nod before she snuck out Pinky on her heels. There was only so much pregnancy blubbering a woman could take. They hung out in the lobby, waiting for Kisy to get dressed.

A few minutes later, Crush and Pinky lifted Kisy up into their arms. Each of them had an arm around her back and another under one of her knees, and Kisy's arms over their shoulders.

Butterfly had made some comment about carrying the sass queen around, which sent Kisy in a fit of laughter as they entered the clubhouse.

Trailing behind them were the rest of the Ol' Ladies and Ginger.

"What in the hell did you do to my mate?" Dragon asked as they sat Kisy down on the table in front of him.

"Nothing," Crush said on a laugh. "We didn't want your lips rubbing all over the Howlers colors."

Dragon's lip print was one of the tattoos Kisy got. The other tattoo was the Howlers logo.

Pinky snorted. "Could you imagine Dragon kissing the Howlers' asses?"

And just like that, the whole lot of them devolved into giggles.

Dragon locked gazes with Kisy. "Explain. What in the fuck are they talking about?"

T.S. Tappin

"It'll be easier to show you," she commented and pointed down to her legging-covered thighs.

Curious, Dragon stood and scooped her up. As he carried her out of the room, toward the restrooms, Crush and Pinky chuckled as the rest of the girls hooted and hollered.

Thirty minutes later, Crush was sitting with Pinky and a few other Claws members at a corner table in the clubhouse, when BonBon, Dragon's mother, walked in.

She halted just inside the main room of the clubhouse, and her head ticked to the side. Crush knew why. They had heard the noises and voices coming from the women's bathroom since Dragon and Kisy went in there. Crush wasn't about to speculate on what Dragon was doing to Kisy, but from what they heard, it was effective.

Crush and the rest of the people in the room — several members of the Howlers, the Claws, and the Ol' Ladies — watched as BonBon crossed the room and stepped down the hallway. She stopped at the door to the women's restroom and knocked, before she called out, "While I've been there and understand what is coursing through your veins right now, you have quite the audience out here, kids."

"Be right out, Mom," Dragon loudly growled out from inside the restroom. Crush and most of the others in the room were shifters, so they could hear him clearly.

There was humor in his mother's voice when she replied, "Thanks for making my son so happy, Kisy."

"Mom," Dragon barked.

"Okay! Okay. It's just sex, but fine. Hurry up."

As BonBon came back into the main room, Crush and the rest of the onlookers were cackling. BonBon wasn't like most moms, but she was one of the best.

Lucifer

In the following days, Lucifer went with Crush to the site of the demolished club a couple of times and with Trip once. As he watched the faces of the club members who were trying to clean up the site, Lucifer felt their despair and anger. The Hell's Dogs did more damage at that site than just destroying a building.

Yeah, they were furious about the destruction of their property and their business, but they were also upset that their employees were left swinging in the wind, and they weren't sure what to do about that.

To Lucifer, that was the easiest problem to deal with, or at least, it was the problem they could solve the quickest. As he helped the Howlers and the Claws with cleanup, he thought on how to fix that.

When he and Crush got back to their apartment and she plopped down on a stool at the island, Lucifer hated the stress he could see in her face and the tension in her body. He sidled up behind her and began to rub her shoulders and upper back.

He hit a particularly tough spot between her shoulder blades, and a moan came from her mouth, making him smile for a moment.

"The HDMC bullshit never ends, huh?"

She sighed. "It feels that way."

He continued to rub and work out any knots he found. "Would it help if we broke the giant situation into smaller, more manageable problems?"

She was quiet for a moment. "What do you mean?"

"Not that it's any of my business, but… it seems to me that the most immediate issue is finding work for your employees, right?"

Crush let out another deep sigh. "Yes."

"We could… Well, you could offer them to help with cleanup and rebuilding the site. I'm sure some of them would like to help restore the place. The rest… I'm sure there are places within the other business where they could help. Sure, you might end up being over-staffed in some areas, but it's better than your employees suffering."

Crush looked over her shoulder at him. Her expression showed interest and contemplation with her drawn brows and focused eyes. "I'm listening."

He moved his hands up to her neck, forcing her to face forward again as he worked on her tense muscles there. "For instance, the bartenders and wait staff could help in the clubhouse or the diner. The dancers could help in the merch shop or maybe work the counter at the tattoo shop, so the artists can focus on their work. Maybe some of the dancers have some experience working in salons or have office experience that Kisy could put to good use."

At that point, Crush was nodding a bit as he spoke, so Lucifer continued, "I think taking that off your shoulders would help with the stress load and free you up to focus on what you plan to do with the club."

"I've been thinking… The Claws are half owners of Heat. Yet, we don't have much say in how it's run or what it is. That needs to change."

"I agree."

"I need to talk to my club and figure out if we want to keep things the same or change things up," she mumbled as her head bobbed from the loosening of the muscles in her neck and shoulders and his ministrations.

He grinned. "My badass mate is about to put her boot down with the Howlers, isn't she?"

Crush snorted a laugh. "Something like that."

"The employees might be able to help with that, too," he said, not giving a damn if he was stepping over the line. Too often owners of companies forgot that their employees knew more about the day-to-day functions of the business and might have important insight. "They could tell you what was working and not working. They might have suggestions on how to improve business or what Heat was lacking."

Crush swung around on her stool and stared up at him. Her brows were still drawn, and she seemed to be contemplating what he had to say.

"I'm just saying you might as well make improvements now, if improvements are needed, and they would be the best source of that information."

"Think you can handle gathering that info? I know you're working with Trip, but—"

"Give me a list of names and numbers for them, and I'll get it done."

Lucifer was surprised she was taking in what he had to say without a fight, but he wasn't about to question it. His woman wasn't stupid. She obviously felt like he hit on something that needed to be addressed, since she was so willingly accepting his point of view.

Unable to help himself, he grinned and bent down toward her, nipping her bottom lip. "Is there a reward in it for me?"

Her arm shot out, and her hand cupped his balls through his jeans. "I might hold off slicing these off of you for being an annoying fuck for a few more days."

Lucifer chuckled. "I'm a lot of things when I fuck, but annoying is not one of them."

With her hand still cupping his balls, she took his lips in a kiss. "Thank you… for the massage and the suggestions."

"You're welcome. A blow job will be payment enough."

When her hand tightened, he winced.

"Always have to press your luck, don't ya?"

Crush

Feeling a lot looser after Lucifer used his strong hands to work out her tension in more ways than just giving her a shoulder massage, Crush walked through the open door of Axle's office and plopped down in the chair across the desk from him.

Axle's eyes shifted up from the screen of his laptop and over to her. His raised brows invited her to tell him what the hell she wanted.

"We need to put our Heat employees to work."

That brought his full attention to her. He slowly shut the laptop. "Okay."

"It's not fair to them that our shit took away their day-to-day employment."

"Ideas on where to assign them?"

She nodded. "Lucifer suggested we could offer to let them help with cleanup and rebuilding."

Axle sighed. "I can't have untrained employees working on a construction site."

"So, train them." Crush shrugged. "We could also place them in other businesses. The waitstaff might be interested in helping at the diner... or even in the clubhouse. Same with the bartenders. The rest we could offer to have them man the desk and the tattoo shop or the salon... or work shifts at the merch shop. Some of them might have office experience and can help Kisy at PM. Hell, how do we know we don't have a mechanic hidden in the club staff?"

Axle gave a nod and a shrug. "All good points and suggestions."

"Lucifer," she said, simply.

"Diamond in the rough, that one."

Crush grinned. "Mine."

Axle chuckled. "Glad you finally see that."

As Crush rose from her chair and headed for the door, she shot him the bird, causing his laugh to intensify.

"Are you handling job placements, or am I?"

She turned around at the door and faced him. "What if we let one of the Ol' Ladies handle it? I'm learning that we don't have to shoulder everything."

Axle's brow lifted again, but the smirk on his face told her he approved.

"Butterfly," she suggested.

He gave a nod. "Talk to your sis-in-law."

Chapter Twenty-Four

Crush

Crush found Butterfly at the salon, getting her nails done. Plopping down in the chair next to her, Crush let out a deep sigh.

"Well, that was an ominous start to whatever this conversation is going to be," Butterfly commented but smiled at Crush.

After rolling her eyes, Crush asked, "How bored have you been lately?"

Butterfly snorted a laugh. "Will buildings blowing up and our family fighting in a war and people dying… I've been *so* bored."

"Smart ass," Crush mumbled.

"I have time. What do you need?" As usual, Butterfly cut to the chase.

"I need to find places in our other businesses and buildings to put our Heat employees to work. I'd like to offer them jobs to do in the meantime, so they at least have money coming in. I know many of them won't accept hand-outs and will want to work for what they're given, so we need to accommodate that."

Butterfly started nodding halfway through Crush's explanation. "Okay. Do we have a list of available jobs, or are we just creating jobs?"

"Both," Crush answered. "Talk to the managers of our businesses to see where they could use help, but if needed, create jobs. Lucifer suggested even having some of the bartenders or wait staff helping at the clubhouse."

Butterfly nodded again. "Okay. Get me names and numbers for the employees. I'll take care of it."

"I have Pumps compiling a list for Lucifer, since she worked there the most. He will be contacting them about something else, so I'll have him get with you."

"Oooo... I get to hang with Lucy *and* talk shit about the Welles siblings? I'm in."

Crush rolled her eyes again and left the shop. Lucifer and Butterfly were going to have a blast with this.

Lucifer

Lucifer was just finishing lunch the next day when he received the text from Pumps.

Pumps : Got the list ready, bro. Where you want it?

He took a drink of his pop and typed out his reply.

Lucifer : I'll be back around 5. Can you meet to give me a rundown of the people and what their jobs were?

Her reply was almost instantaneous.

Pumps : Meet you at the clubhouse. Bring food.

Lucifer chuckled and sent her a thumbs up before he slid his phone back into his pocket.

"Who was that?" Trip stacked up their dishes on the diner table.

"Pumps. Crush asked her to get me some information. She was letting me know she has it."

Trip nodded. "Is this about the employees from Heat? Heard you were working with Butterfly to get them taken care of and stuff."

Lucifer nodded. "Didn't know I was working with Butterfly, but yeah, essentially."

Trip chuckled. "Well, you're working with Butterfly. Now, ya know."

"I don't mind. I like Butterfly. Might drive Bullet insane, but that's just the cherry on top."

"If you treat Butterfly well, you'd be surprised what that would do for your relationship with Bullet. That man is obsessed with his woman."

Lucifer raised a brow. "Aren't we all obsessed with our women?"

He watched as Trip's eyes unfocused, and a grin grew on the man's face, proving his point. Trip was most definitely thinking about Darlin' and enjoying whatever visual that brought to his mind's eye.

"Exactly," Lucifer said and stood, ready to get back to work.

Crush

At three o'clock, Crush was sitting in her seat at the table when her club filed into church. She wanted to have church earlier in the day, but Kitty had been the only waitress scheduled at the diner and couldn't get away. As much as the club came first, Crush would never put a business in a tough spot for a meeting that wasn't an emergency, so they worked around things.

When everyone was seated, she pounded her fist on the table to bring church to order. "Okay. Heat. We own half but haven't acted like it. That needs to change."

The murmurs of approval sounded around the table.

"First question: Do we want to have a strip club, or do we want to switch things up?"

"Is this connected to the list you wanted me to put together for Lucifer?"

Crush looked over at Pumps and nodded. "Yes. He's going to ask them about suggestions for improvement, what was working, and what wasn't working."

Pumps nodded. "Why can't we build a space big enough to have Heat on one side and something for us on the other? I mean... let the Howlers run Heat. It's lucrative, and we have a good number of loyal regulars, but there's enough property out there for a bigger building. We could start a new business on the other side or... I dunno."

"No, I like where you're going, Pumps," Pinky commented. "There has to be a market for something geared more toward women or other people who aren't into the strip club scene."

"Burlesque," Ginger suggested. "Or at least theme nights."

"Yesssss," Kitty pointed at Ginger and nodded. "I like that."

Crush smirked. "So, you're saying I have to go head-to-head with Axle and demand we have our say? Oh, darn."

Pinky chuckled. "I know that will break your tender heart."

"Is a vote necessary?"

Crush was not surprised when half of the table flipped her off, and the other half said, *No,* in unison.

"The other issue... we need to figure out a way to resume the classes that were offered at the club. How difficult would it be to set them up somewhere else?"

Kitty shook her head. "Not difficult at all. As long as we have the poles, we only need a day to install them. The rest is just buying the mats and equipment and finding a space big enough."

"Would the free space on the other side of this floor be big enough?"

At Nails's question, Crush looked over at Pumps and waited for an answer.

Pumps shrugged. "Might have to split the classes into small groups, but we could make it work. I could talk to Trip about installing the poles... or maybe Dragon. He's the one who installed the ones at Heat."

"You won't be talking to Dragon about shit," Kisy uttered and sent a glare down the table at Pumps.

After rolling her eyes, Pumps replied, "You can't tell me who I can speak to or who can speak to Dragon. He's a grown man."

"Watch me, Bitch," Kisy growled and stood.

"Ooo... Cat fight," Halo blurted.

"E-fucking-nough," Crush bit out. "Kisy, ask Dragon if he has time to help install some poles. Pumps, worry about gathering supplies. And you two need to get over this fucking shit. Dragon is Kisy's Ol' Man, and I hate to tell you this Pumps, but she *can* tell you not to talk to him." When Kisy shot Pumps a smirk, Crush huffed out a breath. "And you have to stop jumping down Pumps's throat just because you don't like her. You're supposed to be fucking sisters."

Kisy's smirk faded, and she crossed her arms over her chest in frustration.

"Axle's right. It's like herding toddlers," she mumbled as looked between the two.

Lucifer

After getting the rundown from Pumps, and a play-by-play of her annoyance with Kisy, Lucifer tracked down Butterfly in her room with Bullet in the apartment building.

He knocked on the door and waited. When the door swung open and Bullet was staring out at him with a glare on his face, Lucifer grinned. "Need to talk to Butterfly."

"About?"

"Nothing you need to worry about."

Bullet crossed his arms over his chest and tried to stare Lucifer down, but he wasn't intimidated. They could stand there all day in a stare-off if that's what Bullet wanted to do. It was entertainment to Lucifer.

It didn't last long. Thirty seconds in, Bullet was shoved to the side by Butterfly who was shaking her head. Then she smiled at Lucifer. "Is it time to gossip about the Welles siblings and plot ways to make their lives hell?"

"How did you know?" Lucifer asked with exaggerated cheer.

She giggled and lifted on her toes to give Bullet a kiss. "Dial back Tony and get over it. We're family."

Bullet grumbled against her lips. "We won't be if he's dead."

Butterfly dropped down to her heels and rolled her eyes. "You're not going to kill your sister's mate, and we all know it." Then she stepped out of the apartment and shut the door in Bullet's face. Looking over at Lucifer, she put her hands to her hips. "You two are acting like dogs fighting over the same steak, except there's enough to share."

Lucifer chuckled as they made their way to the stairs. "I just think it's funny when he thinks he can intimidate me. I'm mated to *Crush*. If she doesn't scare me, what makes him think any of the Howlers are going to?"

Butterfly and Lucifer spent a couple of hours compiling a list of jobs available and possible placements for employees before they called them and scheduled a meeting with the group for the next day.

The meeting was being held at the clubhouse, but Lucifer talked to Axle about closing the clubhouse to members for a couple of hours. That way, the employees could feel safe to speak freely. Since the main topic of the meeting was to find out what Heat could improve on, honesty and bluntness were going to be important.

The main complaint was that there wasn't a place for women to go that catered to their enjoyment. Heat and Bobby's Bar were the only drinking establishments in Warden's Pass, and both of them were designed and run with the male gaze and enjoyment in mind.

Besides that, there was talk about a more conductive layout of tables, and better music and choreography for the dancers. One of the bouncers suggested they have a room designed specifically for keeping an eye on patrons without having to always be in the mix. That way, it would be easier to catch patrons doing things on the sly. The dancers nodded as he spoke, which made Lucifer irritated that the Howlers weren't protecting their dancers as much as they thought they were. That shit couldn't stand.

After discussing improvements and suggestions, Butterfly shifted the topic of discussion to temporary employment. Within an hour, they had all but three of the employees in new positions within the HTC businesses. The three who declined had already found temporary employment, but made it clear they wanted to return to Heat or whatever it became when it was finished.

Lucifer was happy to see that the loyalty of the clubs had leaked out to their employees. The family wasn't made up of only the members and their families, it also included employees and friends of the club. It still boggled Lucifer's mind the community the Howlers and the Claws were able to create, and it made him proud to be a part of it.

After the employees had the names and numbers of their temporary bosses and directions to call for shifts and hours, the clubhouse emptied out, leaving Butterfly and Lucifer sitting on the bar top.

T.S. Tappin

Lucifer held his hand out, palm facing Butterfly, and waited. After a moment, Butterfly slapped his hand in a high-five.

"Nice work," he told her.

"Same, bestie," she replied with a giggle.

"Will you do me a solid and tell your mate that we cuddled?" Lucifer grinned at her.

Butterfly burst out with laughter. "Uh… no. I would hate to be the reason you took your last breath, because if Bullet doesn't kill you, Crush will."

"Touché," he said through a chuckle.

Lucifer spread his bent knees, digging his heels into the bed, as he slammed his hips up to meet Crush on her downward strokes. His thumb was circling her clit, and her nails were digging into the flesh of his chest as her orgasm built inside of her. He was riding the edge, ready to blow at any moment, just waiting for her to reach her second climax of the evening.

"Give it to me," he growled, punctuating his words with a harder thrust, almost bouncing her off his cock.

"Earn it," she shot back, scraping a nail across his nipple, almost making him shoot before her.

Lucifer flexed his abs and pulled himself further up so he could latch on to her nipple and took it between his teeth. Biting down, he gave her the shot of pain needed to push her over the cliff.

"Yes," she moaned as her head flew back, and she dropped down on him and grinded.

"Thank fuck," Lucifer breathed and allowed himself to go.

Once they both came back down to earth, he wrapped his arms around her and rested his forehead against her chest, enjoying the rare moment of cuddling his mate was giving him.

"Love you," he mumbled into her skin.

"Fucking love you, too, even if you keep trying to take over in bed."

Lucifer pulled his head back and smirked as he raised a brow at her. "You were the one riding, Sugartits, but I was holding the reins."

Crush snorted a laugh and climbed off of him. He followed her as she went to the bathroom to clean up. Once done, they went back to bed and lounged. When Crush settled on her back, Lucifer shifted and laid his head on her stomach.

Circling her nipple with his fingertip, he told her, "The employees had a list of suggestions. I took notes and left it on the island."

She nodded. "Did you get them in jobs?"

"Yeah. Butterfly and I made sure they all had their new boss's number before they left. There were only three who had already found employment, but all of them said they wanted to come back when Heat was done… or whatever it turned into."

"I appreciate your help on this."

Lucifer turned his head and circled her navel with his tongue. "Glad I could help."

"Now… you want to tell me why my brother sent me a text promising to kill you if you didn't learn your place?"

Lucifer chuckled against her skin. "Your brother is easy to manipulate."

Crush quietly laughed. "Try not to get killed. It would be a shame to have to go back to using my vibrator."

"Is this a *single* vibrator… or are there more players in the game?"

Crush's grin had his cock twitching, even though she just rode him to completion like a fucking beast. "I believe in teamwork."

"So do I… which is why I need to know where my team resides. We have plays to write and game plans to strategize."

When her eyes shifted to a small wooden treasure chest sitting on top of her dresser, Lucifer grinned and hopped off the bed. Like a kid opening presents on Christmas morning, Lucifer swung open the top of that chest and rubbed his hands together.

"Oooo… this is going to be fun."

Chapter Twenty-Five

Crush

The next morning, Crush headed to Axle's office to discuss the plans for Heat. As she took her seat in the chair across the desk from him, she winced at the soreness that had yet to dissipate. That was what happened when your mate spent *hours* experimenting with every toy in your treasure chest and eeking out as many orgasms as he could.

The proud smile on his face when she climbed out of bed that morning had her nipples tightening. She may be exhausted, but they were remembering their time with Lucifer fondly.

"Sore?" Axle's smirk let her know he guessed why.

"Shut the fuck up."

He chuckled, and his eyes dropped to the pendant hanging from around her neck. He gave a nod. "Good for you. Now, why'd you want to meet?"

Crush ran through what Lucifer learned from the employees and which employees were assigned where. When she was done, she met his gaze and announced, "The Claws have voted. We'll be taking a more hands-on role in the club from now on."

Axle's brows lifted. "In what way?"

This was it. He would either be all for it, or he would fight her on it. "We think the building needs to be bigger, and we want to add another venue to the other side that is more geared toward women and patrons who don't necessarily want to see strippers."

The sigh that came from Axle annoyed Crush, but she waited for him to speak. "And where is the money coming from to fund this venture?"

Crush glared at him. "We are equal partners, Axle. Half of the insurance payout belongs to the Claws, so I'd be really careful how you approach this conversation."

"Heat is a proven moneymaker, Crush. What you're talking about is something brand new."

She shrugged. "It's been voted on. If we need to reevaluate ownership, I'm sure the Claws would be willing to pool their money and buy a percentage from you to make this happen."

"Now wait a damn minute." It was Axle's turn to glare. "I'm not turning down your idea. I'm just trying to figure out how we could manage it."

Crush gave him a humorless smile. "That's the problem, Axle. You think you have a right to turn down a demand from the Claws in a business where we're equal partners. You. Do. Not."

Axle rolled his eyes and huffed out a sigh, but he threw up his hands in surrender. "Okay. Fine. We'll expand the building and designate a space for the Claws to do with what they will. However, a budget is going to have to be laid out for the insurance funds and approved by both clubs. We can't be at odds over this, and we can't just go at this with a fuck it attitude."

"Well, no shit, Sherlock," Crush replied. "I'll put together a group of three members to work with three of your members to decide a budget and work on the plans. Deal?"

"Fine. Deal," Axle grumbled, obviously pissed, but Crush didn't give a damn.

It was time the Howlers learned that they weren't in charge around there.

As she left the office, she thought about who could keep their cool when going head-to-head with the Howlers. She decided Ginger and Kitty would be the best options. With a grin, she mentally added Kisy to the list, for shits and giggles.

Two days later, Crush and Pinky stood in the hall outside of the room in the tattoo parlor while Kisy laid on her stomach on the table without a shirt on. She took a deep breath and slowly exhaled and looked over at Ginger sitting on the other side of the table from the door.

Ginger gave her an understanding smile and asked, "Full-back?"

"How about half that size and on the top half... like in the middle?"

Ginger gave a nod. "Okay. I'll make the stencil and put it on you. Then you can tell me if it works for you. Deal?"

"Yeah."

Ginger placed a hand on her shoulder. "If it's the pain you're worried about, this won't be as bad as the inner thigh. If it's the permanence of the club colors, you already accepted that. This is just a visual representation of your commitment. You have to get the club colors, but the size and the location is up to you. We can make it smaller and put it in a different place if you don't like the stencil."

Kisy nodded and took another deep breath. While Ginger went about doing what she needed to do down the hall, Crush watched as a variety of emotions crossed Kisy's face, but it ended with a private smile.

"Seems our Kisy just worked through the nervousness," Pinky commented as she and Crush walked into the room.

"Ginger, she's good," Crush called down the hall. "Smiling like a loon in here."

Kisy's smile turned to a grin. "Just thinking about Dragon's pierced cock and how well he can use it."

Pinky whistled as Crush chuckled and uttered, "Yeah… she's fine."

As they watched Kisy get her tattoo, Crush thought about the conversation she had with Lucifer about getting his name inked into her. She made a note to schedule an appointment with Ginger before she left.

Hours later, and appointment scheduled, Crush headed across the street to the clubhouse to have celebratory drinks with Kisy and the rest of the girls.

Lucifer

Watching Crush celebrate with her sisters, Lucifer sat at the bar and sipped his beer. It warmed his heart that she had such a great support system in them. Crush wouldn't ask them for help, but they knew her well enough to identify when she needed them. Hell, they were there whether she needed them to be or not. That was the sisterhood every woman needed.

It was the type of relationship he had always longed for, and what drew him to the biker culture to begin with. The men weren't always saints or as morally sound as the Howlers, but loyalty and camaraderie were almost guaranteed.

Growing up with little to no support from a family unit, it was a surprise that he would yearn to create one for himself. It was a blessing in disguise that the HDMC was decimated by the Howlers. In the end, it was the catalyst for him finding where he was supposed to be, for him finding *who* he was supposed to be with.

T.S. Tappin

A cheer and the sound of women talking over each other pulled him out of his thoughts. The women were shouting at Dragon as he set a tall glass of water in front of a very tipsy Kisy.

Lucifer chuckled. Kisy could stand on her own two feet and go head-to-head with Dragon, but now she had a whole pack of bitches to back her up. That man was in for it, but Lucifer had a sneaky suspicion that Dragon loved every minute of it.

Like Lucifer, Dragon thrived on the tension, the snarkiness, the fight. Where Crush was grumpy and aggressive, Kisy was bratty and strong-willed. The outcome was the same — Their men loved trying to fuck the fight out of them. Whether they succeeded or not wasn't important. It was all about the journey.

The next few weeks flew by. Rebel and Rock both claimed Ol' Ladies. Rock's claiming wasn't a surprise. Diamond, previously known as Mary, wasn't a new addition. The two of them had been dancing around each other since before Lucifer came to town. Rebel's mate was a newcomer to the biker world, but she slid right on into the family like she'd always been there.

Ruby, previously known as Bri Cooke, was the town's librarian and had been taking pole-dancing classes at Heat for exercise. Surprisingly, she hadn't ever come across the path of any of the Howlers until

Rebel saw her at the library and immediately fell for the sweet and sassy woman. She was perfect for him.

During their courtship, a group of townsfolk had banded together with the intention of pushing the Howlers and the Claws out of town, but that went over about as well as a lead balloon, especially when the idiots started vandalizing local businesses and pulling funding from the library. One of them even broke into Ruby's townhouse and tied her up, promising to 'cleanse' her from being tainted by shifters. That ended with the man stabbed by Ruby and killed by Rebel when he arrived at her place in the middle of it.

The Howlers cleaned up that mess and went about organizing a carnival to raise funds to replace the rescinded donations for the library. There was no way they were letting the town bigots shut down the library just because they didn't like who the librarian chose to love.

It was almost the weekend of the carnival when Lucifer entered the apartment and found Crush sitting at the island with several pieces of paper scattered in front of her. She had one arm bent and was leaning on her elbow with her head in her hand, looking stressed. He stopped behind her and bent his head down. Kissing the side of her neck, he asked, "What are you doing?"

"Trying to figure out who to assign where for this carnival." She sighed. "The Howlers handled the set-up, so I volunteered to be in charge of the job assignments."

"Can I help?"

She shook her head. "I'm almost done, but a sandwich wouldn't be unappreciated."

He nipped the skin he had just kissed and rounded the island to prepare his woman a sandwich. He grabbed two slices of the bakery bread from the bread box and put them in the toaster. While it did its thing, he compiled the ingredients on the counter — Turkey, ham, Colby Jack cheese, lettuce, tomato slices, pickle slices, mayonnaise, mustard, salt, pepper, and the potato chips he'd watched her layer on her sandwich the week before. After retrieving the toast and putting together the sandwich on a plate, he cut it in half and slid the plate over to her, setting a can of pop next to it.

She finished up what she was doing on the papers and piled them together. "You are an angel."

"That's why they call me Lucifer," he said with a wink.

"Sure, it is," she replied as she picked up half of the sandwich and took a bite.

He smiled when she moaned at the taste. "So, the hunter academy... is that a real threat?"

She nodded as she chewed. "We have to assume it is. Axle has a plan for the hunter they discovered in town, but that's club business."

Lucifer nodded. He wouldn't push her on it. He knew how that worked. "If there's anything I can do to help, you know you can tag me in, right?"

She winked at him and nodded as she chewed.

"I need a shower. Am I showering alone? Or should I wait for you to finish eating?"

Crush finished chewing her bite of sandwich and swallowed. "Part of the deal when I mated you, Lucy, was you never get to shower alone again."

He grinned. "Okay. Then which one of us will spend it on our knees this time?"

Crush took another bite of her sandwich. As she chewed, she pointed a finger at him.

CHAPTER TWENTY-SIX

A week later... Axle

Axle brought church to order. Once his club brothers quieted, he ran through the few things they needed to address, which didn't take long, before he brought up Lucifer.

"I think it's time to address the Lucifer situation." Axle took a deep breath and exhaled, preparing himself for any arguments. Most of the members agreed with him that Lucifer had earned a prospect patch if not a full membership, but there were a few members, specifically Bullet, who had reservations.

Trip nodded. "I am willing to sponsor him."

"If Trip doesn't," Siren began, "I will."

T.S. Tappin

Bullet huffed out a breath, glaring at Trip, then at Siren. "Why does he need to become one of us? Isn't it enough that he's family?"

Siren leaned forward and met Bullet's stare. "He saved the life of my woman, *my mate*. He had no obligation *or* responsibility to stick his neck out for us, *for her*, but he did it anyway. He fought at our side in the war when he had no responsibility to do that. Hell, he told us HDMC's plans against us before he even knew anything about us. So, no, it isn't enough that he's *family*. He's fucking already one of us, Bull."

"Sorry, brother," Trip said, quietly, and Axle could see he didn't like that he was going against Bullet's wishes, but Trip knew it was the right thing to do. "Siren's right."

Bullet's jaw hardened as his eyes shifted down.

"You need to let your reservations about him go," Axle told Bullet.

Bullet's eyes didn't move from the table, but he growled, "Respect, Pres, but don't fucking tell me what I need to do with my reservations."

Pike huffed out a breath. "I fucking quit." He stood and started yanking at the edge of his *Sergeant at Arms* patch. "Being SA, I quit."

Axle rolled his eyes, before he glared at Pike. "No, you don't."

"Yes, I do," Pike insisted.

"Well, I don't fucking accept. Sit the fuck down."

Pike plopped back in his seat and crossed his arms over his chest. "I barely keep Dragon from killing Trip.

Now, you expect me to keep Bullet from killing Lucifer? I'm only one fucking man, Ax."

Axle chuckled and shook his head. "Bullet isn't going to kill Lucifer. He's too scared of Crush."

"Fuck." Dragon shook his head. "Aren't we all?"

"So, let's vote. Are we letting Lucifer prospect?"

Even with Bullet's reservations and grudge against Lucifer, the vote was unanimous.

"When are we letting him know?" Skull asked.

Axle shook his head. "I think we need to give Bullet some time to get used to it, but soon."

The Next Day... Halo

As Halo laid on the floor of his kitchen, blood seeping from the cut on her cheek and her body aching all over, she knew Patrick had just sealed his fate. She couldn't hide this from her sisters. She had tried, but she knew they saw the swollen eyes, the healing cuts, and how she would try to hide the limp as she walked. *Damn shifter sight.* She also knew they were just waiting for her go ahead to really make Patrick's life a living hell… or non-living as it might turn out if she knew her president at all. Factor in Nails's bloodlust, and there was no way that they would allow him a quick or easy death.

He had spent the last thirty minutes ranting and raving about whatever the fuck, while dragging her around by her hair and beating the hell out of her. She tried to fight back, but with the hold he had on her hair, she wasn't able to do much. At some point, she managed to grab onto his junk and squeeze for all she was worth, which is how she got the gash on her cheek. He backhanded her with his right hand, the hand he always wore his class ring on. That was when the pain really began.

As soon as she was on the floor, he had done his best to make sure no part of her went untouched. She couldn't even think of the number of possible bruises or injuries. There wasn't time for that. She needed to get out of there before he killed her.

Taking a deep breath, and immediately regretting it when her ribs protested, she started to climb to her feet. When he reached down and took a hold of her bicep to help her, she yanked her arm out of his grasp. "Don't touch me."

"Come on, babe," he cooed, regret in his voice. She knew that voice. It was the one he used to reel her back in. It wasn't going to work this time. "Don't be like that. I didn't... I didn't mean to hurt you. I just... You know I don't like it when men hit on you."

Finally on her feet, she flipped him the bird as she made her way over to the countertop next to the back door. *One step at a time, Halo.*

"Halo! If you would just *blah blah blah*" She stopped listening as she reached into her purse and palmed the handle of the knife Crush had given her as a birthday present the day she turned eighteen. Halo had taken it everywhere with her for the last three years since she got it. Too bad it had been in her purse and out of her reach when she needed it.

She pulled it out and kept it in her hand as she slid her purse onto her shoulder, ignoring the way her body ached with the movement. There would be time to feel the pain, but now wasn't that time. Now was the time to get out of the house alive and back to her sisters. Once she reached the compound, she would be safe, and hell would begin for Patrick.

When she reached for the knob of the back door, Patrick headed for her. She held the knife up, pointy end pointed at him, and ordered, "Don't."

He stopped in his tracks and put his hands up. Not taking her eyes from him, she left the house and made her way around to the front. Without her bike, she didn't have a choice but to walk the three blocks back to the compound.

It wasn't the longest and toughest three blocks of her life. She had plenty of time to think about all the ways she could have stopped it from happening and all the ways she could have trained harder to ready herself to fight back harder. Halfway to the compound, she let out a shallow sigh, hearing Crush's voice in her head.

This wasn't your fault or your doing. This isn't the result of your choices. It's the result of his choices.

An asshole was an asshole. His choices were his own. All she could do was stay away from him and let him take the consequences of his actions.

When she reached the clubhouse and stepped inside, all the strength she had left seeped out of her, and she collapsed on the floor, knife still in her hand.

Crush

Crush had just finished clearing out space in her dresser for Lucifer, sick of seeing his clothes stacked in piles in the corner, when her phone went off with a message from Axle, immediately followed by a message from Pinky. Hearing each of the two distinctive ringtones, Crush knew something bad had happened.

Cursing under her breath, she crossed the space and snagged her phone from the island. Checking Pinky's message first, she was worried.

Pinky : Emergency. Clubhouse. Ours.

When she checked Axle's message, pure rage filled her.

Axle : Halo collapsed in clubhouse. Bleeding and bruised.

Crush slipped her cut on her shoulders, grabbed her gun from the nightstand, and slipped it into the holster built into her cut, before she ran out of the apartment, headed for the clubhouse.

She had barely stepped through the door before she saw Halo's prone body passed out on the floor.

Shoving Howlers aside, she knelt down next to Halo and shook her shoulder. "Halo!"

From Halo's other side, Pinky said, "Ranger and Siren are on their way. She woke up for a second and said the name Patrick. Isn't that—"

"The motherfucker who drives the lifted truck? Yes," she hissed and ran her hand gently over Halo's dark brown hair. Crush was a bit relieved to know Siren and Ranger were on their way. Siren was an EMT, and Ranger had been in the special forces. Between the two of them, they were the best crisis medics a girl could ask for.

Halo was so small, barely over five feet, and skinny as shit, but that didn't mean she was weak. The fact that she made it out alive meant she held her own, but Patrick was over six feet tall and had to be over two hundred pounds of muscle. Halo was only a human, after all. There was only so much she could do when faced with a much larger opponent, which is why Crush bought her the knife that was currently laying in Halo's open hand.

Crush looked at the blade and didn't see any blood. She suspected Halo didn't use it.

"We'll take care of him, Crush," Dragon growled from over her.

"No, you fucking won't," Crush said and glared up at him.

"Crush—"

"No!" She straightened on her feet and pointed a finger in his face. "This is *not* your business."

She heard Axle's voice from behind her say, "Crush, be reasonable. Let us help."

Crush whirled and glared at Axle. "This is *not* a Howler issue. This is *not* your business. We will handle it the way *we* decide to."

Axle gave a nod. "Yes, but we are offering backup."

She let the growl roll up from her chest. "We don't fucking *need* the men to come in and *save us*, Axle. This is Claw business, and you *will* back the fuck off."

After staring at her for a long moment, Axle gave a nod. "Just let us know if there's something we can do to help."

Crush took a deep breath in an attempt to calm herself, looked back at Halo, and then back to Axle. "Will you take care of Halo?"

"Consider it done," Axle promised.

She could tell by the understanding look in his silver eyes that Axle hadn't taken any offense to her demands, and he was finally understanding it was time for him to stop butting in and taking over when it was Claw business. They had the talk more often than was probably necessary. She also knew it was taking a lot for him not to order his men to give Patrick the beating he deserved, but he didn't need to worry. Patrick would get his beating… and he was going to get that beating from a bunch of women.

"Claws! Mount up!"

Axle

After watching Crush storm out of the clubhouse with the Claws in tow, Axle let out a sigh and pulled his phone from his pocket. He sent Dr. Gloria Janson an emergency message to let her know they needed her assistance as soon as possible. Siren and Ranger had enough medical training between them to keep Halo stable, but she needed a doctor.

With the cut on her face, Axle knew both of the men would hesitate to do the stitches. They could do it, but it wouldn't be pretty, and they would feel horrible about any ugly scar that would potentially be left behind. No, it would be better to have Dr. Janson take care of it.

The anger he felt at seeing Halo beat to hell was almost more than he could control. Yeah, he offered the Howlers services as backup, but the truth of the matter was he wanted to beat the hell out of the piece of shit just as much as Crush did. She may not be in his club, but Halo was family.

He wanted to avenge her, but he didn't want to overstep Crush's authority. As much as he hated it, Crush was right. It wasn't a Howler issue. It wasn't their business unless *she* made it their business. The offer of help was out there, and she rejected it. The only thing he could do was make sure Halo received the medical help she needed.

"I don't know what the fuck her problem is," Bullet grumbled as he helped Dragon lift Halo carefully up and moved her to the top of the pool table. "I get that she thinks we take over sometimes, but we're trying to help."

Axle let out a sigh. "I'm sure she has her reasons."

Halo

Halo could hear male voices, but it was as if she was listening through a thick door. They were muffled and seemed to be coming from a distance.

She knew she was moving but she wasn't sure how until the feel of hands on her body told her that she was being carried. With every movement, her ribs screamed at her, and her head pounded angrily.

Crying out from the pain of it, she was too weak to stop them from moving her. All she could do was suffer through it and pray that it didn't last long. She didn't even have the strength to open her eyes to see who was carrying her.

When they finally stopped moving her, she tried to figure out where she was, but she couldn't. All she knew was it was a hard surface. It could be the floor, the bar top, the pool table. *The pool table.* That would explain the slightly scratchy fabric-covered surface rubbing against the back of her arms, exposed by her sleeveless tee and her hands.

As soon as she began to focus, a new part of her body began to scream in pain, stopping her from being able to think. It was as if she was experiencing the world through a fog or through deep water. Nothing was sharp or clear, except for the pain.

A warm weight on her shoulder caught her attention, then she heard who she assumed was Axle say into her ear, "Try to relax, Halo. You're safe. Dr. Janson's coming."

Knowing she was truly at the clubhouse, and she hadn't dreamed of making it home, Halo took the first relaxing yet painfully shallow breath as tears slid away from her eyes and disappeared into her hair.

Lucifer

After working late, Lucifer had returned to the compound to find numerous Tiger's Claw members leaving on their bikes. Crush looked pissed, judging by the expression on her face and the tension in her body, but she did give him a nod. He was curious about where they were going, but he figured he'd find out when Crush returned. Shrugging off his questions, he headed inside the clubhouse to have a drink and wait for her to return.

As soon as he stepped through the door, he figured out why Crush was tense. Halo, a younger member of Tiger's Claw MC, was lying on top of the pool table, talking to Dr. Gloria Janson, the doctor they always called at times like that, while Siren and Ranger cleaned and wrapped injuries.

"What the fuck?"

"Her boyfriend beat her up," Bullet said from his seat on a stool at the bar.

Lucifer turned his head and looked over at Bullet, only a few feet away. "Is he breathing?"

Bullet shrugged. "For now."

Lucifer thought about going over and checking on Halo, but she looked to have all the help she needed. He didn't want to be in the way, so he moved over to the bar and took a seat on the stool next to Bullet.

They weren't exactly friends, but Lucifer figured they should probably get used to each other, basically being brothers-in-law. Whether Bullet liked it or not, he wasn't going any damn where.

"You need to talk to your woman," Bullet said with a huffed breath. "Maybe you can talk some sense into her. Axle and Dragon both offered the assistance of the Howlers. We would have had their backs, but she's stubborn."

Lucifer thanked Rex, who was behind the bar, and grabbed him a beer, setting it in front of him. He thought about the situation from Crush's position. If Axle just offered their help, Lucifer couldn't see Crush shooting them down completely and abruptly. There had to be more to the story. Curious, he asked, "What exactly did Dragon and Axle say to her?"

Bullet gave Lucifer a more in-depth rundown of what happened, and it all became clear. As Bullet talked about Crush getting in first Dragon's face and then Axle's, Lucifer started nodding. He could practically guess Crush's thought process.

"You gonna talk to her?"

After taking a sip of his beer, Lucifer set the bottle down in front of him and glanced over at Bullet. "Nah."

Bullet stared at him for a long moment, his brows pulled together. "You're too fucking calm about this. Your woman just took off to confront a woman-beating bastard with no back-up, and you're sitting here, calm as shit, like she just ran to the store for milk."

Lucifer met Bullet's stare, head-on, and replied, "She has back-up. *Her club* is her back-up. And from what you've told me, she didn't turn down an offer from Axle, she told Axle and Dragon to mind their fucking business, because they had every intention of having her sit here like a *good little woman* and let the *big men* take care of *her* business. Nah. Fuck that. My woman doesn't play that shit. You should know. She's your sister. And as her Ol' Man, it's not my job to get in her way or tell her how to run her club. It's my job to be here when, or if, she asks for my help… kind of like her brother and ally club should be doing."

"That's not—"

"Stop." Lucifer slid off his stool and turned to face Bullet, who got to his feet, obviously feeling threatened. He had no intention of threatening Bullet, but he was done with the conversation. "Look. I know you don't give two shits about my fucking opinion, but you're getting it, anyway. I've watched the way the Howlers treat the Claws. You say you work together, and that you're equals, but when push comes to shove, it's expected that they take your lead… and that's bullshit."

"That's not—"

Lucifer shook his head. "If you can't see it from their fucking point of view, you're being deliberately blind. If for no other reason than your sister, you need to open your fucking eyes. I'm fucking done."

Before he ended up throwing hands with his brother-in-law, he walked away from Bullet and went to check on Halo. When Crush returned, he wanted to be able to give her good news. It was the only way he thought he could help her at that moment.

Chapter Twenty-Seven

Crush

After parking their bikes in the alley behind Patrick's house, Crush stormed for the backdoor with seven of her sisters behind her — Kitty, Pumps, Ginger, Kisy, Nails, Pinky, and Lushess. Foxy and Shortcake were at one end of the street, watching for cops. Vixen and Minx were at the other end, doing the same thing. Nova and Raven stayed with their bikes, and Beretta and Goddess headed for the front of the house to keep watch.

If she were thinking straight, Crush would be grateful that the fuckwad lived in an area of town where houses were rundown and abandoned. Fewer witnesses to worry about.

Crush didn't bother knocking. She just kicked the door in. It slammed against the wall, the noise jarring Patrick on the other side of the room, causing him to drop the mop. As it clattered to the floor, Crush advanced on him, stomping through the blood and water. *Halo's blood*.

"Crush," he breathed and held out his hands in front of him. "Wait! Hold on. You don't understand. We had... there was a misunderstanding."

Crush let out a humorless chuckle. "I don't understand? You beat the fuck out of Halo, and *I* don't understand?" She shook her head, not giving one fuck that her eyes were glowing greenish-gold light. "What the fuck kind of *misunderstanding* leaves our sister *unconscious* on the floor?"

Being the first time he had seen any of them show their shifter abilities in person, his eyes widened in shock. Hell, Crush wasn't even sure she believed that shifters actually existed. She tried to remember if he was at the town hall and didn't recall seeing him in the audience, but that didn't mean much.

"What the fuck?" Patrick started backing away from her, tripping over the discarded mop but catching himself before he hit the floor.

As he righted himself, her sisters surrounded him. Crush grabbed him by the throat with her left hand and pulled him close. "You like to beat on women, do ya?" She swung with her right hand and slapped him across the face like the bitch he was. "Come on, tough guy. Show me what you got."

He stood there, dumbfounded.

"Yeah, Patrick, show us how Halo got that handprint bruise on her side," Kitty said through gritted teeth.

"I… I caught her… kept her from falling. She said she was fine and that it didn't hurt." The man stuttered out his terrible lie as his eyes wildly scanned the room. He was probably looking for a way out. No fucking way in hell.

"Ooh, while you're at it. Maybe you can show us how you bruised the side of her neck when it was definitely *not* a hickey," Kisy added.

Crush, no longer giving a shit about hearing what he had to say, tightened her grip, unsurprised when he started pulling at her arm, trying to dislodge her hand. She unleashed her claws, but only let them break the skin a bit, letting him know of the danger.

His eyes widened even more as it registered in his brain that he wasn't dealing with a group of women. He was dealing with a group of predators.

"You're… mon… sters," he choked out.

Crush gave him a full-tooth grin, letting her fangs elongate just the slightest bit, and answered, "Boo." She loosened her grip, but not enough for him to get away or take a full breath.

"I th-thought… they… made it… up."

Stepping up next to them, Pumps let her fangs slide down and hissed. The smell of urine permeated the air and made all of them curse out loud.

T.S. Tappin

"*We're* supposed to be the pussies, you fuckwad," Kisy said through gags as she headed back toward the back door, no doubt to get some fresh air.

Patrick began to tremble and tears filled his eyes. "I'm sorry," he pleaded. "I shouldn't have hurt her. I shouldn't have. I'm sorry."

"Yeah, well, that doesn't mean much, now does it? She's hurting, and you should be, too," Pinky taunted from behind him. "This is going to be fun."

Pinky was usually the voice of reason. It was the main reason Crush had her as her VP. Her ability to keep Crush from killing folks was a very useful tool. If Pinky was in for torturing the piece of shit, there wasn't much hope for Patrick.

From somewhere in the living room, Crush heard Nails begin humming *Gunpowder and Lead* by Miranda Lambert.

"Please," he whimpered through his sobs.

Crush was disgusted. She fucking hated it when men acted all big and bad but crumbled when faced with someone tougher. If you're going to act like a badass, you better own that shit, not cower in the face of true toughness.

"Don't bother begging for your safety," she told him, her hand tightening again around his neck. "We will take a pound of flesh for each and every ache you made Halo feel. When we're done, you'll beg for us to end you. If I'm feeling charitable, we'll give you that… But you're going to suffer first."

Lucifer

As Lucifer approached the pool table, he heard Dr. Janson say, "You'll be okay. You gotta take it easy, though, and follow the concussion protocols I gave you. I'll pass the info on to…" Dr. Janson looked around.

"You can tell me, Dr. Janson. I'll make sure she gets looked after."

Dr. Janson looked back at Halo. When Halo gave a nod, her gaze swung back to Lucifer and ran through what needed to be done to take care of Halo. He listened carefully to make sure he could pass the information on to Crush with confidence.

After giving Halo's hand a squeeze, Dr. Janson walked away. Lucifer gave Halo a smile and tried to figure out a way to break the ice. He wasn't close to Halo, but he needed to figure out a way to relay that she would be safe with him. When she glanced up at him, she softly returned the smile and started to sit up. He took a couple quick steps toward her and slid his arm around her back to help her.

"Thanks," she mumbled, and let out a deep breath.

"You thirsty? Hungry? Want help getting to your room?"

"Water would be good. Maybe some crackers."

Lucifer nodded. "On it." He looked around for someone to hang with her while he got what she requested.

Siren was a few yards away and started heading for them. "Go. I have her."

Lucifer nodded and made his way to the cafeteria area of the clubhouse. Nodding at Top, who was sitting at one of the tables, eating a sandwich, he entered the kitchen. He grabbed a bottle of water from the refrigerator and looked in the pantry for something light for her to eat. All he could find were cheese crackers. Shrugging, he grabbed the box and left the room.

Approaching Halo and Siren, he held up the box of crackers. "This is all I could find."

Halo gave him another smile. "I'll take it."

He handed her the bottle of water and began opening the box. "Doc said sip that. Don't guzzle."

Siren nodded. "He's right."

Halo rolled her eyes, winced, and then nodded. She took an exaggerated sip and looked to them as if she was waiting for their approval of her sipping skills.

"Smartass," Siren commented with a quiet laugh. "If you need me, I'll be right over there." He pointed to a table where Sugar, Trip, and Ranger were sitting.

"Lucy has it covered," Halo said and patted Siren's hand.

Siren's gaze shifted to Lucifer. He stared for a long moment, contemplative, before he nodded and walked away.

"I don't think they'll ever trust me," Lucifer said with a grin.

Halo shook her head. "They already do... well, maybe with the exception of Bullet."

"You think?" Lucifer knew the Howlers were appreciative of his contribution to the war as well as his efforts in saving Sugar from her ex and the drug lord her ex's father was in business with. Sure, the Howlers were less watchful of him, especially after Crush mated him, but they weren't exactly welcoming him into their brotherhood.

Halo nodded. "If they didn't, things would be a lot more hostile toward you. It's been months since anyone besides Bullet threatened your death."

Lucifer chuckled. "That's true."

After taking another sip of her water and eating a few crackers, Halo expressed, "I'm happy Crush has you. She may not admit it to you, but you make her happy. You're good to her. She deserves that."

"She makes it worth it." He gave Halo a wink. "Even when she's threatening to use her claws on my balls, she makes me happy, too."

"I know things can get tense between the Claws and the Howlers, but honestly, that does a lot for their outlook on you. Axle holds Crush's opinion of things as fact. If she trusts you, Axle does, too. Give it time."

Lucifer shrugged. "Either way, I'm not going anywhere." He grabbed the front of his property cut and gave her a wink.

Giggling, Halo grabbed a few more crackers from the box and winced. As she wrapped her free arm around her waist, Lucifer understood the wince and felt bad for making her laugh, since her ribs were probably reminding her that laughing wasn't a good idea yet.

T.S. Tappin

Crush

Using her grip on Patrick's neck, Crush lifted him off the ground, turned, and slammed him onto his back on the floor. A loud crack sounded as his head hit the linoleum. It was a beautiful sound, in Crush's opinion. As he moaned and rolled on the floor, Crush pulled her leg back and kicked him in the gut.

"Bet you hurt her ribs," Crush said, almost conversationally.

"They always go for the ribs," Pumps commented, sounding bored.

Pinky crouched down by Patrick's head and grabbed a handful of his hair. Forcing him to look at her, she bit out, "She's our baby sister. You picked the wrong one to fuck with." She pulled her other hand back and swung forward, striking him on the cheek in the same place Halo had been bleeding. When his skin didn't break, she released a claw and dug into the flesh of his cheek, sliding it down, creating the same wound.

As soon as he saw the claw, Patrick panicked and tried to get away, but Crush, Kisy, and Pumps held him down while Pinky did her thing. His screams didn't faze any of them as he cried and begged for mercy. Too bad none of them were named *Mercy*.

Crush searched herself for any signs of empathy or regret, but all she found was a blood-thirsty tiger, pride in her club, and loyalty to her sisters.

"Get him up," Crush ordered and stepped back as Pinky and Pumps grabbed him by his armpits and hoisted him up. Kitty swung first, catching him in the jaw, precisely in the place where the first bruise was that he had given Halo weeks ago. Kisy was next, giving him a jab to his left eye. Pumps continued to hold him as Pinky punched him hard in the chest, making sure to catch a few ribs.

After taking turns throwing a few more punches, making sure to connect with his other eye and his nose, one of the girls kicking him good and hard in the dick, Crush wrapped her fingers around his neck again and squeezed as she stepped in close. Unleashing her claws, she stared into his scared blue eyes and stabbed those claws into his gut. As he began to scream again, she put her mouth close to his ear. "I'm feeling charitable. I feel the need to make sure you *never* get the opportunity to take your inferiority out on another woman." She pulled her claws out of his gut and moved her hand down.

Gripping his balls, she didn't give two shits that her claws were digging into sensitive places. She squeezed with all of her might and watched his eyes roll back in his head as he screamed when she felt one detach, followed by an immediate burst of blood. For good measure, she crushed it like a grape and let out a low snicker when his screaming only ended when he passed out. As his body slumped in her grip, Crush smiled. She let go and watched his body drop to the floor. After turning on her heel, she walked over to his kitchen sink, twisted the knobs of the faucet, and wet her hands and claws. She looked for soap or dish soap but found nothing. Scoffing with disgust, she did her best to scrub the blood and skin from her claws.

Once done, she dried them on her jeans as she watched Nails reenter the room, screwing a silencer on the end of her gun.

"My turn?" Nails looked giddy at the prospect.

"Have at it but wake him first. Make sure he knows *exactly* who ends him," Crush replied and headed for the back door, "then scour the house for anything worth anything while you clean up. I'm going to check on Halo."

"I'll stay and make sure everything is taken care of," Pinky commented.

Crush gave a nod and stepped outside, sending a text to the rest of the members.

Crush : Dinner is cooked. Head home.

Taking a deep breath, she felt her tiger purr at the thought that they avenged their baby sister.

As she crossed the backyard, heading for her bike, she grinned. "And the town was worried about the Howlers," she uttered to Nova and Raven.

Nova snorted a laugh. "Let them think the Howlers are the real danger."

Raven put on a sweet, innocent facade and cooed, "We're just weak women, emotional and innocent."

As they all laughed, they climbed on their bikes and took off.

Adrenaline and the rush of satisfaction from avenging her sister was running through her veins as Crush stormed into the clubhouse. When she entered the main room, she was surprised to see Lucifer sitting on top of the pool table with Halo. Her surprise was quickly replaced with relief when Halo quietly chuckled at something Lucifer was saying.

Watching the two of them interact had Crush overwhelmed with gratitude for Lucifer. Even though part of her was still scared shitless, he would try to take power in their relationship, she was finding that he didn't just give her the sexual release she knew he would. He gave her *so much more*. He was supportive in ways she didn't expect, like taking care of her sister when she wasn't there to do it.

She didn't think he could be sexier than when he was inside of her, but the proof that he could be was staring her in the face.

Approaching the pool table, her gaze met Halo's, and she lifted her hand to check Halo's temperature. "You okay?"

Halo nodded but winced. "Yeah. Concussion, bruised ribs, bumps, bruises, stitches in my cheek… ya know… just another day."

Crush smiled. Halo was a tiny woman and a full human, but she was tougher than most men Crush knew. "Piece of cake." Her smile faded. "Gonna have Ginger take care of you when she gets back, though."

"I figured," Halo said on a sigh.

Moving her gaze to Lucifer, Crush took a deep breath and slowly exhaled. When her gut was telling her to hold back, her tiger was pushing her forward, and Crush decided to ignore her gut and focus on giving Lucifer what he deserved. Her fear and hesitance would be a detriment to their relationship if she didn't learn to give a little. With that in mind, she bent forward and pressed her lips to his.

The kiss wasn't wet and urgent, like normal. Instead, it was a brush of lips meant to let him know she appreciated him. When she pulled back and saw the pride in his eyes, she knew the message was received.

"Thank you," she whispered.

He gave a nod and took her hand. Giving it a squeeze, he replied, "You don't need to thank me, Sugartits. Just taking care of my sis, here."

Crush rolled her eyes and walked away, letting the smile grow inside of her as her tiger purred.

"She has the best ass," she heard Lucifer utter behind her, which made Halo giggle.

Biting the inside of her cheek to keep from smiling, Crush approached Axle standing at the end of the bar. "Thank you for taking care of Halo."

"I had Doc Janson come." He sighed. "Crush, I… We…" He cursed under his breath. "When I offered our backup, I didn't mean that you couldn't handle it. I'm sorry if that's how it came across. Same with Dragon. We don't mean to diminish your abilities."

Crush just stared at him. She'd heard it before.

"After what Lucifer said to Bullet, I guess... we didn't realize how it came across. So, I'm sorry. In the future, we'll wait for you to ask for help. Just know you have a standing offer from us."

Crush gave a nod in acknowledgement. "What did Lucifer say to Bullet?"

Bullet walked up and stopped at their sides. "That I need to pull my head out of my ass and see things from your point of view. That my club and I have always expected the Claws to take our lead, and that's fucking bullshit because you are capable of handling shit and making decisions. And he was right." Bullet sighed and shook his head. "I'm sorry, Sis. In an attempt to protect you, I went overboard... we all have."

"I love you, Bull, but I don't need your fucking protection," she said and crossed her arms over her chest, staring her brother down.

"I forget sometimes."

"Well, stop fucking forgetting." She turned her head to look over her shoulder at Lucifer, who was still hanging with Halo. "Excuse me." Without waiting for a reaction from them, she headed over to Lucifer and grabbed his hand. When she began to pull, he willingly climbed off the table.

"Guess I'm needed," he said on a chuckle as he followed her through the room and down the hall.

T.S. Tappin

Crush shoved through the door of the women's restroom and started looking under the stall doors. Finding it empty, she nodded to the door. "Lock it."

Chapter Twenty-Eight

Lucifer

Lucifer wasn't sure what was happening, but he was curious enough to do what Crush said. Still holding on to her hand with one of his, he used his free hand to turn the lock on the bathroom door.

As soon as the bolt of the lock slid into place, Crush was on him. She let go of his hand, and her arms went around his neck as her lips slammed against his. With a groan, he wrapped his arms around her and cupped her ass in his hands. His cock instantly hardened as her teeth bit down on his bottom lip and pulled.

"Fuck," he moaned when she released it. He took her mouth in a deep, wet kiss, letting his tongue dive deep and play with hers, while he turned them and pressed her against the back of the bathroom door.

Her hands fisted in his hair as she tilted her head and let him make love to her mouth. He loved the bite of pain from her yanking on his hair or biting his lip or clawing at his skin. It amped up his pleasure and made his need for her grow.

When he broke the kiss to breathe, he uttered, "Not that I'm complaining, but what brought this on?"

"You told my brother off." She nipped at his jaw.

Lucifer grinned. "I'll tell him off every day if this is what I get for doing it."

Crush didn't reply. Instead, she dropped to her knees in front of him, and Lucifer nearly swallowed his tongue at the sight of her looking up at him.

As she went to work on unfastening his jeans and pulling them over his hips, along with his boxer briefs, Lucifer cupped her face in his hands and ran the pad of his thumb over her bottom lip. "Christ! You're fucking beautiful," he breathed.

Crush sucked that finger into her mouth, sending bolts of pleasure through him as she wrapped a hand around his erection and gave it a stroke. As he cursed from the feel of it, she released his thumb and leaned forward. Looking up into his eyes, she opened her mouth and slid him inside, making sure to let her tongue caress all the sensitive spots on his dick.

Lucifer let out a loud moan and slid his hands back to fist them in her hair. She was *perfection*. The suction and the warmth of her mouth felt like heaven, but when she took him all the way back and kept going, he

Crush's Fall

thought he would blow. Clenching his teeth, he fought against the rising climax.

After getting his cock wet and playing a bit, she pulled off and sucking him down again, setting a steady rhythm. As she took his breath away with her mouth, she lifted a hand and cupped his balls, giving them a gentle squeeze.

Lucifer groaned loudly and thrust his hips forward, unable to help himself. Her greenish-gold eyes shined that gorgeous fucking light as she leaned into the thrust and took him deep into her throat.

"I love the way you look with my cock down your thr—" His words were cut off with a moan as she swallowed around him.

The roar they heard from the other side of the door had her laughing with his cock still in her mouth. Lucifer groaned. "Sugartits, I'm going to come if you don't stop that, and I'd rather do it in your—"

Axle shouted, "If you break that fucking door down, Bull, you're paying to repair it!"

As Crush pulled off of him and swallowed him down again, they heard Bullet growl, "It would be fucking worth it!"

Pike called out, "Fucking hell! Dragon, could I get some help?"

"I dunno. I think you should let him," Dragon said, sounding calm as can be.

"That's enough!" Axle sounded fed the fuck up. "Everyone away from the hall! Now!"

Chuckling, Lucifer used his grip on Crush's hair to pull her off of his cock and to her feet. Kissing the hell out of her and loving the taste of himself in her mouth, he went to work on her jeans. Once he had them open, he shoved them down to her knees, growling when he saw she was going commando, and forced her to turn around.

"I want it hard and fast, Lucy," she ordered, and bent over the edge of the counter.

He slapped her ass, hard, and met her gaze in the mirror, loving the way the sting from his hand made her bite her bottom lip. Gripping her hip in one hand, he lined his cock up with her entrance. He slammed home and soaked in the moan that came from his mate's mouth, along with the contraction of her pussy around his cock.

"Fuck! You feel so damn good."

"Fuck me, Lucy," she demanded, and pushed her hips back.

"Your wish is my command, Sugartits." Then he pulled out and slammed in again.

Crush left the bathroom first, and Lucifer followed her in a euphoric daze. His muscles were loose, and his head was a bit foggy, exactly the way he liked it. Sex with Crush always did that to him.

As Crush passed Bullet standing at the end of the bar, she reached up and wiped the edge of her mouth.

It took everything in Lucifer not to crack up laughing. Instead, he winked at Bullet and smacked Crush on the ass.

Bullet's eyes flashed in anger, but Axle stepped between them. "We need to talk to you," he informed Lucifer.

Lucifer's euphoria waned as he stared back at Axle. "About?"

"Club business," Axle replied and pointed to the stairway that led up to the Howlers church room.

Lucifer suspected he knew what it was about, but instead of questioning further, he just nodded and followed Axle up the stairs. He wasn't surprised at all when he looked behind him and saw the rest of the men coming with them.

Crush

Grinning from ear to ear, Crush walked over to the table Pinky, Nails, and Kisy are sitting at. She plopped down in the chair next to Pinky and grabbed Pinky's bottle of beer from where it was sitting on the table in front of her. After taking a drink, she handed it back and let out a sigh.

Her girls were chuckling at her as Butterfly took the empty seat next to Kisy and smirked at Crush. "You know you're doing your brother's head in, right?"

"Yup," Crush replied.

"Thought so." Butterfly grinned. "It's good for him."

"Sounded like Lucifer was having the time of his life in that bathroom," Nails commented, and waved to the prospect behind the bar to bring over another round.

Crush shrugged. "I was just giving him what he earned."

"Good boys get good rewards," Kisy said, causing Butterfly to snort a laugh.

"I'll make sure to let Dragon know you said that," Butterfly promised.

Damn, Crush loved these women.

Lucifer

As the Howlers took their seats, Lucifer stood next to the door and crossed his arms over his chest. Before he met Crush, he would have thought it was a sign of weakness to be wearing a property cut in a room full of patched members of a club, but he felt nothing but pride wearing Crush's property cut. There was nothing to be ashamed of. His woman was a badass and was hot as fuck. The men in that room knew Lucifer was a lucky bastard, and Lucifer was willing to shout that shit to the moon.

He just waited patiently while the other men settled in their seats. Eventually, Axle slammed his hand down on the table and cleared his throat.

"We brought you in here to talk to you about prospecting for the Howlers. Since you arrived here—"

Crush's Fall

"You mean since I was kidnapped and brought here?"

Axle gave him a hard stare, but continued, "You've spent months proving that you are willing to put our family above yourself. That is rule number one of this club. Our family should always be protected. If it wasn't for you, we might have lost Sugar. And you fought next to us in the war when you had no responsibility to do so. Because of all of that, and the fact that you are mated to the president of our closest ally, we are extending the offer to you to prospect for the Howlers. Keep in mind, the prospecting period will most likely be shorter than most since you've already proven yourself."

"I will be your sponsor," Trip added. "Do you accept?"

The smile on Trip's face told Lucifer that they expected him to be grateful and excited. They were about to be disappointed.

Lucifer shrugged. "I'll have to think about it."

Axle blinked hard. "What?"

"I said I'll have to think about it."

As Bullet started angrily mumbling under his breath, Skull asked, "Is there a reason why?"

"Yeah." He looked around the room, making sure to meet the eyes of each and every member before he said, "I won't be a part of a club that questions the strength of my mate or her club. You all have a habit of expecting them to cow to your decisions, to depend on your guidance, to let you *handle* things. They don't

347

need that. They are capable women, who, quite frankly, could teach you a thing or two if you took your blinders off long enough to pay attention. So, yeah, I'll have to think about it. In the meantime, maybe you should think about how good of an ally you've been to them. When you can promise me that you'll learn to be better allies, I'll promise my loyalty to you."

Without waiting for an answer, Lucifer turned and walked out of the room, knowing he could have just destroyed any chance he had at being patched in to the Howlers MC and completely at peace with that.

Crush

Sipping her beer, Crush was surprised when Lucifer returned to the main room without a Howlers MC prospect cut on. She had been positive that was what they wanted to talk to him about. When he stopped at her side and looked down at her, she met his gaze and raised a brow in question.

"I'll explain." He nodded to her hand wrapped around the bottle. "We need to clean those up."

Crush glanced at the cuts on her knuckles and shrugged. "They're already healing."

Staring hard into her eyes, he replied, "Humor me."

It wasn't often that Lucifer was serious about anything. Curious, and a bit concerned, Crush nodded and released the bottle. She stood and followed him out of the clubhouse, continuing to follow him all the way to their apartment. Once inside, he pointed to the stool by the island in the kitchen area, indicating he wanted her to take a seat.

She had been sitting there for only a few minutes before he walked out of the bathroom with a couple damp washcloths and a small, white box in his hands. The red logo on the front of the box let her know it was a first aid kit. He set his bounty down on the island and sidled up next to her side.

Letting him lift her hand in his and get to work on cleaning her already healing wounds, Crush examined his face. His jaw was tight, and his brows were pulled together. It could have been concentration, but she suspected it was more than that. She was just about to ask him what was wrong when he opened his mouth.

"They offered me a prospect cut with the understanding that the prospecting period would be shorter due to what I've already done for the clubs and the family."

She nodded, not surprised at all.

Wiping away the dried blood with a washcloth, he said, "I told them I had to think about it."

That surprised her. "What? Why? Think about *what*?"

He set aside the washcloth and pulled a packet out of the first aid kit that looked to contain an alcohol swab. After ripping the package open and pulling out the wipe, he met her gaze and answered, "I told them I didn't want to be a part of a club that would disrespect my mate or her club. I told them that until they could see and treat the Claws as equals, I couldn't promise my loyalty."

"Lucifer," she breathed, suddenly filled with more love and appreciation for him than ever before. "You didn't have to do that."

"Yes, I did." He began to run the wipe over her wounds. She ignored the sting as she waited for him to continue. "My loyalty is to you, and by extension, your club. Making a loyalty promise to the Howlers without them changing the way they treat you and the Claws, that would go against my promise to you. I may be many things, Sugartits, but a liar and someone capable of betrayal are not among them."

"Fuck. I love you," she expressed for the first time without it being practically pulled from her.

The side of Lucifer's mouth lifted. "I know."

"No. I mean... I fucking love you."

He chuckled and set aside the wipe. "I love you, too."

Lucifer had just grabbed the antibacterial ointment when she blurted, "Let's get married."

He froze, only his eyes moving to meet hers. "What?"

She didn't allow herself to back down. Somewhere in her brain, she knew there would come a moment when she wondered why in the hell she blurted that, but she couldn't deny she meant it. She loved him. Lucifer would be the only man for her for the rest of her life. It made sense to get married. It would also save Crush the irritation of being asked a million damn times when they were going to do it. She may be from a shifter family, but that didn't mean her mother wasn't going to want it legal with the government.

"Let's get married. Tonight. We can probably fly to Vegas, since—"

He shook his head, still looking stunned, and mumbled, "I know a judge in GR who would forge the date on the paperwork." He leaned a little closer, staring hard into her eyes. "Are you sure? I'm not trying to push you into anything. That's not why—"

She waved off his concern with the hand he wasn't holding. "I'm sure. Let's do it tonight. I'm not wearing one of those god-awful dresses, though. You can forget that."

Lucifer chuckled. "I don't think I would want to marry you dressed in something like that. If I'm marrying you, I'm marrying *you*. That means I want you in these jeans that hug your magnificent fucking ass and your president patch."

"So… we're doing it?"

He nodded and pressed a quick kiss to her lips. "Can you get your hands on five grand? I'll make the call."

"Got it in my safe." She slid off the stool to retrieve the cash as he pulled his phone from his pocket and began making his call.

Before long, she would be a married woman. Fuck. If you would have told her that a year ago, she would have used her claws to slit your throat. At that moment, she couldn't help but smile.

Lucifer may be an asshole, and an annoying one at that, but he was also loyal, brave, honest, and a great fucking lay. She just might have hit the jackpot.

"Are you telling your club or Bull?"

She removed the framed Tiger's Claw MC logo from the wall in her living room area and began punching in the code for the safe. "Nope." When it buzzed, she put her thumb over the sensor. After a moment, it dinged, and the lock mechanism released. She turned the handle and pulled open the safe door. "I'd rather it just be us. They can find out when we get back."

"Sounds good to me. Are you actually going to ride on my bike with me?"

After grabbing the stack of cash and closing up the safe, she looked over at him with a smile on her face. "I guess... but don't get used to it."

As she hung the framed logo back over the safe, she heard him chuckling.

"Judge Bowen, Brooks." There was a moment of silence. "Yeah, sorry. I know it's late, but I need a favor... a favor I'm willing to *reward*." Another silence. "A favor that will only take ten minutes of your time."

Crush made her way to Lucifer's side.

"A fast-tracked hitching for five large... trailers."

Crush snorted at the ridiculous way Lucifer was asking the judge to marry them.

"Can be there in an hour and a half at the most." Silence. "Great. Thanks."

When Lucifer ended the call and grinned at her, Crush rolled her eyes. "You look like a kid who was just told he could go to Disney World."

He took hold of her hips and pulled her against him. "Makes sense. Isn't that the place where dreams come true?"

T.S. Tappin

CHAPTER TWENTY-NINE

Lucifer

Shocked would be an understatement when describing how Lucifer felt when Crush suggested they get married. Sure, it was an antiquated tradition, and he was far from a traditional type of guy, but there was a part of his caveman personality that wanted to be legally tied to his woman. He wanted to be able to declare to the world that his wife was the badass president of the Tiger's Claw MC. He was more than proud to have her on his arm.

It probably had something to do with being raised a human. There was a ridiculous importance put on *getting married* and *settling down*, something that went against the biker badass in him. He had always bristled at those words and demands from his elders until Crush. Fuck. He'd do anything she wanted.

Lucifer was pretty sure she thought she had no power over him and was worried he'd try to wrench control of her and her life. It couldn't be farther from reality. *Crush* was the one who had all the power, and it had nothing to do with her shifter strength.

She was his kryptonite, but she was also the nourishment that kept him alive and breathing. She was his air and his poison. Whether he lived life to the fullest or died a slow, painful death was solely in her hands.

One touch, one kiss, one look from her had his body primed. And if she got anywhere near the mating mark she left on his shoulder, he was ready to come in his jeans. She knew it. That's why she chuckled after she gave the mark a lick when she was climbing behind him on his bike. Riding with an erection was uncomfortable, but he was willing to do it if it meant giving her what she wanted.

The ride to Grand Rapids was the best and worst ride of his life. He loved having her wrapped around him, her hands sometimes clutching his shirt, sometimes exploring. The problem was her hands on him had him ready to pull off to the side of the highway and fuck her brains out, which he would have done if going to jail for indecent exposure wouldn't have delayed getting them to Judge Bowen.

When they pulled up to the ridiculously large home in the high-class end of Grand Rapids, Crush let out a low whistle. "My mate has high-class connections."

Lucifer shrugged. "He may live in a big home and have money in the bank, but he's a lecher. Try not to kill him, okay?"

Crush snorted a laugh. "Yeah. Okay." She climbed off the back of his bike.

Lucifer slid off the bike and took her hand in his before he headed for the front door. Before they could even knock, the door opened and an older woman in an all-black uniform with tight white curls in her hair rushed them into the house. Obviously, Judge Bowen was worried about the neighbors seeing biker scum on his doorstep. Lucifer rolled his eyes as he stepped into the marble foyer.

"Wait here," the old hag grumbled, and hurried away.

"The hospitality is astounding," Crush commented.

"You still want to get hitched?" Lucifer smiled at her.

"You ain't getting rid of me, so why not?"

Feeling overwhelmed with love for her, he cupped her face in his hands and pressed his lips to hers. It didn't take long for the kiss to spiral out of control and for his tongue to snake past her lips and tangle with hers. Crush was gripping his property cut and pulling him closer when they heard a clearing of a throat.

"Get control of yourselves, and let's get this done," Judge Bowen grumbled. "You're interrupting my wife's birthday party."

Crush looked around. "Party? It's as silent as a tomb in here."

"Unlike some people, we're civilized," the judge sneered and turned on his overpriced heels to head down a hallway.

Flipping him off, Crush followed. Lucifer snorted a laugh and brought up the rear. Fuck. He loved that woman.

Crush

After saying their vows and signing the necessary paperwork, they decided to get a room for the night and headed downtown. Crush laughed at the looks the two of them received when they walked into the Amway Grand. She was surprised the manager didn't immediately ask them to leave, but that probably had something to do with the wad of cash Lucifer had pulled out of his wallet.

He paid for two nights just in case they decided to extend their honeymoon. The desk clerk fast-tracked their check-in and handed them their room key with a smile. Taking her hand, Lucifer led them to the elevator with his head held high. As they passed a couple in designer clothes and perfectly coiffed hair, the woman looked scared to death of them. Because she was a bitch, Crush winked and grinned, which only made the woman clutch her pearls.

When they stepped into the elevator, Lucifer pulled her into his arms. "That wasn't very nice, Mrs. Brooks."

"I'm a bitch," she replied with a shrug and a smile.

"Nah… you're just a pussycat," he said against her lips, before he took them in a deep kiss, making her toes curl in her biker boots.

By the time the elevator dinged that they had reached their floor, Lucifer's hand was down the back of her pants, cupping her ass. He didn't bother pulling it out as he turned her and led her down the hall to their room, instead giving her ass a squeeze every few steps.

She used the key on the door to their room and opened it. As soon as they stepped inside, Lucifer was pushing the door closed and pressing her against it.

"I want you right here," he growled against her lips.

"I've told you before, Lucy. If you want something, you're going to have to take it."

In response, he nipped her bottom lip and pressed his hips against hers, letting her feel how ready he was for her. She could feel his hard cock against her lower abdomen as his free hand slid into the hair at the back of her head and fisted. Yanking her head back, he lowered his and sucked on her neck, making her moan.

She was just about ready to start yanking off his clothes when he dropped to his knees in front of her and went to work on her boots. Not wanting to waste time, she unfastened and unzipped her pants. Once he had her boots and socks off, he reached up, gripped the sides of her jeans, and yanked them down to her feet. She barely got a foot out of them before his mouth was on her pussy, and his tongue was swirling around her clit.

"Lucy," she moaned and gripped his hair, using it to keep him against her, afraid he'd suddenly stop what he was doing.

Instead of stopping, he added two fingers sliding in and out of her cunt, curled and hitting her g-spot on every stroke, sending jolts of pleasure through her.

Her tiger was pacing and roaring, tail swishing, as Crush let her head fall back against the door with a thud. She tried to hold off her orgasm as long as she could, but her man knew exactly how to drive her over the edge.

As soon as her core began to contract around his fingers, he used his free hand to hike her leg up on his shoulder, giving him better access. Quickening the pace of his fingers, he latched onto her clit and sucked. Light exploded in front of her eyes, and every muscle in her body seized as she let out a loud moan and rode the wave of pleasure that washed over her.

He kissed and licked her slit as she recovered from her orgasm, causing her to twitch every time he came close to her clit.

"Fuck. You taste like motherfucking heaven," he moaned against her.

She released her grip on his hair. Instead of gripping it, she ran her fingers through his hair as she stared down into his dark brown eyes. "Now, where do you want me?"

One of his dark brows hiked, he grinned up at her. "Is my wife allowing me to have a say?"

"Your wife was giving you an opportunity to be in charge for once, but I can rescind that offer if you plan on throwing it in my face."

Lucifer chuckled and stood. "Naked. On your hands and knees on the bed," he ordered, his voice deeper and more gravelly than she'd ever heard it before.

Lucifer

As he watched Crush get into the instructed position on the bed, Lucifer undressed, leaving his clothes wherever they fell, except for his cut. He laid that over the top of the dresser.

She glanced over her shoulder at him, and his brain almost exploded. The sight of her naked, round ass in the air, her smooth back, and the greenish-gold light shining from her eyes had his breathing labored and his gut clenching. She was the most beautiful woman he had ever seen in his life. He couldn't believe that she was his, really and truly his, forever.

"Fuck. I love you," he choked out as he fought the stupid tears that lined his eyes.

Her face softened for a moment before she began to shake her ass at him. "I would love it if you fucked me."

"Your wish is my command, Mrs. Brooks."

"Then I *wish* you'd stop talking and start moving, Mr. Welles."

T.S. Tappin

As soon as she finished her sentence, Lucifer moved onto the bed and gave her ass a slap, hard enough to make her shift forward and moan his name. When she caught herself and moved back into position, his cock was there, ready to slide inside of her. He groaned as her pussy enveloped him in wet heat.

When her breath caught in her throat, Lucifer couldn't stop the masculine pride that welled up inside of him. The fact that he was able to make this strong, aggressive woman gasp was like he was given a billion dollars and the title *sexiest man alive* all at the same time. *Fuck.* She was the key to everything — his happiness, his desire, his life.

The pace he sent was unrelenting, hard, forceful. Gripping her hip in one hand to hold her in place, he slid his other hand up her back and fisted it in her hair. Forcing her head around to look at him, he gazed into her glowing eyes, loving the raw pleasure there, before he took her mouth in a deep kiss.

He kept kissing her until the force of his thrusts made him unable to keep contact with her lips. When he broke the kiss, he moved his mouth to her ear and whispered, "Your pussy feels so good clenching around my cock. So hot and wet and tight. When you come, it feels like you're strangling my dick, and I love every fucking second of it." He released her hair and slid that hand around her and down to her clit. Taking it between his fingers, he pinched the nub. "Now fucking come on my cock, Sugartits."

She screamed as her orgasm overwhelmed her. Her pussy clamped down on his erection, making him unable to keep thrusting. Giving in, he slammed inside of her and let himself go.

The last thought he had before he was swamped with pleasure was, *This is how I want to spend the rest of my life.*

Reclining against the headboard, Lucifer watched as his naked wife chowed down on a piece of pizza. She was sitting at the foot of the bed, facing him. His gaze was so fixated on her, his own piece forgotten in his hand.

His wife. Fuck, that felt good to say. Finally, she was his in every possible way.

"Stop staring at me and eat your pizza," Crush said around the bite she just took. She was the least ladylike woman he knew, and he fucking loved it.

Grinning, he took a bite and chewed, keeping his eyes on her. That was how he caught her fingering the pendant he gave her. She did that a lot, but he was pretty sure she didn't realize it.

His tiger was just a pretty kitty down deep.

Lucifer's brows pulled together as he continued to chew his food and watch his woman. After he swallowed and set aside the crust in the nearly empty pizza box, he said, "Are you really a tiger... or just a house cat?"

T.S. Tappin

Crush froze mid-chew, but her gorgeous greenish-brown eyes shifted to him. "What?" she mumbled around her mouthful of food before she started chewing again.

He shrugged. "I've never seen you shifted. You *claim* to be a tiger shifter, but... are you *really*?"

Crush rolled her eyes. "You're stupid."

Lucifer swallowed down his chuckle. "Are you worried that Bullet is a prettier kitty than you are? Don't worry, Sugartits. You know I'll always think you're prettier."

She scowled at him. "I don't give a fuck if you think my tiger is prettier than Bullet's."

"I think you do. It's the only reason you wouldn't shift in front of me. I mean... I know my opinion means a lot to you." Her hiss made him grin. "I just want to put you at ease, Sugartits."

"I was at ease until you opened your fucking mouth and started speaking."

"Now, Sugartits, we both know that's true. Nonetheless, it doesn't change the fact that you haven't shifted in front of me. And unless you can prove otherwise, I will keep assuming it's because you're nervous to find out my opinion of your tiger."

Her eyes flashed that greenish-gold light seconds before she shoved the open pizza box off the bed and shifted. In the blink of an eye, he was face to face with a fully grown tiger female, hissing and snarling at him.

She was fucking gorgeous in her tiger form. The many colors in her fur and the long whiskers sticking out from her face were mesmerizing to him. But if he didn't know she loved him, he'd be pissing himself at the sight of those fangs. Her head was at least four times the size of his. He assumed her body was, too, but he couldn't see it since her snarling teeth were only inches from his face.

Not one to show any fear, and truly not afraid of her, Lucifer reached up and ran his hand through the fur on the back of her head. It was somehow soft but coarse at the same time, a lot thicker than he expected, and had an oily coating to it.

"Why am I so turned on, right now?" Slowly he moved his hand forward, giving pets, until he reached the tuft of fur behind her ear. Lifting his other hand, he gave her scratches behind her ears and murmured, "You really are just a pretty kitty, aren't ya? Yeah, my pretty kitty."

She leaned into the scratches for only a few moments before she hissed and shifted back.

Lucifer chuckled as he watched her subconsciously rub the spot behind her human ear.

"Shut up," she grumbled.

"That was possibly the hottest thing I've ever experienced," he said, and motioned to his erection, tenting the sheet over his lap.

Crush rolled her eyes, but he didn't miss the fact that she bit her bottom lip. After a few moments, she yanked the sheet back and threw her leg over him. Straddling his waist, she leaned forward and scowled at him.

"Are you going to glare at me or fuck me?" He grinned.

She didn't verbally answer, but the fact that she reached between them, took his erection in her hand, and lined his cock up at her entrance was all the answer he needed.

Chapter Thirty

Crush

The sun shining through the window woke Crush from the deepest sleep she'd had in years. She was warm and cozy, wrapped around a hard body. Opening her eyes, she looked into the sleepy eyes of her mate. The smirk on his face had the memory of the night before rushing back into her brain.

She was a married woman. Holy shit. She actually married Lucifer… without telling anyone. When they got home, their family was going to kick their asses right before they kicked off an impromptu celebration, unless Lucifer got his shit together and finally accepted what the Howlers were offering him. Then it would be her girls kicking off the party, while the men handled business.

While she was grateful for Lucifer's loyalty and willingness to put his foot down in her honor, Crush knew he wanted to be a Howler. It was something he wanted in his core. He needed the colors to complete him, make him happy outside of what she could provide as his mate.

"You need to take the prospect offer," she said as she shifted up on a bent elbow.

He shook his head as if her words caught him off guard. Then he blinked and uttered, "Okay. I'm not sure how I feel about the Howlers being the first thing you think of when you wake up in my arms."

She rolled her eyes. "I wasn't thinking about them. I was thinking about you. You want it."

He slid himself up until his back was to the headboard and sighed. "I won't accept it without them agreeing to change their ways with you."

Crush smiled and shifted closer, so she was once again pressed against his side. Sliding her hand down his chest and abdomen, she said, "Once my mate is a member, I have full faith that he'll make sure they don't keep doing the same shit. After all, what better way to change things than from the inside?"

As she wrapped her hand around his morning erection, she heard his breath catch.

He cleared his throat and replied, "True."

She started stroking and ran her tongue around his nipple. "Just reiterate your stance on it and accept the offer. I want you to have it because you want it."

"At this moment, what I want is my wife to climb on my dick and give me a show."

Crush rolled her eyes, but she threw a leg over him and shifted until she was straddling his lap. "One last ride before we head back home."

Biting his lip, he fisted his cock and held it up for her to slide onto. As she began to roll her hips and bounce on his dick, he cupped her breasts and bent his knees. "One last ride before we go get rings. Then we'll head home."

She stopped mid-bounce. "Rings?"

He looked at her like she lost her mind. "Yeah. We're married. If you think for one second that you're not wearing my ring, you're fucking wrong, Sugartits."

She returned to her rhythm and rolled her eyes again. "Fine. Whatever. Shut up. You're distracting me."

Pinky

"That bitch," Pinky hissed as she watched her best friend walk into the main room of the clubhouse hand in hand with Lucifer. The light glinted off of a rock on her bestie's ring finger, letting them know she got engaged sometime in the previous twenty-four hours.

After the meeting with the Howlers, Lucifer had whisked Crush out of the clubhouse, and no one had heard anything from them since. She wondered what they were up to for that long, but now she knew.

T.S. Tappin

"And when in the hell were you going to let us know you got engaged?" Pinky demanded as she stood and faced Crush.

"If I had, I would have told you," Crush replied.

"Hello! Rock on your finger!" She pointed at the offending rock.

Crush rolled her eyes. "Hello! Wedding ring," Crush shot back.

The entire room went silent. Everyone turned to look at Crush with shock evident on their faces. Pinky completely understood. "Wedding? What?"

Lucifer chuckled as he held up his left hand, flashing the black band around his ring finger. "We went and got hitched."

Bullet finally had something to say. "Fuuuuuck. Mom is going to kill you."

Crush shrugged. "She'll get over it."

"I would have liked to be at your wedding."

"Wedding? If that's what you want to call standing in front of a judge's kitchen counter while he said some words, then sure."

Pinky was still stunned, but a thought hit her and fueled her anger. "You didn't let me throw you a bachelorette party! You bitch!"

"Fuck," Lucifer cursed under his breath as he stared at Pinky.

"Ryker! Bring a bottle and shot glasses!" She pointed at Crush. "You!" She swung her pointing finger to the chair next to her. "Sit! We're getting trashed!"

Lucifer

As he watched his wife bicker with Pinky, Lucifer approached Axle standing at the mouth of the hallway. "Can we chat?"

Axle gave a nod. "Me or the club?"

"The club."

Axle let out a loud whistle. When heads turned toward him, he shouted, "Church."

The lot of them and Lucifer filed up to the church room, each of the members who passed him giving him various looks. Some of them were curious, some of them annoyed. He expected that. He knew his words offended some of them, but he didn't care.

After talking the situation over with Crush, he felt comfortable giving them his promise as long as the Howlers promised to try to do better when it came to the Claws. Like Crush told him, the Howlers didn't *intentionally* disrespect the Claws, they were just clueless men who needed to learn. Lucifer figured that he could be a positive influence in that education once he was a member.

Inside the church room, Axle waited for everyone to take their seats, except for Lucifer, who was standing off to the side. Then Axle uttered, "Go ahead, Lucifer."

Lucifer cleared his throat. "If I have the promise of all of you to do better regarding the Claws, I would like to accept the prospect cut."

The sound of a chair being pulled out sounded near the end of the table. Brute motioned to the chair next to him, directing Lucifer to take a seat. He did, and for the next hour, the table discussed what Lucifer meant and the many ways they could honor that promise.

Wearing the prospect cut and a smile, Lucifer carried his property cut in his left hand as he descended the stairs with the Howlers. They were going to make him do shit jobs for the next however many months, but eventually, he'd earn the colors and rockers, and be able to call himself a Howler. To him, it was worth it.

When he reached the mouth of the hallway, he heard his wife call from across the main room, "Luficer! *There* you are!"

Bullet chuckled next to him. "Welcome to the family. She's your problem now."

As his brother-in-law gave him a rough pat on the back, Lucifer grinned. "Not a bad problem to have."

Axle gave his shoulder a squeeze. "Since it looks like you're going to have your hands full tonight, you can start your prospecting time tomorrow."

"Thanks," Lucifer said through a chuckle as he headed for Crush.

"Lucy No Fur, because you're not a shifter," she slurred, obviously having spent the last hour doing exactly what Pinky ordered.

The table of her club sisters burst out laughing.

"Feeling good?" he asked her and bent down to kiss her lips.

She gripped the front of his prospect cut and nodded. "Loofah, Sir, I'd like to rub you all over me."

He snorted a laugh. "Drunk Crush is a barrel of laughs, I see."

"If you mention it tomorrow, I'll deny it," she mumbled as she yanked him down to her again.

Lucifer kissed her again. "I think your impromptu party might be over, wife."

"Boo," her girls shouted as he scooped his woman into his arms and headed toward the front door.

"Congrats," the Howlers called after them.

The next day... Crush

Crush knocked on the frame of Halo's open room door in the apartment building and stuck her head in. She saw Halo lounging against the headboard of her bed. "Hey."

Halo waved her in. "Hey."

Crush sat on the end of Halo's bed, folding her legs in front of her. "How are you feeling?"

"Like I got ran over by an entire club of bikes," Halo responded.

After sighing, Crush reached out and took Halo's hand in her own. "We need to talk about your taste in men."

Halo groaned. "Do we have to? I think I learned my lesson."

"Did you? Is this the first time he's gotten violent?"

When Halo's gaze shifted to the side, Crush knew she hit the nail on the head. "That's what I thought. We are going to start giving self-defense classes again. I want you to join them."

Halo rolled her eyes. "Okay."

"I'm serious, Halo. I want you able to protect yourself. One time is too many. You need to remember that. If he'll do it once, he'll do it again. You're not alone. I thought I taught you that, but obviously, you need a reminder that your sisters have your back. You can lean on any of us to help you out of any situation. No judgment. No questions if that's what you need."

"I know," Halo mumbled and stared down at their clasped hands. "I promise I'll come to you the first time, if something happens like that again."

"Thank you," Crush expressed, and she meant it.

When they took Halo in as a runaway and gave her a place to belong, she became a baby sister to the entire club. While they did their best not to baby her, she was young and needed a bit more guidance. And in Crush's mind, if Halo was hurt, she failed in her duties to protect her. Right or wrong, she would always shoulder the blame.

"It's a good thing I have a pack of badass sisters behind me," Halo said with a smile.

"Badass and bad-tempered," Crush replied, grinning.

CHAPTER THIRTY-ONE

Bullet

After parking his bike behind his father's SUV in his parents' driveway, Bullet headed in through the front door. He knocked and waited a moment before he stepped inside, though. He didn't need a repeat of the scene he walked in on years ago. It had been about two years after Crush moved out, and Bullet came over to grab something from his old bedroom. When he opened the door, he found his father mounting his mother on the steps in the foyer. He still couldn't look at those stairs without feeling nauseous.

When he stepped inside, he looked everywhere but at the stairs as he called out, "Mom! Pops!"

"In the kitchen," his father shouted back.

Bullet made his way there and smiled at his mother, who was stirring something at the stove. Giving her a kiss on the cheek, he took a deep sniff and groaned. "You making chicken and dumplings?"

"It's fall, Liam. Of course I am," she replied with a proud smile.

He made his way over to where his father was sitting at the dining table and took a seat across from him. "Hey Pops."

"Bull. This is a surprise visit. Where's my daughter-in-law?"

"She has a volunteer shift at the children's hospital." Bullet met his father's stare. "Got a second to chat?"

Taking the hint, his father stood and headed for his study. Bullet followed. Once they were shut in the study, his father leaned back against the edge of his desk and crossed his arms over his chest.

"I need to talk to you about Crush's mate."

"Husband, from what I hear," his father grumbled, his brows pulled together in disapproval.

Bullet nodded. "Yeah. They did that without telling anyone." He sighed. "Listen. I know she'll be bringing him over soon, and I wanted to give you my opinion before you meet him."

His father's stare turned curious. "I'm listening."

"You're going to want to hate him," Bullet admitted and plopped down in one of the leather chairs facing his father's desk. "And it would be easy to. He's abrasive and crude and an asshole."

"You're not singing his praises, here, Bull."

Bullet shook his head. "That's how he is. He's like that with Crush, too, but... Pops, he has her back in ways none of us can. He pushes her when she needs it. He backs her up without taking control. He will go head-to-head with anyone who even thinks of disrespecting her. As much as I don't want to fucking say it... Lucifer is good for Crush. I've seen her smile more since they mated than I've seen her smile in years. And if you tell her I said any of this, I'll fucking deny it."

His father chuckled. "Okay. I'll give the fucker a chance."

Bullet nodded. "All I can ask."

Crush

It was lunchtime when Crush got the text that the police were at the compound and looking for Halo. Crush set down the ledgers she was going over for the business she managed for the clubs and headed down to have Halo's back.

She was expecting the police to show up. A man died. His girlfriend would be the first person they wanted to speak to. It would be suspicious to them that Halo was beaten to hell and he mysteriously died, but that wasn't Crush's problem. She knew there wasn't any evidence to link to any of the Claws. The Claws specialized in cleanup.

T.S. Tappin

She approached the two suits standing out front of the clubhouse and crossed her arms over her chest. "Detectives."

"I'm Detective Hank Wilson, and this is my partner, Detective Brian Kolche." He held out his hand to her but Crush just glanced at it.

Detective Wilson was a creepy man in his thirties with greased back dark hair and a suit he bought to make him look pulled together, but it somehow made him look frumpled and unkempt. It probably wasn't the suit's fault, Crush decided. It was probably the slime that seemed to ooze off of the man.

His partner was more pleasant to look at. His hair was cut in a short, businesslike manner and his face was clean-shaven. His suit seemed to be quality and fit him properly. He looked like a man doing what he was meant to be doing, instead of playing dress up like his partner.

"What can I help you with?" Crush tried hard not to sneer, but it was a struggle.

Detective Wilson dropped his hand to his side and replied, "We're looking to speak with Kinsley MacDonald. Her last known address is listed as the clubhouse address."

"She lives here. Let me see if she's up to talking to you."

"*Up to* it?" Detective Wilson's eyes narrowed.

"Yeah." Crush didn't elaborate. She wasn't about to hand information over to them. They could do their jobs

Crush's Fall

and find it out for themselves, but that wasn't a likely outcome.

"Is she ill?" Detective Kolche asked.

"Something like that." Crush pulled her phone from her pocket and dialed a number. She put the phone to her ear and waited.

"What's up, Boss Lady?"

Halo's voice in her ear sounded normal, which vibed with the condition she found her in earlier. While Halo was sore, she was a tough cookie, and it would take a whole lot more than a douchebag to bring her down for long.

"You up to chatting with a couple detectives? Not sure what they want, but they're asking for you by name."

"Damn. Yeah, I guess, since I doubt they'll listen if we tell them to kick rocks."

Crush chuckled. "Clubhouse?"

"I'm in the cafeteria. Thought food would be good."

"See you soon." Crush ended the call and held out a hand toward the clubhouse. "This way." Then she made her way up to the front door.

As they walked through the main room of the clubhouse, members from both clubs stood and followed them into the cafeteria. Crush bit the inside of her cheek to keep from laughing at the expressions on the detectives' faces when they noticed they had a tail.

"Can we do this somewhere more private?" Detective Wilson asked.

Crush shook her head. "I won't force Halo to move more than necessary, and neither will you. This is a public space, so I won't be ordering anyone out, either."

"We could demand to bring her in for questioning."

Crush raised a brow. "Not unless you plan on arresting her. I can have a lawyer here in less than five minutes. Is that going to be necessary, Detective?"

They stopped next to the table where Halo was eating a grilled cheese sandwich with a side of tomato soup. Halo looked up at the Detective and waited for an answer to Crush's question.

Detective Wilson let out a sigh. "Not yet... unless she wants one."

Halo nodded to the empty seats across from her. "Would you like to sit down?"

As both detectives sat, they looked around. Crush nearly lost her battle with holding back her laughter when the seriousness of the situation they walked into dawned on them. Behind Halo and Crush stood a large group of Claws and Howlers, all prepared to back Halo if necessary.

"Miss MacDonald," Detective Wilson began, a slight waiver in his voice, "I'm sorry to have to share this news with you, but... Patrick Aikok was found dead this morning."

The snort of laughter coming from the group of club members at the mention of Patrick's last name wasn't appropriate, but they were bikers. When were they ever appropriate?

Halo stared back at the detectives and, in a monotone voice, uttered, "Oh no. That's too bad."

"Weren't the two of you dating?"

She nodded. "We were until he decided to use me as his favorite punching bag. I decided that wasn't something I was into."

"Is that how you were injured?"

Halo pushed away her plate and crossed her arms over her chest. "It is."

"Where were two nights ago, late evening?"

Halo pointed to her black and blue face and stitched up cheek. "In bed. Recovering. I have around fifty witnesses who can attest to that."

The Detective's stare narrowed on her as he asked, "Do you think it's odd that you would end up injured and he would die so close together?"

Halo shrugged. "If it were anyone else? Sure, but Patrick had a way with pissing people off. Who knows who else he may have pissed off. Could have been anyone."

"Are you saying you had nothing to do with his death?"

"That's exactly what I'm saying," Halo replied, nodding.

"Do you know who could have killed him?"

"We weren't that close. Fucking and fighting do not equal a devoted relationship. I didn't know many of his friends. I never met his family. We didn't exactly have deep, meaningful conversations."

After that blunt answer, the detectives asked a few more questions and didn't get any new information. When it was clear they had weeded out everything they were going to, Detective Kolche brought the interview to an end, handed Halo his card, and requested that she call if anything else came back to her.

"Don't leave town," Detective Wilson grumbled as he followed his partner out the door.

"I'll do what I want, Detective Wilson, unless you show up with a warrant to prevent that."

The glare Halo received in return was humorous to the clubs if the laughter he was met with was any indication.

Mr. Welles

Hearing the roaring sound of the pipes from motorcycles coming down the street, he moved to the window in the living room and looked out. It was an unseasonably warm day in Warden's Pass, and his wife had insisted they open the windows and air out the house one last time before winter would demand they remain closed for months.

Through the open window, he watched and heard as his daughter and her mate parked their bikes in the driveway and immediately began bickering.

"Okay. Now, listen. Don't be... you," Meredith ordered.

Lucifer climbed off his bike with a grin on his face and smacked Meredith on the ass. "Me? I'm a delight."

"Sure. And I'm Mary Fucking Poppins."

"Relax, Crush. I'm not going to disrespect your parents," he said as his hand slid onto her ass and squeezed.

She slapped his hand away and glared at him. "None of that at my parents' house."

Lucifer snorted a laugh. "If you think your father hasn't done that to your mother, you're delusional. I've watched Bullet do the same to Butterfly in the middle of a room full of people."

"Not. The. Point."

"Exactly the point," Lucifer argued as they climbed the steps to the front porch. "Fine. I'll try to limit the feels I cop."

"They are so damn cute," his wife and the mother of Meredith and Liam said as she pressed into his side.

Mr. Welles sighed but smiled. "Yeah. Let them in."

As he followed his wife to the foyer, he thought about what he just witnessed and decided his son was right. Lucifer was brash and a bit of an asshole, but he was exactly what Meredith needed.

A wave of parental pride washed over him at the knowledge that both of his children had found their mates and were settling in to mated life.

When Meredith entered the house and came over to him, he wrapped her in his arms and whispered in her ear, "He'll do."

T.S. Tappin

Glimpse at What's to Come...

Halo

For months, Halo had taken every class Crush had wanted her to take. She even hired a therapist to talk to about what Patrick had done to her. Halo thought she was well on her way to putting Patrick and the attacks behind her, but the fear in her gut at that moment proved otherwise.

While jogging down her favorite trail in the woods just outside of Warden's Pass, she instantly knew when someone was following her. The person was pretty good at not giving their presence away. There was no snapping of twigs under feet or heavy breathing, but Halo's radar for what was around her was stuck in overdrive.

She needed to call Crush or text her. While she better learned how to protect herself, she was under no illusion that she could take on anyone, no matter how big or strong. After the attack by Patrick, she had made a promise to Crush to call for backup if she thought she might need it. Halo was determined to keep that promise.

Maintaining her pace, she reached down and unzipped the pocket on her fanny pack. The Howlers had given her shit for wearing it, but she liked it. It was rainbow-colored and had a Bluetooth speaker in the front that could connect to her phone if she decided to listen to music. When she was running, she liked to wear it because it was big enough to hold her phone, her keys, and a bottle of water.

Once it was unzipped, she pulled out her phone and held it in her hand as she approached a side trail that would bring her back to the parking lot instead of continuing on with the same trail.

Her heart was racing, and her breathing was more labored than usual on her runs as she made a left onto the side trail and kept running, hoping beyond hope that the person following her would keep running.

Lining both trails were thick woods and brush, but the paths were packed, relatively smooth dirt. Looking down at where she placed her foot on each stride, she listened hard for the person to keep going.

"Miss!"

Fuck! Halo picked up her pace as she sent an *SOS* text to Crush, knowing that they had tracking applications on all the members' cell phones.

"Miss! Hey!"

Halo's heart was pounding so hard she could barely hear the man's call over the sound whooshing in her ears.

"Hey! Your keys!"

What? Halo slowed her pace only slightly and tried to figure out what the man had said.

"You dropped your keys!"

The man sounded closer. As his words finally registered, Halo shoved her hand in the fanny pack, searching for her keys. What she found was her half-empty water bottle and a hole in the bottle corner of the pack.

Slowing to a stop, Halo let out a sigh of relief and turned to wait for the man to catch up. Trying to catch her breath, she put her hands on top of her head and paced back and forth on the trail.

When the man came to a stop a few feet from her, Halo looked over at him. He seemed to be in his late twenties or early thirties and had long blond hair pulled back in a messy man bun on the back of his head. His eyes were a deep turquoise, so rich in color that they looked as if they had been enhanced in some way. Her keys dangled from long fingers that connected to a strong hand, which made sense. The rest of his body looked to be in great shape, muscled, fit. She wouldn't call him bulky, but she had no doubt that he spent a great deal of time focusing on his physical health.

Halo reached out and took the keys from his hand.

"Didn't want you to have to search for them," he commented and gave her a small smile.

"Thanks." Halo's eyes didn't leave his as she hooked her keys to the hole in the pull of the zipper.

He gave a nod and stared back at her for a moment. Then he chuckled. "Have a good day."

Halo watched as he turned around and headed back to the main trail. Her heart had finally calmed, and her breathing had returned to normal, but her nerves were frayed from the jarring shot of fear that had entered her system before.

Once he disappeared around the bend of the trail, Halo looked down at her hands and found them shaking. Frowning at the sight, she took a deep breath and released it slowly, trying her best to calm her system. After a moment, she looked at her phone and saw the reply text from Crush.

Crush : OMW

With her heart full of love for Crush and the rest of her family, Halo sent another text to Crush.

Halo : False alarm. Leaving the trail now.

With another deep breath, she turned and headed for the parking lot. She wasn't surprised when she left the woods to find Crush and a handful of her fellow Claws waiting for her. Their bikes were parked around hers, and her club sisters were standing in a group near the mouth of the trail.

"Finally," Crush breathed and pulled Halo into a hug. "You good?"

Halo nodded. "I just overreacted."

Crush pulled back and shook her head. "It's never an overreaction if you are taking precautions to protect your safety." She crossed her arms over her chest. "What happened?"

"I'll explain when we get back."

Sulien

Sulien Ignatius Flint was excited for his mission. It was the first time that Ordys or Raghnall trusted him enough to head a mission. Okay, fine, he wasn't technically heading the mission. Ordys was, but Sulien was the middleman between Ordys and the Howlers. With Ordys undercover at the Black Forest Academy and unable to contact the Howlers directly without suspicion, it was Sulien's job to pass on any messages to Axle Weber from Ordys and vice versa.

When he arrived in town, after being in the car for twelve straight hours, Sulien had needed to run. He had always been high energy and active, and immediately went on a run as soon as he found a trail. Besides the cutie he saved from having to search for her keys, there wasn't anyone else on the trail. It was perfect. He did his run, climbed back in his car, and headed for the Howlers compound.

He had never been there before or had met any of the members of the Howlers MC or the Tiger's Claw MC. He'd heard from Ordys that they were unlike anyone he'd ever met before, but that could have been good or bad. Ordys never clarified.

Curiosity and excitement coursing through him, he parked in the lot where he was instructed to by the GPS. Turning off the ignition and pulling out the keys, he looked around. It was like a little mini city. They had an apartment building, a meeting place, and several businesses, and all the buildings appeared to be well-maintained and clean. Even the parking lot of the auto shop was neat and orderly. There were no scattered parts, no beat-up, or rusted vehicles left forgotten in back corners.

Sulien climbed out of his car and headed for the front door of the clubhouse. He needed to make contact with the Howlers before he started looking for a place to stay. When he reached out to pull open the front door, it came swinging out at him. He stepped back and out of the way as the woman from the trail came strutting out with her head turned, talking to another woman.

"Trail Girl," he uttered with a chuckle.

The woman stopped and looked over at him with fire in her eyes. "I'm not a—" Her words cut off suddenly as her eyes landed on him. She cleared her throat and tried again. "I'm not a girl."

He gave a nod. "You're right. Sorry. Trail *Woman*."

"What are you doing here?" She crossed her arms over her chest and stared at him with narrowed eyes. The woman she had been speaking to had stopped at her side.

"I'm here to speak with Axle. What are you doing here?"

She unfolded her arms and pointed to a patch of the front of the leather vest she was wearing. *Tiger's Claw MC*.

"Oh." He chuckled. "Well, I guess we'll be seeing more of each other. I'm Sulien." He held out his hand to her.

"Halo," she replied and took his hand to shake it.

The second her hand touched his, his inner dragon went wild and the word *mine* shot to the front of his brain. His breath caught, and he couldn't pull his eyes away from hers.

Her honey brown eyes widened as a sizzle of energy bounced back and forth between their hands. Her dark brown hair framed her face and fell down her back, begging for him to run his fingers through it. She was tiny, petite, but clearly carried herself like she had a spine of steel.

"What the hell," she breathed as she stared back at him. Then she yanked her hand from his and stormed away.

"What in the fuck did you do," the other woman demanded, her greenish brown eyes glaring at him, her brown hair with purple tips pulled back into a ponytail. His eyes dropped to the patches on her leather vest and read the word *President*.

"I didn't do anything."

The woman looked over at Halo's back and returned her gaze to him. "Axle's inside." She started to walk away and called over her shoulder, "Watch yourself."

Confused, Sulien yanked the door open. Halo was his mate, his destined partner. As he entered the building, he let that information settle inside him, then he chuckled. Halo was *his mate*.

FIND HER ON THE WEB:

TikTok: Booksbytt
Instagram: Booksbytt
Goodreads: T.S. Tappin
YouTube: Books by TT
BookBub: T.S. Tappin
Website:
www.tstappin.com
Merch Store:
www.booksbyttstore.com
Any emails can be sent to
Booksbytt@gmail.com

T.S. Tappin

ABOUT THE AUTHOR

T.S. Tappin is a storyteller who spends most of her days playing chauffeur to her children (Tyler, Gabby, & Hailee, not to mention all of Hailee's friends who also call Tara "Mom"), strong (probably stronger than he wanted) partner to her significant other (Mark), emotional support human to her American Bulldog/Pitbull (Champ), or cleaner of other people's messes (at work and at home). Reading and Writing are her favorite ways to spend her spare time, but she doesn't have much of that with three busy teenagers in the house. She loves every moment of it. She's that mom in the stands yelling and cheering and generally making an embarrassment of herself. She's a very proud Wrestling-Baseball-Softball-Dance-Cheer-Theater-Robotics-QuizBowl-DECA-Esports-Choir-NHS-Rockstar-Crew-Rockstar Mom!

FOR MORE INFORMATION

On the Howlers MC or Tiger's Claw MC, go to www.tstappin.com or find T.S. Tappin on any social media using the handle BooksByTT.
Your honest review would be appreciated. This book is on Amazon, GoodReads, and BookBub.
If you have any questions, T.S. Tappin can be reached at BooksByTT@gmail.com

Thank you for Reading!
Dream Big. Dream Often. Dream Always.

Printed in Great Britain
by Amazon